The V8 Ford Blues

Gordon Donnell

Writers Club Press
San Jose New York Lincoln Shanghai

The V8 Ford Blues

Published by Writers Club Press
an imprint of iUniverse.com, Inc.

For information address:
iUniverse.com, Inc.
620 North 48th Street
Suite 201
Lincoln, NE 68504-3467
www.iuniverse.com

ISBN: 0-595-01075-X

Printed in the United States of America

Chapter 1

A miniature tornado ambushed me as I trotted to beat the traffic light, swirling up from the gutter and sandblasting me with fine grit.

The TV weather report had a satellite loop showing a late October storm moving in from the Pacific and a computer graphic of the Los Angeles basin to explain the blustery wind.

I knew better.

This was the night I had taken the cleaners' plastic off my good raincoat. I was wearing a freshly pressed flannel suit, white shirt, silk tie and polished wingtips. I wanted to look prosperous, for a change. I was on my way to an exclusive supper club to find out what a legendary gambling boss wanted with a generic skip tracer.

The entrance door of the Crown Colony was a perfectly hung slab of varnished teak on which a pair of fearsome dragons faced off in low relief. The black iron hardware was cold. A pneumatic closer produced a progressive muting of wind and traffic noise. A soft, satisfactory thud sealed me away in a hushed foyer. Languid music rose pleasantly muffled from somewhere below.

The attentive personality on duty was a brunette Caucasian doing her best to look oriental in a high-necked dress with a pair of gold ideographs embroidered over a prominent left breast.

"Do you have a reservation with us tonight, sir?"

"Not exactly," I said. "But I think I'm expected."

Two carats of diamond solitaire decorated the third finger of the hand that held my business card while she clicked a cursor down a brief computer screen of people who wouldn't have to pay cover tonight.

The ring started me wondering again how I had reached mid-life without finding the right chick. That wasn't the real question, of course. It was just a stand-in for a bigger and hazier anxiety over where the years had gone, and what I would make of what I had left.

The brunette found my name before I could turn morose. "Thank you, Mr. Spain."

She gave me a Chinese pari-mutuel ticket in exchange for my raincoat. I wondered what would happen to the coat if my dragon didn't come in.

Ornate carpeting flowed down the curve of a wide stairway and issued out into the club proper. Tough Tommy Lipton's ill-gotten gains had been spent lavishly there, blending the elegance of a Far Eastern Governor's residence with the intimacy and intrigue of a Macao dive.

The club was built on two levels. The higher, where I paused at the base of the stairway to get my bearings, held a bar sunk into the length of the rear wall. It seemed to exist largely for under-funded social climbers who wanted to be seen in the right places.

Guarding the only passage to the lower level stood a tanned and white-haired gentleman of sixty. He had a back as straight as the barrel of an Enfield and blue eyes as remote as the harbor at Singapore. Flanking him were silk divans. On crowded nights, protocol undoubtedly required the old gentleman to ignore the near-rich and not-quite-influential for a suitable space of time before condescending to guide them down to a table among the privileged.

No one was waiting at the moment, but the club was still doing excellent business for this early in the week. A rangy blonde whose sapphire eyes weren't impressed by my outfit passed me doing a final touch-up on her way from the powder room. She tucked a compact into an evening clutch, got her hips up to cruising speed and moved down among dim-lit tables, where tailored suits sipped and savored and talked about gilt-edged investments and corporate acquisition rumors and how their close personal friends expected to make out in next week's elections.

The fact that the polished dance floor wasn't drawing any action didn't discourage the five-piece band on stage. They were doing some nice work on the kind of instruments they didn't have to plug in. Their repertoire was about as oriental as the aroma of New York steak on the air. I listened to a muted horn luxuriate sentimentally over *Pledging My Love* until a bartender got around to me.

"May I get you something, sir?"

He wasn't impressed either, but his tone of voice left open the possibility that if I asked politely, paid cash and didn't wet the carpet, he might actually mix me a drink.

I put a business card on the bar. "I have an appointment with Tommy Lipton."

I had never met Lipton, unless you counted trading telephone recordings. I don't know why I called him Tommy. The bartender had a Ph.D. in phony. He took it for name-dropping.

"I'll let Mister Lipton know you've arrived, Mr. Spain."

He took the card back to an alcove, holding it delicately at some distance so he wouldn't contract anything unpleasant, and used a phone left over from *The Shanghai Gesture*. He was back in a minute, handing the card across the bar with a smile.

"Mr. Lipton regrets that he will be tied up for the next few minutes, Mr. Spain. Anything you care to drink while you wait will be complimentary."

There was some activity on stage while he was making me a Bacardi and Coke. Nothing spectacular. They wouldn't go in for that sort of thing here. It was all smooth and correct and restrained. The music faded away and the bandleader stepped up front with a slim hand mike to introduce the club's featured attraction. He called her Miss Jean LaBostrie with the proper level of subdued excitement in his voice, then backed up a couple of half steps to lead the diners in some polite clapping.

Miss LaBostrie made her entrance in a full evening sheath that showed less than you would see on a cold day in the secretarial pool. One of those unemphatic gowns designed to tone down women who could bring the Atomic Age to critical mass without the right kind of shielding. She opened with a rhythm and blues standard: *There Is Something On Your Mind.*

I hadn't heard it done live in years. I couldn't remember ever hearing a woman do it. She sang in a rich husky contralto that flowed up from somewhere below sea level. The band stayed back in the shadows, putting each note to sleep as she finished with it. She closed the number under a heavy round of applause, some of it mine.

I turned back to claim my drink and discovered I had acquired some company. I was surprised I had missed his arrival. He was at least as gorgeous as the singer. A couple of inches taller than my six feet, mid twenties, bleach blond Prince Valiant hairdo. A fine poster boy for steroid abuse, but he didn't belong in the Crown Colony.

His muscles did their bulging in a purple suit with too many individual touches, like it wished it had come from Hugo Boss instead of Made-To-Measure Max. A pink shirt and a tie full of dark purple flowers reminded me of the ads you had to browse past to get to the interesting parts of high-tone girlie magazines. The ones that suggested today's man ought to be sure enough of his manhood to wear the clothes that showed the real him. They were the kind of literature Prince Valiant could take seriously.

At the moment, he was taking me seriously. There was a strong hint of resentment in his scrutiny, as if someone had stolen his last can of hair spray, and I was the prime suspect.

"Your name Henry Spain?" he asked.

"That's right," I said, and got set to learn which of my many faults was really irritating him.

"Okay, Dude. Just making sure." He went off down the bar.

I spent a moment looking stupid, then asked the bartender, "Who was that?"

"That was Mr. Calland, sir. He works for Mr. Lipton."

"Doing what? Comic relief?"

"I really couldn't say, sir."

The bartender moved off down the bar. Everyone was going off down the bar. That was fine with me. It left me alone with music that brought back aching memories of a shackled down '57 Ford and twin scavenger pipes ripping a velvet California night. Miss LaBostrie had time to finish her routine and an encore number before Calland came back.

"The Man will see you now," he announced gravely.

"You should work South Central," I said. "You speak the language like a native."

He tried for a little more resentment, discovered there was a limit to how frosted he could look and had to content himself with repeating what he had said.

Chapter 2

Calland led me to a door screened by a potted ginger tree. The concrete floored passage beyond was an abrupt reminder that we were in the basement of a seventy-year-old office building. A door at the end hissed open to reveal a freight elevator padded like the inside of a psycho ward. Twenty floors lit up one after another on the indicator panel.

The penthouse lobby was a black marble mausoleum dripping oppressive silence and subdued light. Calland used a magnetic security card to open a heavy teak door. The relentless eye of a closed circuit camera watched us cross a reception area, unstaffed at that hour. Calland knocked respectfully on an inner door then opened it for me. I stepped through into a room that felt more like a rich man's study than a business office.

A wild starless sky outside the tall windows made the warm silent blue of a gas log seem appropriate. Two massive leather armchairs were drawn up half facing the fire, half facing each other. Monopolizing the rest of the room was a desk the size of the British Empire, with carved lions facing out from the front corners.

A man leaned cross-ankled with his hips against one of the lions in a calculated pose that took six inches off his height, so any visitors he might be expecting could look down at him a little and feel relaxed. Posture aside, he was distinguished in executive blue flannel and freshly trimmed gray hair. Green eyes, crinkled at the corners, had a look of intelligence that went well with the clearly defined line of his jaw and the hook of his nose. He smiled patiently while he waited for Calland to remember his manners.

"This is Henry Spain, Mr. Lipton."

"Thank you, Ricky."

Tommy Lipton had a quiet, cultivated voice that could put eloquent inflection on the most trivial words. Trot along now, young fellow. Call you when I need you. There's a good lad. I heard the door close reluctantly behind me. Lipton straightened from the desk.

"Sorry to have kept you waiting, Spain," he said cheerfully, and stepped forward to offer a strong hand. "I'm showing off some rather fine Napoleon Brandy, for which I was recently allowed to spend a young fortune. How do you like yours?"

"Does neat apply to anything that costs over twenty dollars a bottle?"

He chuckled politely and offered me one of the chairs at the fire. It was a piece of furniture I could sink into any way I wanted, without worrying that I was sabotaging six thousand man hours of orthopedic engineering. It had the aroma of fine old leather, a subtle suggestion that in places like this the very best would be just barely adequate.

Lipton brought two snifters with viscous liquid swirling at the bottoms of their huge bowls. He gave me one, settled into the other chair and half raised his drink to me. I returned the gesture in the interest of customer relations. His brandy was warm, and good enough to roll around in my mouth before I swallowed it.

Tough Tommy Lipton seemed to have come a long way.

"How much do you know about me?" he inquired.

I put my snifter on a side table, dug an envelope out of an inside pocket and read aloud from my scrawl on the back.

"Terrence Llewelyn Stafford, called Tommy Lipton, or Tough Tommy. Born in Singapore in the early 1930's, of British parents. Brought to Los Angeles at the outbreak of World War II. Enlisted US Army, 1950, as part of an agreement to win severance from a gambling conspiracy trial on grounds of age, contrition and limited involvement. Scope of criminal activities not known with certainty but rumored to be extensive. Subpoena issued 6/17/51. Could not be served. Subject hospitalized overseas as a result of wounds suffered in Korean conflict.

"That much was buried in a couple of paragraphs of the 1951 California Crime Study Commission Report. Arrested again September 1953, for murder. Nolle prossed. No arrests of any kind since 1957. Never convicted of anything. Triple A commercial credit rating. Politically active. Widely known restaurateur. Owns the Crown Colony."

"I also own this building," Lipton added, intimating that I might as well know everything about him. "Do you usually research prospective clients?"

I put the envelope away. "It pays to know a little about them while they're still prospective."

"Well, as your sources correctly point out, I haven't been suspected of anything naughty in forty odd years."

"My sources are the credit bureau and an acquaintance with morbid interests. He thought you hadn't been arrested in forty odd years. I wouldn't want to draw any inferences from that."

My skepticism drew a good-natured laugh. "In 1957 you weren't old enough to notice girls."

I shrugged uncomfortably. When you're right, you're right. And he was right.

"You're looking at an anachronism, Spain. A man who has outlived an age you're not old enough to remember. When I first came to L.A., gambling was an industry. Everywhere from back rooms on Sunset to a rust bucket anchored out beyond the limit. It was only three miles in those days. Then, after the war, some people had a bright idea called Las Vegas. Like most bright ideas, it flopped in the beginning. But in the fifties air service got better, the highways improved, cars were more comfortable and easier to drive and customers started showing up. A lot of people who had been mixed up in L.A. gambling found out they weren't any more. Not because of any epidemic of morality, but just because there wasn't that much gambling left to be mixed up in. Most of them drifted to follow the play. I stuck around and put what money

I'd made into some real estate and eventually a supper club. The old days were as dead as the phosphorescent jukebox."

Lipton raised his snifter to drink a final, private toast to them. The blue of the gas flame reflected in the curve of his glass; a liquid luminescence fronting the lilt of *Sentimental Journey* drifting from unseen speakers. I didn't say anything. I wasn't in a position to hold Lipton's past against him.

"Let's talk about you," he suggested. "You've a reputation as something of an outsider, haven't you?"

My shrug had more eyebrow than shoulder in it. "That's a little hard for me to judge. Reputation is what other people think of you."

"You left a national investigative agency after too many years of the kind of jobs they didn't like to send family men on and opened a one man office."

I just nodded. My departure had been at the agency's request, but that was ancient history. I didn't see any point in mentioning it.

"You're known primarily as a field investigator. Background and skip trace. No special witness qualifications. Would you call that a fair appraisal?"

"As far as it goes," I allowed. It was the sort of synopsis lawyers liked to base their hiring decisions on. Which explained where he had got it, and why I didn't work for many lawyers.

"I didn't pick up the background just to be nosy," he said. "I specifically wanted a man who doesn't have secretaries or clerks or associates, and doesn't have a regular clientele he has chatty business lunches with. The job I have involves information I want held as closely as possible. It wouldn't be the end of the world if it got out, but it could cost me money, and maybe a nice business opportunity."

"I limited myself to some receptive nodding and a muttered, "Mm-hmm". He seemed to be getting down to cases, and I didn't want to interrupt.

"It used to be that you made your contributions and your interests were protected," he went on. "That's another thing that's changed. Today, any chiseler with a nickel's worth of inside information can make a pile on another man's investment. All nice and legal. The hell of it is you still have to write the checks. All they buy you is someone to run interference against men like Ben Osborne, if you know what I mean."

All I knew about C. Benton Osborne was that he'd made a lot of money pioneering computer applications in the advertising business, and a name using his electronic organization to save California from ideas and politicians he didn't like. I wouldn't have known that much if his heart hadn't tried to give out on him at a primary election celebration the previous month, practically on live television. He got a lot of editorial play as a kindly old patriarch, which was what editors called political bosses they happened to agree with. I also remembered some sly winking to the effect that he had once been a ladies' man. Nobody had mentioned any men like him.

If Lipton's reason for watching me was to get a reaction, he was probably disappointed.

"What did you think of the girl down below?" he asked.

"If you mean the singer, I'm no judge of talent. Is she the reason you had me cool my heels?"

"And the reason I asked you to stop by after business hours. I hope you don't mind?"

"Uh-uh. I enjoyed the performance."

He nodded confidently, as if that was as expected. "I need someone to look into her background for me."

"Is she the business opportunity?" I probably sounded skeptical.

"She has been singing here about five weeks," he explained in a voice that found my suspicions amusing. "She's drawn a lot of reaction, including customer inquiries about buying souvenir tapes or CDs."

"You make that sound unusual."

"Enough so that I had two separate recording company executives in to hear her. They were both impressed. On their advice I also took a poll from last week's reservation list, to see who remembered her and who might have bought her output, as souvenirs or off a store shelf, if any existed. The end result was that she might do fairly well, if someone fronted the money to get her the right sessions, distribution and publicity."

"You're thinking of putting up the money yourself?"

"That's in strict confidence."

"I must be missing something," I said. "I thought the recording companies had that sort of thing sewed up."

"They aren't about to put their imprint on anyone they don't think is good, or at least marketable. But like most businesses, they don't have the working capital to take advantage of every possibility that turns up. If a private investor comes along with someone acceptable, and the wherewithal to do a first-rate taping and promotion, they'll provide their facilities and organization on a cost plus basis. The costs are grossly inflated, of course. If things work out, they also get a nice percentage. If not, the investor eats the loss."

I had never heard of an arrangement like that, but Lipton wasn't your average California sugar daddy. As the owner of a high profile nightspot, he could easily rate special consideration from an industry hungry for places to showcase fresh talent.

"Nice system," was all I said.

"Nice for them. It leaves me with a girl who has the talent to make me some money and a past I don't know the first thing about. I'd like to cut the odds a little, before I place any bets."

"The odds against what, specifically?"

"The girl is unmarried. She has no family in L.A., that I know of. There have been a lot of changes in this town over the years, but I don't imagine the possibilities in a situation like that are among them. I'm not so much worried about scandal magazine material, though I'd like to know if you find any. Mostly I want to know her business history. Agents, managers, that sort of thing. There are a lot of sharpies working the music business. They'll sign these kids to representation contracts with lifetime clauses that don't surface until one of them makes it big. Anything like that, just so they get a free ride in case somebody clicks. It doesn't do any good to ask the kids about it. They never know until it's too late." He looked at me interrogatively, to see if I was getting his drift.

"Personal background means nothing to you, beyond the possibility of a little free publicity," I summarized. "I'm to concentrate on the business angles, to make sure you won't be carrying any freeloaders if things do go for you."

"If you find anyone you think isn't kosher, keep after him until you're sure. The trick will be to do it without tipping off the project. I guess I'll have to trust your judgement there." He wasn't the first client to sound nervous about that.

"Does your singer know she's going to be investigated?"

"She's agreed to sign a waiver of privacy. My lawyers are stalling a couple of days on the wording. Probably to justify the bill they're going to send me. Will there be any problem starting without it?"

I shook my head. "What can you tell me about her?"

"Not much beyond what I already have. She gets along well enough with the people here, though I don't know of any special friends among them. Never misses afternoon rehearsal, never late for a show. I get the impression she fancies herself a bit of a hard case, but a lot of girls do nowadays."

"A deposit is normal for this kind of assignment," I told him.

"I never doubted it. How much?"

"One thousand advance fee, five hundred advance expenses."

He started to lift his eyebrows at me, then decided it wasn't worth the bother. Sound muscles brought him effortlessly to his feet and he went to the desk.

I stood up, toying with an idea. "Was this originally going to be Calland's job?"

Lipton looked up from the memo pad he was writing on. "I don't think he knows about it, beyond the fact that he wasn't to bring you up until the girl finished. Why?"

"He seemed to resent me a little more than our short acquaintance called for. I thought that might be the reason."

Lipton chuckled and went back to writing. "Ricky tried to date the girl when she first came to work here. I never did get the blow by blow, but we had to send him in for X-rays to make sure she hadn't broken his foot."

"It's none of my business, but why keep a turkey like that around?"

"If I don't give the ladies something to tickle their fancy, they'll put the bee on the boyfriends to take them someplace else."

Lipton tore off a square yellow sheet with some hopeless scribbling under the club ideographs.

"Take this down to the business office. They'll issue the checks. You can get the girl's address and phone from the files."

I promised to bring my standard contract form around the next day. "If you want, I'll hold up cashing the checks until you've approved it."

"That won't be necessary."

We shook hands on it.

Lipton escorted me out to the elevator lobby, installed me in the freight car and waited smiling until the door closed. It was a neat touch to polish off a flawless performance. I hadn't a clue why he had wasted it on me. The job was a straightforward piece of legwork. One of his lawyers could have filled me in just as easily, and chiseled down my advance at the same time.

Chapter 3

The business office was an oversized closet, tucked away where the decorators had missed it. A bored waiter in a tuxedo stood on the worn linoleum in front of a gray metal desk. His lips worked furiously smoking the last cigarette he would probably enjoy for a while, if he were enjoying that one. A small, serious man in a gray swivel chair worked up a customer's tab on a credit card reader.

Supervising things was a cruiser weight alley cat who sat in the top tray of a double decker routing box with his orange tail wrapped around his legs. The cat was the only one who noticed my arrival. He measured me like a loan shark eyeing a customer who was two weeks behind in his interest payments.

The waiter stubbed out his butt and took back a charge slip and the card in a leather wallet. He noticed me when he turned to go. He couldn't have been more startled if he had come face to face with Godzilla. He recovered in less than an instant and went around me on noiseless feet.

The little man noticed me too. He stood up. He was five feet four and didn't look heavy enough to anchor a stack of petty cash vouchers. His neck was too small for his shirt collar and his eyes were too big for his face, bulging in their sockets and giving him a permanent expression of probing curiosity. They blinked at me through a haze of remaining smoke. He had no chin to speak of, so the questioning smile that formed by uncertain stages monopolized the lower portion of his face.

"May I help you, sir?" he asked in a tentative voice.

I gathered they weren't used to strangers back here. I handed over Lipton's note by way of introduction. The little man had no trouble deciphering the Sanskrit.

"It says here that you are Mr. Spain, and that I am to make out certain checks to you."

"Two of them would help keep my books straight. One for a thousand, the other for five hundred."

He seemed relieved at my knowing those amounts, as if they had been the other end of an impromptu challenge and password. He put the memo on the desk over by the cat.

"What do you think of that, Wilbur?"

Wilbur looked disdainfully down at the scribbling, as if he weren't particularly impressed by the transaction, but didn't want to go to the bother of refusing to approve it.

"Would you like to sit down, Mr. Spain?"

"Thanks." A padded gray chair squeaked under my weight. The little bookkeeper massaged the keyboard of his desk computer. A printer came to life on a back table and aligned a thick fold of tractor fed check stock.

"Could I please have the name and address of your firm for the register?"

I handed him a business card. His prominent adams apple rose to the limit of its travel and dropped like a stone. His eyes got about halfway to my face before he thought better of the idea. He fumbled a pack of cigarettes out of a desk drawer.

"Coffin nail?" He shook them up in one end and held the pack in my direction.

"Not since I found out chewing gum was easier on my lungs." Asking the little man what was bothering him wouldn't do anything for my cash flow.

"Anyone can quit," he quipped, plucking a filter end between his lips. "Takes a real man to face cancer."

His wit wasn't very original, but the cigarette seemed to help his jitters. He lit up and got back to the computer. The printer made short work of the checks. He put them through the protector on a metal side table, scooted back and signed them.

They didn't go in for exotic calendars here, and I wasn't a connoisseur of plaster cracks, so I amused myself stroking Wilbur. The cat liked me better now.

"Thanks," I said when he handed me the checks. "I'll also need to see Ms. LaBostrie's personnel file."

He glanced automatically at a gray metal cabinet, and realized his mistake. He forgot about being nervous. He squared sharp narrow shoulders inside his polyester dress shirt and puffed his chest out behind a bargain basement power tie.

"Personnel files are confidential," he informed me.

The little man had gotten tough in a big hurry. It wasn't hard to guess why. I looked at the checks. The signatures were Terrence L Stafford, by Albert Cooper.

"Is this your name?" I asked significantly. "Albert Cooper?"

"Yes, it is." His voice was tight and crisp, but his bright eyes weren't sure what I was getting at.

"Well, then, Albert, are you prepared to take responsibility for refusing to let me see that file?"

The question knocked him off balance. He started to say something, but changed his mind. "Well, if you're sure you have Mr. Lipton's authorization…?" he said with emphatic uncertainty.

I let an impatient stare do my talking. Lipton hadn't actually offered me anything beyond the girl's address and phone number.

Cooper cast a futile glance at the desk telephone. His illusions were leaking out of him like air out of the only balloon a ghetto kid would see that year. I should have felt great. I was in fine form, terrorizing someone half my size.

The spoils were about what I deserved…a manila file folder as thin as my bluff. The contents amounted to a standard performer's contract with a four-week holdover addendum and a personal information card.

I copied Jean LaBostrie's address, phone, social security number, a date of birth that made her twenty four and the fact that she was a native born US citizen into my notebook. Those were the only blanks she had filled in.

"This isn't very complete," I grumbled. "Who's her agent? What about personal references? Who would you notify in case of emergency?"

"Apparently Mr. Lipton didn't think those things were important," Cooper said tartly.

"He does now."

The little bookkeeper arranged the sparse contents meticulously before he refiled the folder. If he were careful enough, maybe no one would ever know. I wanted to tell him it didn't matter. He didn't want to look at me again.

Wilbur began washing his face with his tongue and one forepaw. He was back to giving me the evil eye between strokes.

"Thanks, guys," I muttered lamely. Following a kitchen cart loaded with enough haute cuisine to pay off the national debt got me out to the dining area. I made my way upstairs to the foyer to present my ticket and see if I had won back my coat.

I had, along with a three by five-inch envelope, heavy bond paper, with my name diagonally across the front in neat left-hand script.

Inside was a business card with the name Tod Patrick Grayson centered over the words 'General Counsel.' 'Osborne Associates, Advertising' in a discreet typeface occupied the lower right corner. There was more reverse slanted printing on the back. 'Imperative you contact me immediately. Urgent and confidential.' I turned the card over twice and made a face at it. I didn't know Tod Patrick Grayson from Vera Hruba Ralston. Tommy Lipton had mentioned C. Benton Osborne in passing, but that wasn't enough to stop me from leaning over the check counter and dropping the envelope and card in the attentive personality's wastebasket. I had killed too much time in important people's reception rooms to imagine that any paying business would develop out of a schoolgirl note on the back of an executive giveaway.

Out on the sidewalk the wind had gained a few knots. I leaned back and let it hustle me along to the intersection. The Crown Colony faded to a distant dream. The pompous diners and their pretentious surroundings, the old time gambling boss and his Prince Valiant shill, the little bookkeeper and his cat. None of them seemed quite real. Least real of all was a singer whose voice I couldn't forget and couldn't exactly remember, all at the same time.

I babied my shiny old Porsche up the corkscrew ramp of the parking garage in the next block. A glassed-in booth was manned by a twenty something black in a uniform of gray-blue pants and jacket that looked like the laundry had delivered them five minutes ago.

While he was feeding my card to his clock, Jean LaBostrie clicked in from the sidewalk with the precise heel-and-toe steps of a lady in a large hurry.

She had changed into flat heels and slacks. A three-quarter length coat was buttoned to her throat. A collar turned up against the wind hid the bottom half of a worried expression. She tucked a flat purse under one arm, freeing both hands so she could fold a transparent umbrella without breaking stride. She passed the glassed-in booth and followed yellow wall arrows back toward the park-by-the-month stalls. I could have been one of the concrete pillars for all the notice she took of me.

"In at eight forty five, out at nine fifty," the attendant intoned at my window. "That will be four dollars, sir. Evening rates."

"The lady," I said, moving my head to indicate the direction Jean had gone. "Does she usually leave around this time?"

The attendant smiled down at me, very faintly. "I'm afraid we don't give out that sort of information here, sir."

"It isn't what you think," I assured him. I slipped the corner of a ten far enough out of my wallet for him to see what it was.

"The charge is four dollars, sir," he said in one of those exquisitely careful voices. "If you would care to pay it and leave right now, I just might be able to restrain myself from reporting your license number to the police." He actually looked like his forgiving nature was arm-wrestling with his sense of responsibility.

"Let me guess," I groused. "You're just here working your way through college."

"I've already graduated from college, sir. The difference between the cost of supporting a family and a junior advertising copywriter's salary being what it is...well, I'm sure you understand."

A starter whined back in the hollow chamber of the garage and a light engine caught in a rush of exhaust. I traded the black a rumpled five for a dog-eared single.

"Put me in your first novel," I said. "I'm the old white guy who doesn't get it."

I ran the Porsche out over the sidewalk in an impatient burst and crowded the wind-harried traffic until it gave me enough room for a right turn.

I wasn't being paid for surveillance. There were any number of reasons Jean might be worried enough to hurry out on a blustery night, most of which had nothing to do with her business background. That didn't stop me from pulling into an empty transit zone at the end of the block to watch the garage exit in the mirror.

Chapter 4

Jean popped out of the garage in an older blue Honda Prelude and managed a left turn across traffic without losing any paint. I didn't make any friends using the crosswalk for a U-turn. Jean crowded bumpers and jumped amber lights along Wilshire until she reached the Harbor Freeway. She tailgated a Lincoln in the high-speed lane then she cut across in front of a semi with a loud air horn and led me down the Slauson off-ramp. We wound into an old tract of bungalows packed ten to the acre, where the palms had grown so tall you couldn't see the tops above the street lights. I closed up a little when she slowed to cruise along a street where cars were shoehorned in bumper to bumper at both curbs. It took me a block of rubbernecking to figure out that the cars were overflow from a white frame church up ahead.

All the lights in and around the building were burning. A signboard stood on the spotty grass plot in front; a white window casing on two spindly legs, lit by a hundred watt bulb set up under a bit of protective eaves. I picked out the words 'Charity Bingo Tonight' in block capitals as I rolled past.

Jean found a spot she could squeeze the Honda into in the next block. I passed her as she climbed out, turned the next corner and killed my lights. She locked her car and made for the church with her hairdo inside the umbrella.

My outfit hadn't exactly turned heads at the Crown Colony, but it was liable to raise a few eyebrows in this neighborhood. I needed a new image. Shoved back in the glove compartment was a cigar someone had given me to celebrate the anniversary of something or other. I used the dash lighter to get it going while I located parking accommodations up the road. I peeled off my raincoat, suit coat and tie, climbed out and locked the car. I headed for the church unfastening my collar button and rolling back my shirt cuffs. I had to fight the wind to get the door open, and then to keep it from slamming once I was inside.

Eerie whistling noises filled the deserted antechamber. Through an open set of double doors a tall crucifix fastened on the far wall looked down sadly on an empty pulpit and on obedient rows of empty pews. I followed a series of cardboard arrows thumb-tacked to the walls. The action was down in the basement, in what looked, from a display of childish watercolors, to be the Sunday school assembly room.

Women were packed hip to hip on the benches of all the cafeteria tables it was geometrically possible to crowd into the available space. Housewives of every age and shape, putting the bookmark in Danielle Steel for an evening of reckless abandon. Among them they were wearing the entire Wal-Mart collection, and enough make-up for half a dozen junior proms. Perfume hung thick enough to violate the Geneva Convention. Stale cigarette smoke swirled in lazy eddies around the light bulbs, filtering their incandescence and giving the place the furtive air of a floating crap game.

Play was controlled from a low wooden platform at the far end of the room. A middle-aged man and a younger woman stood one on either side of a cylindrical tumbler cage half full of numbered ping-pong balls. The man spun the cage with a fluid, habitual motion. He was lean, long-waisted, flat-shouldered, with oval brown eyes and curved nostrils that gave his rounded face a shopworn look of Latin sensuality. It was a look the housewives might like. They had probably seen a lot of it. His brown suit looked like it had been to so many of these soirees that it could come on its own if he was ever sick and had to miss a night. He spoke over the light clatter of tumbling balls and the undertones of feminine noise, in a dry voice that reminded me of dice being snicked across felt by a rattan stick.

"Watch-your-cards," he called. "Tu-welve dif-frunt ways to win on each and ev-ery card. Watch-your-cards."

The cage stopped tumbling and the woman, a slim blonde of twenty in an off-the-shoulder frock, took the numbered ball out of the automatic pickup and handed it to the caller.

"N-thirty-four," he announced. "Your number is N-thirty-four."

The blonde stepped back past a stair-step display holding prizes ranging from cheap electric clocks to a small toaster oven. She used a short pole to flip the N-34 plaque on a large marker board that formed the backdrop for the activity on stage. She was back standing by the cage in time for the next spin.

It was all laid out and choreographed as precisely as a television game show. It would have to be. Television had spoiled the suckers. If you didn't package the excitement just the way they wanted it, they'd stay home and watch *Wheel of Fortune*.

"Would you like to buy a card, sir?" a small voice inquired.

A pale, petite woman stood at my elbow. She looked like she might be a minister's wife. Her smile was tentative. They probably didn't get many cigar smokers in Sunday school. I was counting on them not knowing what to do with one when they did.

"Would you like to buy a card?" she repeated, now that she had my attention. She held one out; a professional job with sliding covers over the number windows.

"I'm lookin' for my old lady," I growled at her.

Her smile flickered like a dying candle in a stiff breeze. "Do-do you mean your wife?"

"Where's she at?"

She took a closer look at me, trying to place me and not having any luck. "I-I'm not sure I know her. Is something wrong?"

I snatched the cigar out of my mouth and stared at her. I all but yelled, "Wrong?" then quieted my voice to a wise, conspiratorial rumble. "Look lady, this is my bowling night, see? Only tonight one of the guys ain't feelin' so good, so we don't stop off for a quick one after, like usual. So what do you suppose I find when I get home?"

Before she had a chance to answer, I was brandishing my cigar at her and snarling indignantly.

"I'll tell you what. The kids up lookin' at TV past their bed time, not a goddamn beer in the house and they say their old lady's off playin' bingo. With my hard-earned bread, she's playin' lousy bingo. Now what the hell kinda deal is that?"

A biddy at one of the back tables shushed me. Others craned their necks to check a number that my noise had made them miss. The minister's wife made some jerky movements with her mouth. She looked all over the room, frantically, as if hoping to see her husband somewhere. Fat chance. He'd be off writing the sermon or reading the pronouncements. The sordid details of funding the good works were best left to those of a more worldly persuasion.

The woman ventured, "Well, are-are you sure she came here?"

I had spotted Jean LaBostrie by that time, perched precariously on the end of a crowded bench two tables down.

"That's what the kids said. She probably ducked in the john when she seen me. She's gotta come out sometime. I'm campin' right here until she does."

I marched over and planted myself against the wall a few feet behind Jean's table. The minister's wife stood perfectly still, watching me warily. She wanted badly to go for help, but was afraid of what I might do if she left me alone. At length, when I hadn't done anything worse than a little glaring, she went back and sat on a folding chair beside a card table in a rear corner. She watched me intermittently, between stints at sorting the contents of a small cash box. She was separating food stamps from the money and hiding the stamps under a plastic coin tray.

Jean had bought a card, but she wasn't paying any attention to it. She hadn't taken her coat off. The collar was still turned up against the hard-sprayed perfection of her hairdo. She fingered a pair of dark gloves impatiently. Each time a new number was called, her eyes would dart expectantly around the room and return frustrated when nothing happened.

The fact that she wasn't playing wasn't hurting her chances of winning. Her card had been adopted by the woman next to her; an intense septuagenarian already moving tissue boned fingers over five cards of her own with the speed and accuracy of a welding machine. A night of that kind of play could take a nice bite out of a Social Security check. At a glance, the old lady was ignoring winning combinations to try to black one of the cards out before anyone else completed a line. I had read somewhere that was the big casino in bingo. Like most big casinos, it came complete with a set of prohibitive odds.

On the next number a high voice across the room shrieked, "Bingo!"

The noise level went up twenty decibels. Jean gathered up her gloves, purse and umbrella and came over to stand by my wall while the high voice excitedly verified her line. Composure and poise were habit with Ms. LaBostrie. Only her fine almond eyes bridled at the wait. They were larger than eyes were normally allowed to be, full of quiet determination and maddeningly secure in a consciously chosen level of innocence that coolly dared anyone to try to take advantage of it. They glanced at me once, without recognition and with some distaste.

I didn't need to wonder why. My cigar was beginning to get to me, too. It tasted like the tobacco had been grown downwind from a tear gas factory.

The high voice finished calling back her numbers. She was probably a regular. She chose cash value instead of a cheap clock. The blonde did a runway promenade from the low stage to present her with the money, to a muted chorus of oohs and ahhs. The minister's wife was already circulating with fresh cards and the cash box.

Jean clicked rapidly up to the corner of the stage. The caller ambled over to meet her. His dry voice had taken on a Latin lilt to match the shopworn sensuality of his face.

"Hello, Baby," he purred. "It's been awhile."

Her voice was the husky contralto I remembered from the club. Tension made a riptide of the easy currents. "Where is he, Frank? I've got to see him. I called his house, but there was no answer."

"You mean Brixner?" Frank put a little disappointment into his features. "So he's the one that brings you around. And here I figured it was me."

"Where is he?" she repeated impatiently.

"Still making the rounds, I guess. He was here for fifteen minutes about an hour ago. I got to run some crap up to his place later. He'll be there then."

She muttered something that looked on her lips like "Damnit!" Then she said, "All right, thanks, Frank."

"Say, maybe afterwards you and me could…"

She left him standing there with his mouth working and words coming out and clicked rapidly past me and out the door. Frank shrugged his flat shoulders, gave me an incurious glance and went back to the marker board to reset the plaques for the next game.

I gave Jean thirty seconds' head start and went after her. She was down the street opening her car door when I came out of the lit-up church. The wind had lost some of its gustiness without losing any of its strength or its chill. Black clouds scudded across the night sky. Holly hedges along the block rattled and rustled.

I got rid of my cigar and kept to the restless shadows, hurrying to reach the Porsche. Jean had to do a little jockeying to get her Honda U-turned between cars parked on either side of the narrow street. I was able to fire my engine and back down to the corner before she was up to speed. I lined myself up and accelerated after her receding taillights. She led me back downtown, where she parked in the garage and fought the wind across to the Crown Colony.

I circled the block and parked on a side street with my nose pointed at the garage. Next time I would be ready to turn whichever way she did. I switched on the radio and settled to wait her out.

Chapter 5

Gale force wind was an icy whistle at the window edges. Accident location warnings, trees blocking roads and downed power lines elbowed everything else out of the eleven o'clock news. Football scores were a cursory footnote for anyone who had spent the weekend in suburban Katmandu. An outraged editorial on the possibility that California's lax voter registration laws had opened the door to massive election fraud convinced me to shut it off.

It looked like Jean had come back to the club to do a late show. That gave me some time to kill. I rolled down my cuffs, buttoned all my stray buttons, crawled back into my tie, suit coat and raincoat and climbed out of the car. Loose bits of paper trash skated past like tumbleweeds on the sidewalk. Two couples struggled along with heads down; women huddled close to men for warmth. I was shivering when I closed myself into a phone booth on a bank mall.

There were an even dozen Brixners listed within range of the books. I ruled out Mrs. Astrid C. and Julianne. The barman in a nearly deserted cocktail lounge across the street sold me a couple of dollars worth of change and I came back to try the other ten. Eight sleepy voices told me there was no Jean LaBostrie at that number and no, they didn't know anyone by that name. A fast hand on the receiver prong spared me any slanderous remarks about my ancestors. A ninth voice sounded alert and fairly pleasant, with a television laugh track in the background. He told me confidently that Jean LaBostrie was the French pirate who sold New Orleans to Thomas Jefferson. He wanted to know what contest his answer had won.

The only Brixner who didn't answer was a Mr. Walter O., who lived at 16854 Half Moon Lane. I hadn't the foggiest idea where that was. I tried his number again to make sure I had dialed correctly, then wrote the address. I fought my way back to the car with the skirts of my raincoat whipping and flying.

Within minutes the last stray car on the street started up and left me alone. By midnight pedestrian traffic was down to occasional stragglers headed across from the Crown Colony to the garage. Jean made the trip at twelve five. I couldn't tell from her movements whether she was still in a hurry, or just trying to keep from being blown to Encino. I started the Porsche when she disappeared into the garage. Her Honda nosed out in another minute and turned right. I fell in two blocks back. It wasn't much use trying to keep any of the sparse traffic between us. I was satisfied to have the police busy elsewhere. A brace of sports models running fifteen miles over the limit was red meat to any city cruiser.

Alvarado put us on the Glendale Freeway and that let us off out on Foothill Boulevard. There was rain in the air, but it hadn't made up its mind yet. One minute the wipers had work to do, the next they were scraping bone dry glass. Somewhere before we got out to San Fernando we left the boulevard and started climbing a dark, snaky ribbon of asphalt called Holland Canyon Drive. There was no traffic at all. I gave Jean a one-curve lead. We twisted past lonely private road entrances marked by hooded sets of mailboxes. Far above, dim enclaves of exclusive homes were cantilevered out from the steep hillside, grotesque gargoyle shapes lurking against the night sky. We kept climbing until we ran out of hillside above, and the scattered enclaves obscured themselves in the trees below. I rounded the thousandth curve and almost ran up Jean's tailpipe.

Her brake lights blazed like roman candles as she slowed for a sharp right turn. There was nothing for me to do but keep my foot on it, swing around her and keep going. I caught a glimpse of a sign as I passed. Half Moon Lane. A glow coming faintly up through the trees told me there were houses down in that direction. Two curves up I killed my lights and crept back dark.

Half Moon Lane fell away steeply from Holland Canyon Drive. I eased down the grade in first gear so I wouldn't have to show any brake lights. The narrow paving flattened in a gradual curve that took me around parallel to the hillside. My suspension creaked over something that felt like a speed bump. A dark house as hunched and angular as a nesting pterodactyl clung to a steep yard above. It watched me slip past with a vacant reptilian malevolence in its glass eyes. The scaly sheen of a tile roof snaked along the curve of the lane below. Across that, under a wild, cloud-blown sky, was a night-lit panorama of the Valley that had made everything up here worth building.

Further along a solitary carriage lamp burned against a brick facade above the road, flickering when the wind whipped the intervening vegetation. Its illumination diffused down through exotic landscaping and found Jean's Honda sitting dark beside the road. She wasn't making any move to get out. I switched off my engine. The right side tires crunched quietly on soft gravel as I rolled to a stop at the edge of Half Moon Lane. I set the hand brake, cracked the window to get some air circulation and huddled in my overcoat to wait.

Time was on the graveyard shift. Minutes went by with the leaden slowness of pallbearers. A sudden crack like a rifle shot startled Jean and made her jerk erect inside her car. She calmed down when a flurry of noise told her a wind-broken branch was falling somewhere nearby.

I didn't know what was making her jumpy. I didn't know much of anything, except that we were waiting for a man named Walter O. Brixner who stayed out late, had some connection with charity bingo and lived in a house that could cost several times six figures. Jean undoubtedly knew him better, though not well enough to rate a key. So we waited.

I had a work car in which I usually did this kind of waiting. It was an old Volvo coupe that I bought for the comfortable seats, a little fidgeting room and a price I didn't mind risking in parts of town where you didn't slow down if you still had hubcaps. By twelve forty the classy close quarters of the Porsche had given me a roaring case of claustrophobia.

That was when the first hint of light danced in the upper branches of the trees. A car was turning down from Holland Canyon Drive. I slid as far under the wheel as I could. Light flooded through my rear window. It bobbed around negotiating the speed bump. A sleek new Jaguar sedan went by. The driver braked with a three cornered spray of red and turned up the steep drive of the house where Jean waited. She was already out of the Honda, fighting her umbrella. Mechanism whirred while she climbed a flight of stairs. One of two garage door mouths yawned open, swallowed the Jaguar and closed again. Jean went up through a gateway in the brick facade and got lost in the darkness behind. The neighborhood was still again. The activity had lasted only a minute and had no more effect than the spasmodic twitch of a sleeping cat's tail. The only visible change was the dull aura of a light someone had switched on in the back of the house.

Four pale flashes showed in quick succession behind the curtains in a front window. The hard hollow pops of four pistol shots reverberated out into the night. I had unfrozen myself and shouldered my door open before the wind whipped the last echo away down the canyon.

I was running with the wind slapping my coat collar into my face when Jean appeared at the door of her car. I hadn't been watching the stairs or listening to anything but the memory of the shots. She was inside with the engine running before I could think of anything to yell. She backed the car up the drive to reverse her direction. I plunged up into a yard of low shrubs and decorative boulders to cut her off. A full-grown Honda weighed almost a ton. I had never wrestled one barehanded before, but I had the idea in my head that I was going to stop this one. It didn't work out. Tough heather snarled my feet. I lost my footing on a boulder and hit the drive hard on one knee. Jean never saw me. She already had the car under way. The yard light showed grim concentration on her face. She accelerated away up

Half Moon Lane. Her suspension bottomed over the speed bump and the tires squeaked as they bit pavement again. After that there was only the rising whine of her engine fading up the hill.

I got up gingerly off my knee. It hurt, but it didn't seem to be bleeding, and for once the fall hadn't torn my trousers. I did a little limping to make sure the leg still worked, then settled down to some serious self pity. I was busy picking tiny pebbles out of the palms of my hands when a car door slammed in the distance. The sound came from the direction of Holland Canyon Drive. It caught me completely by surprise. A cold engine caught raggedly after a tortured burst on a wheezy starter. Lights showed in the treetops and began to move. A car went away down the Canyon to the grumbling accompaniment of an exhaust system that was still waiting for reincarnation. The only sound it left behind was the buffeting noise of the wind and the rustle and scrape of vegetation.

I finished brushing of my hands, crossed the drive and went up the stairs. I didn't hurry. My knee hurt, for one thing. But mostly I had a sick feeling that I was already so far behind whatever had happened that it wouldn't matter if I took the rest of the century to reach the house. The stairs brought me up through the brick facade into a small courtyard that held the front porch. Light came dimly from inside the rear of the house and leaked out around the weather stripping to tell me the front door was ajar. I pushed it open and stepped in.

The biting odor of burnt nitrocellulose was there to greet me. I pawed the wall and hit three light switches at once.

Chapter 6

Track lighting cast patterns of brilliance and shadow in a sunken living room. Walter O. Brixner had some money left over when he finished buying the house, and he hadn't spent it on a truckload of the latest high gloss particleboard. The closest thing to furniture was a nine foot ebony Steinway. It was propped open, with music on the trellis and a look of having been played since it arrived. The seating was limited to the cushions of a conversation pit in front of a black marble fireplace. The shelving was West African Iroko, and there was no more of it than was needed for ultra modern miniature stereo components. The only artwork was a framed print of two ducks in sunglasses sitting on a pile of money. It was titled *The Failure of Capitalism,* though I didn't know why. I would have traded places with either duck in a heartbeat.

I stood still, listening. One by one my ears sorted out the muted rush of the wind, the repetitious scrape of a branch on the roof shakes, the more monotonous cadence of a clock. Light leaked from the back of the house. It would be the light I saw come on before I heard the shots. I looked at my hand. It could have been steadier. I limped softly back along a dim hallway into a kitchen full of shadows and formless shimmering. The light came into there through a doorway. A man was sitting in the doorway.

The man was fifty something, medium size and tending to fat. One leg was thrust out in front of him, dressed in the pressed trousers of a charcoal suit, a black and red argyle sock and a black wing-tip shoe. He was sitting on the other leg. The leg under his buttocks unbalanced him, making him look like he wanted to fall over sideways. His shoulder, in a tan raincoat, was pressed against the doorjamb, keeping him upright. His head flopped over to one side, resting against the jamb. He had a round, soft face, with traces of pink in the cheeks. His fine-textured blond hair was cut short; it had started to recede at the temples. Vacant blue eyes stared at nothing through wire rimmed glasses that sat crookedly on the bridge of his nose. He looked like he might have come home drunk and just folded up, except that an irregular pattern of four holes was singed chest-high in his rain coat.

I made my way through a stench of recently burned powder, went down on one knee and felt for a neck artery. The flesh had gone flaccid and pulpy, not yet cold, but lacking the full warmth of life. There was a trace of dampness, but no trace of a pulse. His head rolled when I released his neck, his jaw slacked and a bit of fluid showed at the corner of his mouth. I didn't much like what I was doing.

I lifted his lapels. None of the four neat punctures in his white shirt had drained sufficiently for its stain to mingle with the stain of another, indicating that his heart had quit pumping before his lungs were fully collapsed and inward suction stopped. I extracted a wallet from his breast pocket. It hadn't been hit and there was no blood on it. Inside I found a driver's license, a social security card, a health of insurance card and a bank machine card. All in the name of Walter O. Brixner. I also found a dry cleaner's ticket, a block of four first class postage stamps and fifty-eight dollars cash. I didn't find any credit cards, which struck me as odd for a man of obvious financial standing. I also didn't find anything to tell me who or what Walter O. Brixner had been.

An old alligator briefcase lay on its side on the floor beside him. The case had popped open an inch or so. I put his wallet back and pried the briefcase open another inch for a peek inside. It was empty.

"All right, Mr. Brixner," I said, sounding almost as shaky as I felt. "Why were you lugging this old thing around? Did you have some-thing in it your visitor wanted? Or something you dropped off before you got here?"

Mr. Brixner didn't seem to think it was any of my business, but he didn't object to my looking around. The room he appeared to have come from was big enough to absorb a regulation billiard table without crowding the four stool plumbed-in bar. Light crept up from behind blond oak valences to reflect down from the white acoustical tile ceiling. Along the walls were framed ladies wearing the hairstyles and make up of the early sixties, and nothing else.

The only other door opened past a utility room to a two-car garage. Three liters of deep green Austin Healey roadster stared back at me from the near stall. The car was old only in design. The paint and tires were as fresh as the starch in tomorrow's shirt. That struck a sour note. The Healey's appeal was largely visceral. Even in its day, aficionados had regarded it as a close formation of outdated mechanical components better left to agricultural uses. It was definitely not a collector's item for a man of Brixner's disposable income. I wondered if the late Walter O. Brixner had spent his money preserving a piece of his past, or rebuilding the past the way he wished it had been.

Beside the Healey, dripping water and radiating the aroma of recent running, was the new Jaguar sedan. The Jaguar established Brixner's starting point. I closed the door from the garage and went over to investigate a flat round tin that lay on the bar, cocked up on the front padding. It was an unlabelled film can, cold to the touch, as if it hadn't been in the house long. It contained a metal reel of 16-millimeter footage that looked like it would run about twenty minutes. I found what it would run on by working a bifold door. The projector may have been a dinosaur, but it was every bit as complex and intimidating as the DVD players that now replaced its breed. It was pointed at the far end wall. I tried the first switch on the cabinet console. A motorized screen unrolled down from the valence across the room. I worked the next switch and sprocket covers released, mechanism hummed and a light gave me permission to 'Thread.' I was getting an inkling of how Doctor Frankenstein must have felt. It took me a few minutes to get the film into the machine in the proper pattern. I pushed a green button labeled 'Autostart.' Nothing happened for a couple of seconds. Then the room lights dimmed on their own. The projector bulb clicked on, the mechanism activated and a descending succession of numbers flickered on the screen.

The film would have been considered obscene when it was made, forty some years ago. Which made it pretty tame by modern standards. It was a silent format, in which an amply endowed young lady got mixed up in a game of strip poker with an obvious card cheat. All that was shown of the cheat was a pair of fast hands, French cuffs and a bit of coat sleeve. The viewer was supposed to put himself in the cheat's place and watch the lady lose her clothing, a piece at a time. I had seen versions of it when I was a kid in Hollenbeck. There was an all night grind house on a street of gin mills a couple of blocks from where I grew up. It was a place you could sneak into and hole up when the old man was on a tear and you couldn't go home. Any night but Friday. Friday was the night the college boys came down for a look, while we prowled their cars for beer money.

I snapped off the projector and got the lights on again. There were five film cans on individual shelves in a cabinet under the mechanism. From the neatly typed index of titles taped inside the door, they covered the approximate same subject matter as the one I had in the machine. Curiosity was natural enough in pimple-faced sophomores, but a man of Brixner's age taking that sort of thing seriously could be a sign of unpleasant problems.

I went out to the kitchen and put on the lights. Shadows and formless shimmering gelled into the symmetry of hardwood and appliance fronts. Whoever had shot Brixner had hidden behind a breakfast nook. One shiny brass cartridge casing had landed on the padding, another against the rubber cove molding where it met the floor. Both were from a .32 automatic. I left them where they had fallen. A dirty residue of footprints led me to broken glass scattered over the mottled gold Solarian just inside a rear door. I stepped gingerly and peered out the broken window. There was a steep hillside and probably a path up through the trees to Holland Canyon Drive. I didn't go out to make sure. The rest of the house needed checking.

The master bedroom had no women's clothing hanging in the dressing closet, none of the emergency supplies fast moving bachelors sometimes kept in the bathroom. The suite, in its color and appointments and the possessions that filled its storage areas, was entirely masculine. The remaining bedroom had been converted to an office. Books of every size and shape and binding were grouped by topic on floor to ceiling shelves. By far the largest group covered accounting, financial and tax subjects. The desk held a printing calculator and a microcomputer. Fireproof steel file cabinets flanked a squat, hulking Mosler safe. I tried the safe door and every drawer in the cabinets and the desk. Any secrets in them were locked up tighter than a sorority girl's diary. My last shot was the telephone. The red message light was on.

A man started in directly, without introducing himself. His voice had the tone quality of a block of suet being slapped onto a cutting board. He tried to hide his nerves by sounding mad.

"About that problem we had last month, Walt. The one you said wouldn't come up again. A broad he used to shack up with got a call. Somebody wants her to pass him a message. They'll pay any price for something called the Doomsday Book. What the goddamn hell's going on? Call me at Scheherazade's. Five five five eighty one oh six. Before midnight."

The machine shut itself off.

Offhand I could think of several conclusions to jump to, all of them probably wrong. The only thing that made sense was the caller's question. I decided I had better put it to Jean LaBostrie before I stuck my head any further into this business. I had to get my envelope out to check her address, so I wrote down the phone number of Scheherazade's, whatever that was. I went through the house wiping off fingerprints and turning out lights.

There were no sirens howling up the canyon to indicate that any of Brixner's neighbors had rolled over in bed and called the police. That made his death just a little uglier. It was already ugly enough. Home was supposed to be a place to feel safe and comfortable when you could take time off from arm wrestling the world for a living. There weren't supposed to be gunmen waiting for you in your kitchen.

Chapter 7

Jean LaBostrie had made it only as far as an orphan strip of chic storefronts hunkered at the bottom of Holland Canyon Drive. Her Honda was nosed in under a bit of neon romance (electric blue knight with a throbbing red lance and a foot on the neck of a heliotrope dragon who had fallen asleep with his pilot light on). I put my Porsche in the next stall and went into a combination restaurant and cocktail lounge. The restaurant was dark, closed off by a chain that looked heavy enough to raise a drawbridge. The Round Table Room might as well have been closed too. There weren't enough customers to slay the light bill. Jean sat alone in a high-backed booth. Her coat was still buttoned to her throat.

"I'm waiting for someone," she said when I slid in across from her. It sounded like something she had a lot of practice saying. She didn't bother to look up.

"Someone like the police?" I asked.

Startled almond eyes jumped to my face. They stayed only long enough to be sure they didn't know me, then dropped to read the business card I put on the table.

"So you're Henry Spain." She made it sound like something that slept under a damp rock.

"At least you've heard the name," I said, grateful for small favors.

She ignored me.

A bored cocktail waitress in a serving wench's costume paid us the obligatory visit. Jean's drink looked like a gin gimlet. She didn't like my asking the waitress to get her another, but she wasn't going to encourage conversation by arguing. I ordered a Bacardi and Coke for myself. The waitress went away. I went back to being ignored.

"I had the impression from Lipton you didn't mind him hiring me."

"He never told me."

"No?" I asked skeptically.

She looked up from her drink and gave her head a careless toss. "Oh, he told me I'd have to sign a waiver of privacy so he could check my background. I thought he meant seeing if I had good credit and stuff like that. I didn't expect to have a detective turned loose on me."

"All right, that's between you and Lipton. You and I have to talk about what happened tonight."

"How did you find me here, anyway?"

"I happened to see your car when I stopped for the turn at the bottom of the canyon road."

"What were you doing up there?"

"Following you," I said.

It was like telling her she had bad breath. It was something she hadn't been aware of and didn't want to hear. It didn't help that I was a complete stranger.

"Ever since you scooted out to the bingo game," I said. "Remember the cigar?"

Her expression took on a quality of resigned horror, as if she recognized me as a supporting lizard in the cast of some recurring nightmare.

"You said something about the police...?"

"I thought you might have stopped here to call them. I guess you didn't."

She made it official with a tense, tiny, shamefaced movement that was more like shivering than shaking her head.

"Listen, Jean-do you mind if I call you Jean?-I need to know what went on in that house. I saw you go up and let yourself in. You..."

"I didn't!" she blurted. The throaty vehemence of her voice startled her. She tried again. She managed a nicely modulated tone, but she let words tumble out, falling over one another: "The door wasn't closed-it was closed, but not properly-ajar-it was ajar. I was inside. I was folding my umbrella down when I heard-did I scream? Did you hear me scream?"

"No, you didn't scream."

"I remember my mouth was open. I thought the noise would shake the house apart. My ears were full of ringing. I was afraid I couldn't hear if I was screaming or not."

"You weren't," I assured her pleasantly. "I would have heard you if you were."

"Yes, you were following me." She mulled the idea over while she tried a sip of her frosty gimlet. She made a sour face at the glass. "Following people around and spying on them. God, how does anyone get into a rotten business like that?"

"I grew up in a rotten neighborhood. Why was it so important for you to see Brixner tonight?"

She took her first close look at me. "It bothers you, doesn't it? Talking about yourself."

"Jean, can we focus on Walter Brixner?"

"You go around snooping on other people all the time. How come you're afraid to talk about yourself?"

The waitress returned and set coasters and drinks in front of us. Jean sat perfectly still and watched me pay for them. She probed my face with soft, curious eyes. It made me more uncomfortable than it should have.

"An investigator for one of the big agencies caught me one night when a safe job went bad. He needed some eyes in tough town. I was three months back from Vietnam. I knew a lot of naughty people, either personally or by sight and reputation. The investigator gave me a choice. Go to jail or work for him. Detective work turned out to be more interesting than sweating half the night in the back of some hock shop on the off chance there might be a couple of hundred dollars in the box, if I could get it open. End of biography."

"You don't mean that you were a safe burglar?" she marveled. "And that man gave you a chance to change your life?"

"He gave me a chance to matriculate to strike-breaking and industrial espionage."

"What did your friends do? The naughty ones, I mean."

"They went on being naughty." They were dead now, all of them that I knew about.

"But they stayed sort of friends with you?"

"You can turn off the melodrama, Jean. I don't mind you stalling a little. You've had a bad shock. It may take some time to get yourself organized. That's fine. So long as we eventually get back to Brixner. And why you went to see him."

She drew herself up as haughty as a soap opera debutante. "All right, if you must know the worst. I was Walter's mistress. I saw a coat in Nordstrom's today. I was going to persuade him to buy it for me."

I shook my head. Not very energetically, because it wasn't a very energetic lie. "Brixner's thrills were the kind he could keep on celluloid."

"Pardon me?"

"He never showed you his movies? Or tried to audition you for burlesque?"

"No." There was a hint of impending laughter behind the amazement in her voice. The laughter was gone when she said, "You mean Walter was a...?"

"I think the word is voyeur."

Her reactions seemed legitimate. First a little stunned, the way people get when first told they had been close to something unpleasant or dangerous without ever realizing it. Then remembering little things that hadn't seemed important at the time, but took on a whole new meaning in retrospect. Finally a cold-blooded decision that it must have been true. All without a word from her.

"He's dead, isn't he?" she asked. "You went in and saw him, didn't you?"

"Yes, he's dead."

She nibbled morosely at her drink. I asked, "What was said between Brixner and the killer before the shots?"

"Nothing." She shook her head.

"Are you sure?"

"I didn't hear anything. Just someone who sounded like Walter moving around in the party room. I was folding my umbrella down. I never knew anything was wrong until the shots. There were flashes reflected all over the walls, and the noise. I thought they were happening all around me." She shivered at the memory.

"Did you get a look at the killer?"

"I was frightened. I ran out and down the stairs." She considered her drink and decided against it. She worried her lower lip with gleaming teeth and looked shamefaced into my eyes. "I'm in some trouble, aren't I?"

"Some," I agreed. "How much depends on who killed Brixner, and why, and what your connection with him was."

The unconscious chewing she was doing on her lip dawned on her. She closed her mouth abruptly, like a child hiding a bad habit. An embarrassed flush flirted in the hollows of her cheeks. She poked around in her purse, brought out a compact and inspected the damage, using the mirror inside the lid. She went to work with a tube of lip-gloss, as if repairing her make-up was the most important thing she would do all night.

I wondered if her experience hadn't shaken her more than she knew. I tried my Bacardi and Coke. The drink hadn't been that muscular to begin with, and the melting ice didn't help any.

"I don't know much about Brixner," I said. "I know he must have had money, and some connection with charity bingo. He had a lot of books on accounting, but no membership cards for the professional societies accountants usually belong to. And he had some odd habits. That's all I know about him. I need to know more, and I need to know how you were connected with him."

"I used to work for him." She put her compact away. "Part time. Sort of."

"Doing what?"

"Bingo hostessing. That's what they call it. Hostess. You help the caller and help sell cards and give away toasters to whoever wins. Stuff like that."

"How long did you work for him?"

"Well, it's not like a steady job. It's something singers and actresses and models and stuff do when they don't have any engagements. It's like supermarket openings or boat shows."

"Did Brixner hold the license to operate the bingo games? Or did he work for someone else who did?"

She was blank.

"How were you paid? Cash or check?"

"Uh…check."

"Was there a company imprint on the check? An individual name? What?"

"I…" She glanced fearfully at me from behind a contrite little smile. "I really, truly don't remember. It's like one Sunday I spent fourteen hours giving out hot dogs and sodas at a car place and their name was plastered all over and two days later someone asked me where I'd been and I couldn't remember. All those jobs are the same after a while. You just don't pay any attention any more. Everybody behaved like Walter had lots of authority and he was the one you had to see if you wanted to get on the schedule and be a hostess, but that's really all I can say."

"Why did you want to see him tonight?"

"It wasn't anything important."

"That isn't what you told Frank at the church."

The contrite little smile flickered out. "You talked to Frank Murillo?"

I made a mental note of the name. "I didn't have to. I was close enough to hear most of your conversation."

"How come you followed me? Did he tell you to? Mr. Lipton?"

I shook my head. "You left the Crown Colony right on my heels, like Old Nick himself was after you. I wonder now if that was a coincidence."

"I beg your pardon?"

"You said Lipton didn't tell you he'd hired me. No one else at the club knew about it until I showed up tonight. You heard it from one of them while I was there. The first thing you did was try to call Brixner. When you couldn't reach him, you hustled out to try to find him."

She considered me with troubled eyes. I asked, "What did you have to see him about?"

"About a job," she said after a minute. "I wanted to get on the bingo schedule, be a hostess."

"You have a singing engagement," I reminded her. "And a recording offer."

"I-I didn't know if I wanted them. I'm a very private person. When I heard you were hired, I sort of panicked. I just wanted to get out from under everything."

"Wasn't that a decision you'd have to discuss with your agent? Or your manager?"

"I don't have any of those."

"Jean, you're headlining in a posh club in a big city. That's a long way from the chicken ranch in Sausalito. You didn't make it in one jump. You did a lot of weekenders in places like this to pick up the stage manner and polish it takes to be where you are now. And you picked up one or more agents along the way. You had to in order to get the bookings you needed."

"It was a drugstore in Stockton," she said.

"Who were your agents?"

"I fronted a rock and roll nostalgia band in San Francisco. I just worked where the band worked, like everyone else. They didn't really need a singer, though. Just someone who could do a reasonable imitation of *Latin Lupe Lu* and *Forty Days* and stuff. So I quit and came down here."

"Where you also didn't need an agent?"

She didn't seem to mind my skeptical tone of voice. I was kidding myself when I thought she would even notice. With her looks, she probably had to make a second career of not noticing men, or anything they said or did. I watched her take her sweet time draining the last sip from under the frost in her drink.

"Jean, I know you don't have to answer my questions, but what are you going to do when the police start asking?"

"Can't we sort of report Walter anonymously or something? The police must get a lot of that. People who can't talk to them."

"They're going to interview everyone Brixner knew," I told her. "They're going to concentrate on casual acquaintances, like you, because there is an excellent chance that one of them killed him."

"How do you know that?"

"The killer didn't know Brixner's schedule, or that he would be out tonight. He was waiting in the house long enough for his car to cool all the way down. Even if the police aren't told that, their technicians will find enough subtle indications to put them on the right track."

"Why would a casual acquaintance kill Walter?"

"For the same reason a close relative or a perfect stranger would kill him. The killer has the idea murder will solve some problem. The idea may be coldly rational or totally crazy. It may be his own inspiration or he may get it from someone else. He may think about it for two seconds or two years. But he will think about it to the exclusion of all logic and common sense, until he does something about it. It's not until he's sitting in a police interrogation room afterward, giving a lame recital of the facts, that he realizes how stupid it all was."

Jean's eyes filled with wonder and admiration, and sudden hope. "You really know a lot about that stuff. Couldn't you find out who killed Walter?"

"Jean, whoever killed Brixner waited several hours and shot him cold, four times, without a word. That's not someone I'd care to meet."

Her eyes were very disappointed in me. I was afraid she wouldn't be any more impressed with a couple of middle aged County detectives. As bad as caseloads were, the Police couldn't afford to sit still for the kind of nonsense Jean had been giving me. She was a cinch to have us both locked up in investigative detention before morning.

"All right," I conceded, sounding almost as worried as I was. "Maybe we'd better forget the police for now."

"You won't tell them about me?"

"I won't tell them anything. They aren't fools. If you aren't prepared to come entirely clean with them, the next best thing to do is duck them entirely. Brixner will be found soon enough, and I don't imagine the trail will get much colder than it is already. When they do question you, be courteous and answer in as few words as possible. Stick to the truth. If they press you on sensitive details, tell them you forget. This is a work night. Work nights all look alike after a while. Give them the business about the hot dogs and the sodas if you want. Just for God's sake don't make up any lies to tell them."

"I won't," she promised, too easily.

"When will it be convenient for us to talk?"

"What have we just been doing?"

"I mean about your background, which I'm supposed to be reviewing."

Her shoulders squirmed noncommittally. She collected her purse and gloves. I said, "I've been a long time in the investigation business, Jean. I'll find everything eventually, with or without your cooperation. It's to your advantage to make sure I hear things from your point of view."

"If you're that good," she said demurely, "my point of view won't make any difference."

She knew even more answers than I had when I was twenty-four. I had known too damned many. I put a hand across the table and tugged her purse away before she could make it out of the booth. I opened it and stuck my business card inside. Tucked nose down in a side pocket, half buried under some Kleenex, was a miniature automatic pistol. A hammerless .25 Browning. It would be in working order. I had one at home that had survived two decades of abuse and still shot four inch groups at twenty five yards. I shut the purse and handed it back.

"My home and business numbers are on the card. Call me anytime you feel like improving your lie. Or need any help."

"I actually have to dial?" she asked with mock surprise. "You mean you haven't got my phone tapped yet?"

She slid out of the booth and left with a quiet husky triumphant laugh in her throat.

Laughing at men probably ranked among the more commonplace events in Jean's day. I sat and brooded about it anyway. A career of being used as a cutting edge for other people's schemes had left me touchy on the subject, so I thought of reasons not to go to the police even if she had wanted me to. I was already late, to begin with. Then, too, a witness with liquor on his breath claiming to know as little as I did could raise eyebrows even if he had checked in promptly. Jean getting cute with a couple of homicide detectives could really put the icing on things.

Those reasons, plus my decided lack of influence with the license review board, might have made lying low a gamble worth taking. Except that lying low wasn't what I had in mind.

Chapter 8

I had it in my head that I had put Jean on the spot. It didn't seem to matter that I hadn't asked her to chase around and walk in on a murder just because I'd shown up at the Crown Colony. It also didn't seem to matter that the police would take an immediate interest in anyone who showed any interest at all in the late Walter O. Brixner, that I could get myself into no end of trouble just trying to learn how much trouble Jean was in. It was up to me to straighten things out.

The waitress picked up the remains of Jean's drink. "Maybe she wasn't your type."

I looked up at a woman about half way through her thirties and still in the running. She lounged against the end of the opposite bench in a pose that showed me more thigh than her serving wench's costume was intended to reveal.

"Don't get the wrong idea. Two miles of so-called adult apartments went up down the road. I don't get to talk to many people over twenty five."

I showed a little polite sympathy. "You don't attract any trade from up the canyon?"

"Me personally? Or the establishment?"

"Either way."

"I've been invited on a few field trips. The restaurant gets most of the traffic." She gave me a friendly frown. "Is this casual conversation we're making?"

"Strictly business."

She read the card I handed her. "I didn't know you needed a detective to get divorced these days."

"I'm just doing a background investigation. Credit check, talk to business associates, neighbors, that sort of thing."

"Which was the fox?"

"Ever see her here before? Alone or with anyone?"

She thought a minute before she shook her head. "But it doesn't mean anything. Privacy with a big 'P' is the word in the canyons." She glanced away at a small noise. "Want another drink before I give last call."

"Sorry," I said, wondering why opportunity always picked the wrong time to knock. "My night isn't quite finished."

I lived on a quiet cul-de-sac in the Valley, in a house I bought years ago as a government repossession when the aerospace industry bottomed out so I would never have to move again. I had spent all my years as a kid moving every time the old man got his back up at some union poobah and couldn't get work. I wasn't smart enough to know that the mortgage payments that kept me broke then would be less than the rent on a decent apartment today.

I packed my equipment into a workout bag, filled a thermos with coffee, cranked up the Volvo and headed back toward Holland Canyon. Late or not, tonight was going to be my only shot at Brixner's files. Once the body was found and the police had come and gone, the neighbors would forget all about privacy with a big 'P'. They would jump for the phone every time the slightest murmur came out of that house of murder.

Tonight the citizens of Half Moon Lane still slept as virginal as moths in their double-wall cocoons. I went down with no lights, eased over the speed bump and drifted to a stop below Brixner's. After a minute of listening to wind savaged vegetation to make sure I hadn't attracted any attention, I wrestled my bag out of the trunk and lugged it up the concrete stairs. A flagstone path led around to the rear of the house. Broken glass in the kitchen door hung my jacket up a couple of times before I was able to fumble it open. I snapped the light on as quickly as I could locate a wall switch. Searching a murdered man's files with his body still undiscovered on the premises wasn't a job I wanted to linger over.

My glance at the doorway where I had found Walter Brixner was automatic. So automatic that it took a second for the truth to register. The doorway was still there, but Brixner was gone. I took the shock very nicely. No stupid staring. No sagging mouth. All perfectly normal. Except that my body temperature felt about ten degrees colder than usual.

The briefcase and shell casings were gone too. None of the four bullets that hit Brixner had penetrated to the wall or doorjamb. None of the wounds had drained sufficient blood to leave traces of mayhem. I followed recently beaten down carpet nap through Brixner's play room to the garage door. Brixner wasn't in the garage. He must have been dragged out to a car parked in the driveway. That would have been a struggle for Jean or any other woman. The killer was also unlikely, since he had already made a clean getaway. Whoever it was had needed an excellent reason. Failing to report a fatal shooting was serious enough. Packing up the mortal remains and the rest of the evidence and driving off with it was a major no-no.

It occurred to me that the scavenger hunt might not have been limited to the immediate area of the shooting. I took my equipment back to Brixner's office. The safe, files and desk were still locked. I couldn't remember whether I had left the swivel chair back where it was now, or tucked into the kneehole of the desk. I tried the phone. The message I heard earlier had been erased, the tape reset to zero. A little voice told me I had just shown up a week late for a six-day bicycle race.

I set the UHF monitor to the County Police frequency and poured myself a cup of coffee. The desk lock was an old lever tumbler that took patient fiddling with delicate tools. I was far enough out of practice to feel like a middleweight contender doing needlepoint. The clutter in the drawers included quick reference cards for computer software, a dog-eared amortization book, insurance short rate tables, tax information and depreciation schedules, personal and household business including checking account records showing a current balance close to five figures, and a leather bound degree. The degree was an MBA in accounting. Brixner was a Harvard man.

The locks protecting his file cabinets were straightforward pin tumblers that fell open when I waved a riffle pick at them. The drawers were crammed with neatly labeled manila folders. I started through them, stopping once to refill my coffee cup and once to get an earful of whether the police had finally trapped the Dental Floss Bandit, who had developed a unique method of getting around cheap motel locks. They hadn't, so I went back to what was developing as the bookkeeping for a number of separate bingo operations. There were journals of cash receipts and disbursements, prize inventories, vouchers, charity proceeds, all controlled by a numerical indexing system that ranked with oriental religion for inscrutability. I found a certificate stating that the records had passed an audit by the State.

The last thing I found was a black vinyl binder holding three computer data storage tapes. Brixner's desktop model didn't have a tape drive. It did have password protection though, and it shut itself off after my first half dozen guesses flopped.

I hadn't found any trace of a payroll system, which probably meant Jean had been paid through an independent labor contractor. I also hadn't found either a general ledger or a check register. The general ledger was the book that organized things in the terms that mattered; profit, loss and residual equity. The safe was the only place left to look.

Two thirds of all the safes in existence could be opened with no trouble at all. The half-wits who owned or used them got tired of forgetting the combination, so they scratched it in some clever place close by. I spent ten minutes probing nooks and crannies in the surrounding woodwork with a penlight. I was out of luck. Brixner was no half-wit. The *Safe and Vault Manual* listed a double column of trial combinations for that particular lock and model. None of them worked either.

In spite of the gadgets TV writers dream up, there is no reliable way to open a precision built lock by sound or manipulation. That left butchery. It took me thirty-five nervous minutes to drill the dynamite trigger and punch the curb out. It didn't help my disposition when I finally got the son of a bitch open and saw it was empty.

A yellowing instruction booklet for a compact check-protecting machine was crumpled in a back corner. There were three vertical divisions on one side, where three large books could have been stored. They were empty all the way back. A lack of dust accumulation indicated recent use for all three. Three storage spaces where there should be only two books bothered me. Keeping an extra book, especially if that book turned out to be a general ledger, was outstandingly poor accounting practice. It made it look like you were keeping one book to show the auditors and another for the real figures. Which raised the possibility that the late Walter O. Brixner may have been more than a little bent. He may have been crooked enough to pull corks. Which, in turn, might explain how he had come by the kind of friends who wouldn't want his body or the contents of his safe found by the police.

I thought of all those things, but I didn't know what I was going to do about them at four in the morning. I replaced Brixner's files, all but the black vinyl binder of computer tapes. Getting the contents printed off seemed a faint hope after seeing the empty innards of the safe, but I was too drained to fight the habits of endless years of plugging away after every available lead.

I was also beginning to hallucinate.

On the way home I met a man who leered at me through crooked glasses and told me to watch his house while he went to a movie. I went to a movie. I sat in the back row and peered at a microscopic screen miles away and tried to tell if it was a girlie movie. I wanted the screen to get bigger. It got bigger, and wouldn't stop getting bigger. I was trapped in my seat. The screen grew and loomed until it was all around me. A dancing girl spun out in a swirl of gossamer veils and announced with a wild, mocking laugh that she was Scheherazade.

Chapter 9

Next morning's air was as still as a deadbeat listening for footsteps on the stairs. A cold shower cleared the cobwebs. My breakfast newspaper was full of last night's storm, next week's elections and nothing on Walter O. Brixner. It was probably too early to expect anything, unless someone had been caught playing funeral procession with his remains. I stuck last year's reverse directory CD into the old laptop I kept at home. The number I had taken down from Brixner's tape machine actually did belong to something called Scheherazade's.

The address was six stories of grimy brick a couple of streets off Alameda. Most of the ground floor was a cold storage locker fronted by a faded, jaunty penguin tipping his top hat to three lanes of industrial traffic that had long since quit paying attention. The rest was taken up by a narrow lobby that smelled as old as King Tut's tomb. Once it may have been almost as fancy. A ribbon of mosaic still fringed the worn floor. There was artistry in the wrought iron balustrade of a staircase in the dimness in back.

I was the only one in the elevator wearing a coat. A woman with a mechanical pencil stuck into a wiry perm got off on the second floor where a damaged-freight brokerage was making the usual telephone and office machine noise against a cavernous backdrop of crates and impromptu wholesale displays. On three a custodian was swallowed up in the din of a printing plant. Four was full of intense Asian women and the clatter of sewing machines. Two white men got on blaming each other for late deliveries and rode up to a folding and packing operation on five. The building had the general atmosphere of considerable money being made on a regular basis without much fanfare. An exotic name like Scheherazade's didn't seem to fit in. Maybe that was why no one had bothered to letter it on the pebbled glass of the one door off the minuscule elevator lobby on six.

The door let me into a dingy office. The furniture was as old as the building, and had fought in both World Wars. At the moment it wasn't doing anything but providing storage space for several bundles of morning mail, most of which looked like hand printed merchandise orders, and support for a computer printer with tractor fed orders spilling out the back and fan folded neatly on the floor. They had probably originated from a remote 800 number.

There was a door open in back. My, "Hello!" got lost down the narrow aisles of something that looked like the rear of a discount auto parts store. I never heard from it again. Scheherazade's, if that was what this was, seemed to be as empty as the Sultan's aphrodisiac dispenser on Sunday morning. I could hear the Southern Pacific Railroad yards back behind all the rows of shelves and dividers and bins. I decided to take a look, in case someone was there and the noise had drowned my voice. I didn't get far.

A black man headed my way from the opposite end of the aisle. He was as tall as a freeway lamp post, and had about the same build and candle power rating. The electric bill on his iridescent pink shirt could have bankrupted a small municipality. A skinny gold belt held up a pair of black trousers from a retro zoot suit. A lime green scarf was knotted at his throat. His hat had a wide floppy brim and a crown that would have come close to the hanging fluorescent fixtures even if he hadn't been wearing patent leather elevator shoes under his voluminous cuffs. With his outfit, he didn't need a gun to attract attention. He had one anyway. A pocket sized blue steel automatic that was probably all he could afford after the down payment on his wardrobe. I could think of several reasons for it to be a .32. I couldn't think of anything particularly brilliant to do about it at the moment.

I stood perfectly still. I said, "Hello," again, in the heartiest voice I could manage.

He didn't say anything. He was halfway down the aisle now, about a dozen yards away, and not coming very fast. He took one ponderous step at a time, dragging the soles of his shoes on the aggregate floor. His face was pale; the color of creamed coffee. His eyes, under the brim of his hat, were white all around tiny dark pupils. I was no longer sure they could see me. I was becoming sure something was seriously wrong. The gun slipped out of his hand, leaving the pink insides of his long fingers showing, and clattered at his feet. He didn't seem to notice it. He took one more difficult step and couldn't take another, though he looked like he wanted to.

He said something extremely unpleasant in a harsh whisper. It was all I ever heard him say. Something happened in his throat to choke off the whisper.

He was in no hurry to fall. First he swayed. Then his knees buckled. At the same time his body pitched forward, rigidly, like a fresh cut tree. I had plenty of time to maneuver into position to catch him. It didn't do me any good. The instant I had him under the shoulders, the illusion of rigidity disappeared. His head flopped as though mounted on a lifeless spring, bounding and rolling against my chest, and pushed the felt crown of his hat into my face. His long body sagged under a monumental weight that two of me couldn't have held off the floor. I went down on one knee lowering his head and shoulders to the floor.

I could see viscous blood welling out of two small puncture wounds in his throat. It saturated the lime green scarf and dripped from there to the floor. The pressure and flow slacked visibly. In less than a minute it was a lifeless trickle. I blew the air out of my lungs in a hopeless gust and stood up.

At the far end of the aisle a door swung idly on loose hinges. I wasn't surprised to find it led to a fire escape. Or that whoever had used the fire escape was long gone. I was surprised when I heard another door back in the direction I had come from.

When I got there a young woman in an express company uniform was loading heavy cartons onto a hand truck. They probably had a gorilla out picking up birdseed.

"You ought to talk to the union about that," I said.

"When? They're only in town to get their laundry done between conventions." She didn't look around. She had the sliding door to a wood-floored freight elevator wedged open. I had the idea she wasn't planning to stay long.

"Do you suppose you could knock off for a minute?" I asked.

She knocked off. She put a fist on either hip. She gave me a look that went through me like a Zulu spear, and stuck out a foot in back.

"Look, Turkey, schlepping dildoes and dirty movies may make you a big man in the Chamber of Commerce, but it does nothing for me."

"Fine"" I said in a voice that was just as crisp and a lot more brutal. "But right now there's a dead man back amongst the erotica. I'm going to call the police about it. You stay here. They'll want to talk to you."

The blood was draining out of her face when I stepped into the office. I hadn't been eighteen for more years than I cared to think about. I had long since run out of patience with women trying to protect their pristine bodies from my imaginary advances. The information that Scheherazade's was a mail order porno outlet held limited fascination for me, in light of recent events.

I had forgotten how excited policemen got about shootings. Five carloads descended on Scheherazade's within as many minutes of my call, turning what started as an overly cautious Wyatt Earp style inspection of the premises into a Chinese fire drill. The festivities came to a screeching halt when a couple of well organized plain clothes types got off the elevator.

The senior man was a bulky, deliberate Sergeant named Karlstrom. He had a puritanical face that could have been carved out of white oak. His slow eyes were a blunt suggestion that you would be better off confessing your crimes now, before someone made something really serious out of them. He stood close enough for me to smell his after shave and listened while the first uniform on the scene told him who I was and what I had reported. From what I heard through an open door, his partner was busy thinning the overpopulation of uniform men into a building canvass.

Karlstrom had me take him back for a look at the body. He gave me some more close range scrutiny between deliberate looks at the dead man. We went back for a look at the fire escape. There was a small assortment of personal effects lined up neatly on the dust of a nearby window ledge. Karlstrom used the blade of a pocket knife to flip open a wallet and pry four credit cards out. He made a point of showing me they were all in different names, as if I were personally responsible for that. He used the knife to open a gold inlaid snuff box. He also made a point of showing me the tiny hinged spoon and a small quantity of white powder inside. He didn't bother with a flat designer wristwatch, key case or the lime green silk handkerchief. We went back to the body. Karlstrom put his hands in his pockets, jingled some coins and didn't look happy.

"I'll tell you, Mr. Spain," he began in the tired voice of one contemplating an unpleasant duty, "I can't honestly say I'm satisfied with this situation. I'd like you to tell me exactly what you…" Karlstrom stopped in mid-sentence and took his hands out of his pockets with uncharacteristic promptness.

A man was coming smartly along the aisle, his hard rubber heels making soft noises on the aggregate. At a glance I put his age around fifty. His smooth hair was slate gray, his lean face all angles and planes, slanting down from temples to sharp jaw with the not quite even taper of a hatchet blade. He was wearing a sharply pressed business suit and a business expression.

"Morning, Karlstrom."

"Good morning, sir."

Karlstrom's superior looked thoughtfully at the body and rippled quick fingers against one trouser leg. Then he looked at me inquisitively.

Karlstrom said, "This is Henry Spain. Private investigator's license. He found the body."

The man gave me an economical nod. "Snyder. Acting Captain."

I didn't quite snap to attention.

He addressed Karlstrom. "Preliminary information?"

"Time of death was ten twenty. Mr. Spain was here then. Victim shot some time prior. Twice in the throat. His personal possessions were laid out on a window sill. Nothing we could use for identification."

"Name was Midas Turner," Snyder supplied. "Played some JC basketball. More height than talent. Had a trial date of next Tuesday on procuring charges. Talked a couple of bored Bel Air teenagers into turning out for him. Lead the exciting life of a hooker, that sort of thing. We took him on a complaint from one of the fathers. Turner met the girls through a so-called cosmic temple. Worked there as a second assistant gopher, so they said. They canned him. We couldn't turn up enough to close them down."

"Any connection with this place?" Karlstrom inquired in a deferential tone.

"None that we knew of," Snyder replied, adding significantly, "Maybe we didn't know enough."

"You'll want to be kept posted if we find anything?" Karlstrom presumed.

"Whether you do or not."

Snyder gave Karlstrom and I one nod apiece and went out. We went back to the reception room. Karlstrom's partner was waiting. He was a flashy dresser, even as Latin cops went. A cool cat who emitted his words in an unexpected fast monotone. He indicated the outer door with his eyes.

"Wasn't that the A/C who took over Administrative Vice a couple of weeks ago?"

"Earl Snyder," Karlstrom said.

"You know him?"

Karlstrom put his hands back in his pockets. "Nobody knows Earl Snyder. He's not the type. What did you get?"

"Victim worked here. Has for about a month. Express girl says he hit her up to turn out for him. Little Italian who runs the meat locker below said he showed at eight five this morning."

"Give or take how much?" Karlstrom wanted to know.

"Nothing. Victim's car made enough noise to attract his attention. He looked at his clock because he thought it was a little early for this place to open."

"That car must've been loud, if he heard it and missed the shots."

"Pipes rumbled like Mount Vesuvius with heartburn was the way he put it."

"He heard that on TV," Karlstrom decided sourly.

I had heard a set of pipes like that up on Holland Canyon Drive. The phone number here had come from the late Walter O. Brixner's tape machine. The gun on the floor was the type and probably the caliber that had killed Brixner. The man on the floor would have had a sleepless night if he had done the shooting. Everyone did, no matter how callused they thought they were. The reasons had more to do with mortality than morality, and they sent everyone scurrying to work at the crack of dawn looking for something to take the mind off it. It all seemed a bit much to write off to coincidence. It was also too much thinking to be showing up on the face of a plain, dumb witness. I was glad we had another visitor before anyone noticed.

A short colorless man wandered in, took out an oversize handkerchief and blew his nose. "Can't seem to shake this cold," he said to no one in particular.

Karlstrom said, "Your patient took two in the throat, Doc. Probably .22's. When you get him on the autopsy table, I'd like to know how long he could have lasted after he was shot."

"The transcription might give you an idea. If the penetrations left good palpable tracks, and if a projectile wound was the cause of death."

Karlstrom jingled his pocket change impatiently. "Doc, I'll personally drink every drop of cobra venom you drain out of him."

"Wouldn't do you much harm. Cobra venom wouldn't stand a chance against the acid in a human stomach."

Karlstrom's partner said, "This way, Doc."

The colorless little Coroner's man followed him out, leaving me alone with the big, deliberate Sergeant.

"I can't honestly say I'm satisfied with this situation, Mr. Spain," Karlstrom began where we'd been before Snyder popped in. "I guess I've forgotten what you told me you were doing here."

I wasn't about to tell him that, but Snyder's visit made it obvious that the police had a file on Scheherazade's. Probably a thick one. Karlstrom would check anything I said against it. Since I was already in enough trouble to get my license lifted, I had very little to lose testing a theory.

"I was looking for old striptease films," I lied in a nice bright cooperative voice. "I heard this place occasionally had pieces for sale."

"You're a private investigator, here during business hours," Karlstrom pointed out. "Do you expect me to believe you were on a shopping expedition?"

"I expect you to check the inventory," I said. "My guess is you'll find some merchandise such as I described. If you don't already know it to exist."

"Maybe you're fronting a bashful collector?"

I said nothing.

Karlstrom said, "You're aware of the consequences of obstructing a police investigation, Mr. Spain?"

"I'm not obstructing the investigation," I said pleasantly. "I started it. I called the police and waited until they arrived so I could give them a statement."

Karlstrom let me drive my own car to the division house. I told him all of what I had seen and none of what I thought. I told him I didn't know whether Midas Turner's last words had been a reference to his killer, a snap judgement on my personal habits or a critique of the white race in general. He had my statement typed. It read like a third grade essay on how I spent my summer vacation. I signed it.

"Thank you, Mr. Spain," he said in his quiet, ominous rumble. "We'll be in touch."

I believed him.

Any calls I made from my cell phone were traceable, so I parked in a supermarket lot and found a pay phone in a Plexiglas bubble on the wall inside. Jean LaBostrie's number didn't answer. The Crown Colony was still on answering service. That left the directory set. It had several pages of Murillos; at least thirty of them named Frank. On top of which I was only fairly sure my man would list himself as Frank, and not Francisco or Ildefonso or a couple of other possibilities. As long as I was guessing anyway, I decided to bet my pocket change on the impression that he was also the sort who would put some distance between himself and what the trendy media liked to call El Barrio. That would narrow it down. At a glance there were only four Frank Murillos who didn't have an East L.A. address.

The first owned a plumbing business in West Covina, or so the woman who answered told me. While I tapped out the second, a bakery smell strong enough to float the Metlife blimp wafted out of a nearby alcove. It made me think of lunch.

The line stopped ringing and a dry Latin lilt said, "Yeah?" in my ear.

I put my head into the cubicle to cut as much of the store noise as possible, pushed my voice up half an octave and made it walk on cat's feet.

"Mr. Murillo? Mr. Frank Murillo?"

"Who's this?"

"I am Reverend Matthew Walters, of Mission San Gabriel Presbyterian Church."

"Yeah…uh, yes, Reverend. What can I do for you?"

"Well," I began a bit tentatively, "some of my colleagues in the ministry suggested you as a man to contact regarding the organization of a weekly charity bingo night. You see, our ladies auxiliary is interested in sponsoring missionary work in Ethiopia, and I thought perhaps…?"

I let my voice tail off with a question in it, as if hoping he would spare the poor minister the need to explain further. There was a minute of uncertain breathing at the other end.

"Uh, sure, Reverend. A very worthy project. Have you got a number where me or one of my associates could reach you in the next day or so? We'll have to set up an appointment to discuss the details."

I gave him the number of Scheherazade's. If he recognized it, he wasn't letting any strangers in on the secret. He thanked me so much for calling and hung up.

Something was seriously out of joint in charity bingo. Any competent hustler would have had a firm appointment before he let his pigeon off the line. I wrote down a Venice address.

Chapter 10

Back from the white beach, back from the promenade of thong bikinis and roller blades and wasted street peddlers, the real Venice made its indifferent way into an unclear future. Trash collected in the snatches of canal that remained from the original fantasy. Designer condominiums sprouted randomly, wherever the property owners had contrived to obtain a building permit. Those with applications still pending in the impossible bureaucracy had to be content to lease the surviving bungalows to anyone lacking long range plans. The resulting collection of drifters and dreamers were like the dregs winos gleaned together from discarded bottles. Their presence created a transitory never-never land, while their neglect ate the last vitality out of the old places. And left the house numbers where they fell.

By elimination, Frank Murillo's address was a dusty white stucco with parallel concrete tracks squeezing through a narrow side yard and vanishing in the rear. I parked around the corner, walked back and climbed three questionable wooden steps. I used the knocker and did some waiting in the sultry, stagnant air.

A lock snicked inside and the knob turned. The door moved in a stealthy arc to the limit of the chain. The oval eyes from the church stage peered out at me. They lost their Latin sensuality at close range. Heavy lids gave them an illusion of sleepiness. Beyond that they were moist brown voids.

I said, "I'm looking for Brixner."

Murillo's voice was as dry as I remembered, with an aftertaste of liquor behind the cigarette smoke on his breath.

"What was that name again?"

"Brixner. Walter O. Brixner."

Nothing moved in Murillo's brown face. His oval brown eyes gave me a little study. He brought up a cigarette and touched it to his full lips. Smoke drifted out of his mouth and nostrils in a long, hazy trail with dry words behind it.

"Nobody here by that name. Not even in the neighborhood."

Murillo tried to close the door. My shoulder was in the way. He looked casually at the shoulder then back at my face. I smiled and said, "I didn't think he'd be here. That would be messy in his present condition. I just said I was looking for him."

Murillo's bland oval eyes took time to make sure there was no one on the sidewalk behind me. "The way I get this, you're looking for a party named Brixner? And there's something about his condition?"

"Why don't I come in," I suggested. "That way I won't have to embarrass you by getting specific in earshot of the neighbors."

I gave him just enough shoulder room to slip the chain and followed the door as he walked it back cautiously. It let me directly into a cheerless living room hazy with stale cigarette smoke and rancid from the ghosts of meals past. The walls were soiled plaster laced with webs of settling cracks and spotted with the rectangular memories of pictures that had left with the last permanent resident. A big screen television overwhelmed one corner. Stereo components with the mismatched look of the midnight appliance mart were stacked on a cart. Exposed wires trailed away to speakers precariously mounted on shallow knick-knack shelves. The rest of the furniture had fallen off a Salvation Army truck. I helped myself to a seat on the lumpy sofa and hoped this wasn't the day one of the springs would decide to let go.

Murillo put his head out and looked both ways along the street before he shut and chained the door. He moved crabwise to a window where sunlight filtered in through the rotted remains of drawn draperies. His build was mature enough to look vaguely ridiculous in designer jeans, but his polo shirt was passable. He used a Hush Puppy to nibble a chair out of the kneehole of a flimsy writing desk. He positioned his buttocks carefully against the front edge and drummed his fingers on the front of the single drawer.

I gave him a sly grin, one sharp operator to another. "You don't actually have to pull the gun, Frank. Just tell me what kind it is. I promise I'll be scared."

He wasn't as cool as his poker face made him seem. His hand jerked the drawer open, jumped in and came out with a compact Smith and Wesson revolver. He came erect, stood perfectly still. Behind him, long fingers snubbed out his cigarette in an unseen ashtray.

"Some dude muscles in here, he shouldn't get the idea I won't use the piece if I have to."

"You had some luck, Frank," I said soothingly. "Owning that .38. Brixner was shot with a .32. An automatic."

The muzzle of the compact revolver was a third eye that didn't move from my face. The other two eyes gave me some careful consideration, without reaching anything that looked like a conclusion. I decided a little help was in order.

"The police picked a seven foot black brother off Scheherazade's floor this morning, Frank. The two bullets in his throat came from a .22. It's a good bet they were professionally administered. Talked to any pros lately, Frank?"

Murillo stepped forward and put the .38 under my chin. It happened faster than the dice switch in a furnace room crap game.

"I don't see some ID quick, they'll say the same about the two they find in your croaker."

I would have laughed at him if his Latin eyes hadn't acquired a desperate meanness. I eased the wallet out of my coat and showed him the photo ID that was issued with my license. I didn't know what he was expecting, but a private investigator wasn't it. He gave me a quick pat to make sure I wasn't armed and backed to the desk to give me a little more thought.

"Yeah," he said suddenly and vaguely. "I think I'm getting a flash here. You and Brixner, you must have had a gig going. That's how come you know so damned much."

I wasn't sure what he meant by a gig. "You know more than I do, Frank."

"Yeah," he said with loving sarcasm. "Private cops are righteous dudes, just like on TV. And Brixner never did no hard time for no shakedown. Wake me up when you get to the Easter Rabbit. I always liked that part."

Looking like I had known all along about Brixner's prison term was no chore. It would have been an obvious likelihood, if Murillo hadn't made it fact. I wondered what other little goodies might slip out if I went along with him. It was an idea with fringe benefits, like keeping his gun out of my croaker. I gave him a sheepish grin.

"What can I tell you, Frank?"

He liked my attitude better now. Something still bothered him. "How did you figure it was me that found Brixner? You wasn't working no stakeout up there. I would've spotted you going in. I got a nose for that crap."

"You were the one making the late delivery at Brixner's house." I would have been better off leaving his recall dormant.

"How would you know that?" he wondered sharply. "Brixner didn't know it himself until we talked a couple hours earlier."

Assuming I had been tight with Brixner, there were any number of possibilities. Murillo's brain wasn't quick enough to think of any of them before suspicion made his memory click.

"The LaBostrie broad!" he realized. "That was you in the church when I told her. Cigar and loud mouth. I told you I had a nose. Brixner had you following her. That's it. Sure. I knew there was something funny with those two."

"What did you think it was?"

"Then the LaBostrie snatch did blow him off," he decided, as if that might have been a pet theory of his.

"Bad guess," I said.

"He was scared of her. Plenty. He didn't show it much, but he was. I asked him if it was okay to put a little hustle on her, not wanting to beat the boss's time, and like that. He said both of us better forget it. She'd put either one of us in the County refrigerator and laugh it off an hour later. He meant it, and he didn't scare easy."

"She didn't do it," I said. "The scenario wasn't right, and I talked to her afterward, just to make sure." The remark still bothered me. Jean hadn't shot Brixner, but I had heard her laugh it off an hour later.

"Who then?" Murillo asked.

"The long cool brother from Scheherazade's," I offered. "The one with the .22s in his croaker."

Murillo's oval brown eyes lost their expression and started to study me again. The Smith and Wesson rested against his leg. He wasn't paying any attention to it. I dug out a stick of gum to settle my nerves while I returned the scrutiny.

"I don't blame you, Frank. I'd be worried too. This could put an accessory jacket on you. You got Scheherazade's number from Brixner's tape machine. You passed it on to somebody higher up in the bingo racket. Within ten hours the man who shot Brixner was killed by professionals. Enforcers. That's a long fall, Frank. For everybody involved."

"Bingo is no racket," he said in a low, earnest voice. "That's legit. Audited by the State, a righteous percentage returned to the players as prizes. All legal."

"It's a racket, Frank, but the only way to prove that is by the books, and maybe the peculiar imprint of a check protecting machine. Brixner's boss would know that. You phoned him when you found the body. He gave you the safe combination, and told you what to lift along with the body."

"You ain't bounced that off no cops," Murillo decided. "They'd be dropping out of trees."

"I can't sit on it forever."

"You will if you're smart. Brixner's pals hit town like a heat wave. When they blow in, everything wilts. They handle cops like Tom Cruise handles women."

"Anyone can handle the police, Frank. All they need is a pigeon to take the heat. An anonymous tip, a halfway credible motive, an appointment around the time of death, a blood match from the poor jerk's car." I wrinkled my nose at the living room walls, glanced through a doorway at unwashed dishes in a crowded little kitchen. "Living in a dump like this, you can't be all that valuable to Brixner's friends, Frank."

"I get cheap rent. Mortgage and taxes. No profit."

"Cheap can be a little tough on the old love life, Frank. It must be rugged, a smooth operator like you hooked up with sharp looking hostesses and a crib like this to stage your play."

A pulse started at the corner of one oval eye. "Okay," he said in a tight dry voice, "just this second I'm a mushroom. They keep me in the dark and feed me shit. Only I been around awhile. I seen guys I know make the right connections. I watched careful, so I know how it's done. A dude wants to set himself up, he's gotta learn to see past the next gig. He's gotta lay down some heavy dues. Take some crap to show the right boys they can count on him when the pucker factor goes up. They get to trusting him, the gravy'll come. Plenty. It's tough, Brixner getting it like that. He was good people. But this is the break I been needing a long time."

I couldn't keep a straight face. "Amateur night was last week."

The bland oval eyes just stared at me. I said, "I was there, Frank. I could clear you."

"You'd do that on a subpoena from any public defender that drew the case. You're in this deep enough you could lose your license to hustle if you try any funny crap. You got nothing for me so I got nothing for you. I guess that makes it bye-bye time." The smirk on his features was very superior; calling a tinhorn's busted flush.

I took out a business card and set it on a scarred end table. "Call me when the dues start to get out of hand, Frank. Just don't take too long."

Murillo waggled the gun at me. I stood up. He followed me to the door and saw me out. I went along the walk and turned the corner without looking back to see if he was watching me out of sight. I jazzed my engine a couple of times before I pulled out. This was his turf, and he was the type who paid attention to stray noises. Left turns at two block intervals took me in a wide circle. I parked again where I could watch the dusty stucco front.

My armpits were sticky from the tension of having a gun pointed at me, and knowing what it could do. I spit out the stale gum and spent some time thinking unpleasant thoughts about the things that could happen to a man in my business. Not that it made any difference. I didn't have any other business. I turned on the radio and surfed the oldies stations for something mellow and familiar to keep my mind off it while I waited.

A stooped man in his seventies shuffled out of a little frame house, swept the day's crop of trash off the sidewalk and retreated back inside. You didn't want to breathe too much Venice air if you were still reasonably normal. Little knots of unspoiled children filtered into the neighborhood still under the quiet discipline that school clothes impose. A few minutes later an old brown Ford van came out on the two concrete tracks from behind Murillo's. Murillo was at the wheel, in his brown bingo caller's suit. I had made sure he hadn't seen my car, so I wouldn't have to play him too loose.

He took Venice Boulevard to Olympic and that through Santa Monica. The ocean off Santa Monica was where the gambling boats had anchored when Tough Tommy Lipton came to California, though I didn't know why that popped into my head.

Murillo held to his lane and didn't try to fight the traffic. If he was worried about being followed, he didn't show it. We broke even on the lights through downtown and I heard the Southern Pacific yards, for the second time that day. Tail work was easier in the industrial section. Big vans and grumbling semis jostled passenger cars for road room and kept me pretty well hidden.

Murillo turned through an open gate in an eight-foot hurricane fence. He stopped with the side door of the Ford at the loading dock of a building that loomed over a prominent intersection. Slogans of 'Low Overhead' and 'Easy Credit' were painted one letter on each pane of the building's windows. There was a big 'Bienvenidas' banner and oriental pictographs. According to a huge girder sign on the roof, all three stories of battleship gray glory were devoted to Aserinsky's Discount Appliance Warehouse.

I knew Mister Aserinsky from commercial breaks during the late movie on television. A flashy little huckster making a no turndown credit pitch to newlyweds, servicemen and welfare recipients in a patter as fast as a back country auctioneer. The appliances were a come-on for a little legal shylocking. That was fine for the minimum wage drudges, but I couldn't see a swiftie like Frank Murillo letting himself pay maximum rate and all the finance charges the California Legislature had been persuaded to allow.

A slogan painted on a parked caterer's van caught my eye. 'Eat Dessert First. Life is Uncertain.' I parked behind the van to wait and watch.

Murillo came back out on the dock and opened the side door of the Ford. He and a red-haired kid with mutton-chop whiskers loaded seven good-sized cartons inside. Maybe Aserinsky was schlocking off his not-so-hot lines for bingo prizes. I tried to remember if I had seen his name anywhere in Brixner's account files, and couldn't.

From Aserinsky's, Murillo led me over to Glendale and up to Sunset Boulevard, where the traffic took us into Hollywood. The glamour was long gone and the city fathers were still looking for something to replace it, but the life forms prowling the sidewalks along Highland didn't seem to mind. Murillo found an empty meter near Orange. I ducked into a side lot and got back on the sidewalk in time to spot him going into a run-down office building.

The lobby was a morgue, and Murillo was still standing back in the dimness, watching the needles above the elevator bank. His hands were thrust deep in his pockets and impatience was written all over him. If he noticed the convulsive spasms of the hydraulic door closer, he didn't think the noise was worth a look. I sidled quickly to the cover of a snack stand built into one wall and made a blind grab at the magazine rack. I found myself hiding behind an article explaining to today's up to the minute young woman why nice guys buy sex. The proprietress gave me a tired scowl, put her veined beak back in the *National Enquirer*. Browsers were about as rare as cooling fan breakdowns in buildings like this. I fidgeted around until I had a sliver view across the unappealing leftovers from the day's run of candy bar lunches and nicotine fits. As soon as a car swallowed Murillo and clunked shut, I went back and watched the epileptic needle. It settled on three. The other car opened and disgorged a surly messenger in yellow tights and a bicycle helmet. I stepped in and leaned on a button. The door stuttered through a couple of false starts before it closed. There was a distant sound of ponderous machinery. The slow changing of lighted numbers behind clouded plastic was the only hint of movement. An eon passed before the door opened again on three.

The hall was empty. I drifted along listening to the rise and fall of voices and the monotony of office machine noise. Faded lettering on the corrugated half glass of the doors belonged to hack agents and tired promoters milking whatever advantage there was left in the old address, to places where you sent too many dollars to have your very own soul music composition published, to bombastic political committees with millennial ideas, miniature mailing lists and a few well stroked angels to pay the rent. I didn't think much of my chances of locating Murillo that way. It was his kind of building. He could fit in anywhere.

I selected a strategic piece of wall and parked myself to wait. Time passed. So did a couple of secretaries. They gave me more room than a flasher with leprosy. At length a door opened and Murillo marched out. I needn't have bothered stepping around the corner. He made straight for the elevators without glancing left or right. He looked mad.

When I heard the car clunk shut, I went down the hall. The legend on the glass read: 'Guy Hamilton Agency. Talent and Modeling.' The possibility was too obvious to ignore.

A bored beauty behind the reception desk groomed her nails and watched the clock on the wall above the four chairs and the cocktail table with the copies of *Variety* on it. A lot of dieting had left her with good bone structure and not much else. Her dubious smile didn't do much for my confidence.

"May I help you, sir?"

"Yes, indeed," I said in a big promo voice full of phony friendliness. "I would like to see Mr. Guy Hamilton."

I presented her with a card from my collection. It was the one that identified me as a general agent for Jordan Records in Tacoma, Washington. I doubted anyone here would know the company had been out of business for thirty years.

The card fairly reeked of possibilities. I might even be a paying customer. She put the nail file down. She put some pizzazz in her smile.

"Mr. Hamilton isn't available just now. If you'll wait, I'll tell Ms. Hamilton you're here."

She stood up and swayed through a door marked 'Gerda Hamilton' and 'Private' in reasonably new paint. She was back in two seconds, saying, "Would you care to step in, sir?"

Ms. Hamilton was my age, but the similarity ended there. Three inches of carrot orange hair piled on top of her head gave her that much advantage in height on me. She had green eyes as hard as steel marbles, set in a narrow face that looked like something from an Indian totem pole. She put a bony arm across the desk and offered me a hand that was blood brother to a vise grip wrench.

"You are Mr. Bemis, from, uh"—she read the card—"Jordan Records, is it?"

"Jordan Records," I repeated in my promo voice. "Small, aggressive and always in search of fresh and exciting talent."

She gave me a look that made me wonder if I was overdoing it and let me have my hand back. "Please sit down, Mr. Bemis. What can I do for you?"

I pulled a chair close to the desk. "The home office is very anxious to locate a singer who taped a test session for us last year," I said confidentially. "A little bundle of dynamite named Jean LaBostrie. I understand she is now working out of your agency?"

Gerda Hamilton excused herself. She swiveled her chair and pulled a file drawer open. I pretended to be interested in the display of framed eight-by-ten publicity stills. They were all the face of a youngish man above open shirt collars long out of style. He had the kind of masculine good looks that were enough to get you into a movie studio as late as the nineteen fifties. I wondered if he could be Gerda Hamilton's brother, despite the lack of resemblance. She swiveled back and opened a manila folder with Jean's name typed on the tag. She held it up in front of her so I couldn't see anything inside without climbing over the desk.

"There seems to be some irregularity here," she said. She lowered the folder and scowled at me.

I sat there like a frog on a log and wondered whether it was my bargain basement sport coat or my lousy acting that had blown the charade. I was wrong on all three counts.

"I took over temporary management of the firm from my brother last month," she explained. "His unavoidably sudden departure left the files in a disorganized state. I will have to make a call to verify Ms. LaBostrie's availability."

She wasn't sore at me. She was sore at not being able to turn a quick commission. I said, "No problem," showed her my cosmetic dentistry and sat back to wait.

She closed the folder and looked apologetic, in a grim sort of way. "I have just tried the party I need to contact. I'm afraid he isn't in at the moment."

"Perhaps I should be dealing with another agency?" I wondered out loud. I should have known better.

She drew herself up to full height in her chair. Her eyes bored into mine like lasers. "It would scarcely be ethical for you to try to circumvent this office, Mr. Bemis."

I grinned nervously. "Just trying to do the right thing."

She kept her eyes fixed on mine and danced a set of blood-red fingernails on the manila folder. Something in the file told her she had to call someone before she could book Jean. She had just tried to call, without success. She had also just finished an interview with Frank Murillo. The only common denominator I knew of was Walter O. Brixner. He would be particularly difficult to reach.

I thought briefly about making a grab for the file to check my theory. Two things stopped me. The notations were liable to mean nothing to me, and I wasn't sure I could win the fight to get it in the first place.

"Well, you have my card," I said, and stood up.

"I shall call you," was her chilly promise, "if Ms. LaBostrie is available."

I went out past the bored skeleton on reception, rode the elevator down and bailed my car out of the lot.

Chapter 11

I was in no position to criticize Jean LaBostrie on the basis of her agent's business quarters. My own office was a one bay remainder left over when a steamship company decided they weren't taking any more space than they absolutely needed. Jean was entitled to a cut-rate agent. She was also entitled to her choice of friends and acquaintances. But I felt entitled to wonder when one of them was shot dead and another disposed of the body on instructions from people who blew into town like a heat wave.

I was discarding a photo mailer telling me why it was my duty to elect a long time Los Angeles resident like Mrs. Doris Alexander to the city council when the significance of that activity dawned on me. The undertaking duties had fallen to Frank Murillo because Brixner's associates ran charity bingo from out of town. I grabbed the phone and punched up a number.

"Subscriber assistance. May I help you?"

"Yes, my name is Walter Brixner." I gave her Brixner's phone number. "I'd like to check time and charges on an out-of-area call I made approximately one AM this date."

"One moment, please."

I spent it browsing the day's only skip trace flyer. It was marked: 'Urgent. For Immediate National Release.' A mortgage broker in St. Paul had taken a Winnebago for a test drive three weeks ago. They were still looking for him. He was five feet five, weighed two hundred sixty pounds and sported a red handlebar mustache. He was also bald. Among his possible contacts were two current and five former wives. Some combination of clients and/or creditors had anted up a two hundred dollar bounty for information leading to his return. His partners had kicked in a plea that they would be forced to declare bankruptcy unless he returned with the contents of the trust account and made things right by everyone. Bankruptcy sounded like their best bet. If the joker came back, he was liable to con them out of their fillings, hock the Winnie and abscond with the Prosecuting Attorney's mistress.

The operator came back. Murillo's phone call had taken less than a minute. She verified the number called without my asking. I thanked her and blipped the receiver to try it. The length of Murillo's call gave me an idea what to expect.

"Professional Paging Service."

"What city, please?"

"San Pedro, sir. Which pager number did you wish to reach?"

"Forget it." I hung up.

Murillo's instructions had probably come from a phone booth. As shy as Brixner's friends seemed to be, Jean had likely told the truth when she claimed never to have met them. I touched the number code for my voice mail.

Jean held down the first three spots. She didn't sound happy. She wanted me to phone her at the Crown Colony. The last two were from a Tod Grayson. Most urgent I call him. I had copied the number before I was able to place Tod Patrick Grayson as the name on the card I had thrown away last night. He was doing a little better, but his urgent business would have to wait its turn. I gave my name to a man at the Crown Colony and round filed the last of the advertising circulars while he went to find Jean.

"Where the goddamn hell have you been?" she demanded in a husky, agitated voice.

"Nice talk," I chided.

She was in no mood for criticism.

"I spent half an hour this morning standing outside that stupid office of yours. The people in the ship company said sometimes you didn't show up for two or three days in a row."

"Those smugglers wouldn't recognize honest work if it kicked them in the shins and refused to pay the surcharge."

"It must be contagious."

"What's bothering you, Jean? Aside from the fact that pretty girls don't like to wait outside stupid offices?"

"I have to see you. My dinner break is in twenty minutes. Can you meet me?"

"At the Club?"

"God, no. I'd gain a ton if I ate here. They soak everything but everything in melted butter."

She gave me the name of a department store. I made the mistake of assuring her I knew where it was. She hung up before I could ask her any questions. The woman who answered my call to Osborne Associates informed me that Mr. Grayson was in conference. They usually were. I let her pry a name out of me anyway, to give him when he was free. I fired up my bottom of the line desktop clone, inserted Tommy Lipton's name, his business address and some general particulars of his assignment into my standard contract then ran off two copies on my second hand laser printer. I filled out a deposit slip and stopped at the drive-by window of my bank to drop his checks. Then I took Walter Brixner's black vinyl folder of data tapes into a computer service bureau and rattled off some generic fiction about a bankruptcy investigation I was doing for a law firm to explain why I didn't know the file formats or the source language or have access to a computer system to dump the contents onto greenbar paper myself. I got no sympathy and a very specific affidavit to perjure myself on. All that made me late reaching the store.

I worked my way across a crowded shopping floor listening to the sizzle of cash register print heads and inhaling a crisp aroma that reminded me of fresh roasted peanuts. A flight of stairs took me up to the mezzanine. Jean was holding a booth when I got to the coffee shop. The crisscross dark colors of a tartan outfit went well with the annoyed look on her face. A prosperous young business type was talking to her and looking like he wouldn't mind being invited to sit down. He got an invitation to do something else. His face turned as black as a summer storm.

I clamped a heavy hand on his shoulder. A finger vise on his clavicle kept him from turning on me.

"Hi, there," I cooed in his ear. "Are you a Libra?"

His answer wasn't the sort of thing they said in the executive washroom. He was bigger than I was. He was also a lot stronger. I wasn't going to be able to hold him long. I snapped a short swift kick into his ankle. The narrow glint of hatred in his eyes widened into a flood of agony. He had to choke back a yell to maintain his macho image. It was enough to convince him he had more to lose in a fight than I did. He repossessed his shoulder and went away, trying not to limp.

"That wasn't nice," I told Jean as I helped myself to a seat across from her. "The duck probably wouldn't have liked it either."

"It wasn't my fault," she insisted. "If I hadn't had to wait for you, I could have sat with some nice fashion buyer and talked girl talk." She gave me a drippy smile. "And I did drop several polite hints."

"How many hints did that Calland character at the Club miss before you sent him to the hospital?"

"That wasn't my fault. Ricky wouldn't stop talking about this cosmic guidance place. How they could release the real me, help me develop a real sound. Naturally it was all free if he told them I was a special friend. I finally told him if he was looking for a cheap thrill, he ought to French kiss a wall socket."

Cosmic was probably the second most common word in California, but the last context I'd heard it in bothered me. "What sort of deal was it? The cosmic guidance place, I mean."

"I suppose it's one of those places for bored wives and mistresses. Ricky is the club gigolo. That's the type he attracts."

"Could he have known Brixner?"

The name reminded her she wasn't happy with me. She took a tightly folded evening edition from the bench beside her and put it on the table.

"There hasn't been anything about Walter in the paper," she told me in a low, accusing voice. "I read the morning and afternoon ones and the police part of this one and he wasn't anywhere."

"Is that what has you upset?"

"Did you do something with him?"

"Like what, for instance?"

She didn't like being stalled. "Did you take Walter's body somewhere and hide it so the police couldn't find it?"

"Did you know the body was gone? Or is that sort of thing just standard practice in your social set?"

The muscles of her throat tightened in a ruffled vee of white silk. Her lips slacked apart. The blood drained out of her face, until glistening teeth were the most lifelike thing about her. She watched me with silent, helpless dread. The kind of look that went with hitting the brakes on a wet road and watching the car ahead loom up and realizing there was nothing you could do but wait for the impact.

"Your friend Murillo took the body," I told her. I couldn't tell whether she believed me or not. "While you and I were having our little chat last night. I went back afterward for a look at Brixner's files. It was gone then."

"How do you know it was Frank?"

"He admitted it."

Her hand jumped across the table and caught my sleeve. "You didn't tell him I was there?"

"He knew you were looking for Brixner from your conversation at the church. He drew his own conclusions from that. I had to convince him you didn't pull the trigger."

She took the hand away. She was getting some color back. "Did he take the body because he thought I shot Walter?"

"He took it on orders from the people behind Brixner in the bingo racket. Along with some incriminating evidence."

"Who were the people behind Walter?"

"Murillo was too scared to tell me much about them. Did Brixner ever mention any out of town connections?"

"Did they kill Walter?"

"They killed the man who killed him. A black procurer named Midas Turner. Ever meet him?"

The look she gave me was something women use on fish bait, while it was still wriggling. I said, "It happened this morning, in a mail order pornography outlet called Scheherazade's."

The name didn't seem to register. A bustling motherly waitress arrived and poured coffee for both of us. The waitress knew Jean well enough to guess what she wanted by menu number. She looked at me as if I were something of a novelty, and as if she were positive I wasn't Mr. Right. The dinner menu wasn't in force until six, so I had to settle for a hot beef sandwich. When the waitress bustled off, Jean was staring into her coffee. I had to put a hand on her forearm to remind her I still existed.

"Are you living with a boy friend, Jean? Someone who can keep an eye on you, at least for the next couple of days?"

"Used women are like used cars," she said. "The more miles they have on them, the less the right man will give up for them. And the rougher they get treated after." It sounded like a stock answer she kept ready to fend off girl friends who tried to meddle in her life.

"It's just as well," I said brightly. "The police can offer you better protection."

She made a sour face. "Protection from what?"

"Brixner's friends. The ones who killed Midas Turner."

"I don't even know them. Neither do you. You said so yourself."

"I know a little about them from the way they handled Turner. He was no pussycat. He was almost seven feet tall, and he looked like a street fighter. He was also armed. In spite of which he was carefully searched, probably questioned then shot twice in the throat, all with no sign of a struggle. That, and the fact that it all happened in a crowded building with no one the wiser, suggests some very smooth teamwork. If it was done by one man, I wouldn't want to meet him."

"Do you always talk like the dialogue from some stupid television show?" she asked.

"Faster than a speeding wheelchair. More powerful than tofu. Able to leap garden hoses at a single bound. Can our hero fend off hordes of policemen and solve two murders while he applauds the gorgeous singer with his other hand? Stay tuned for tonight's thrilling episode."

Jean wasn't amused.

"It won't be as easy to avoid the police as I thought last night," I warned her. "I was the one who found Midas Turner."

"What does that have to do with me?"

"I was investigating your background at the time. The police will look for any connection."

"What would I know about some pimp?"

"The police have connected him with something they called a cosmic temple. You mentioned Calland was connected with some sort of cosmic guidance?"

All I got from her expression was a big 'So what?'.

"You never did say whether Calland knew Brixner."

"I guess he must have," she said with an impatient shrug. "Walter came to the Club to see Mr. Lipton lots of times."

"They were friends? Brixner and Lipton?"

She gave me an intense dissatisfied look to say that wasn't quite it. "What's that name for people who tell businessmen how to do their business and taxes and stuff?"

"Consultant?"

She nodded. "That's what Walter was. Mr. Lipton was sort of a client of his, when he had questions, I guess."

"Did Brixner arrange your booking at the Crown Colony?"

She sipped coffee. I was being ignored again. "Come on, Jean. Half the name talent in Hollywood is looking for work. You didn't just bop in off the street and announce you were available."

"I didn't believe he could really do it," she marveled. "He had heard me sing. He said he could get me an audition at the Crown Colony. I didn't believe it until the bandleader called to tell me when rehearsal was. Did you know the band leader played horn with Jay McNeely in"— she scowled at her enthusiasm—"no, you wouldn't care about that."

"Not about the horn player," I agreed, "but I used to go down to the Barrel House when Big Jay played there, back when white boys could still go into Jive Town at night without looking for a fight."

She stared at me and didn't say a word. A note of astonished laughter lay barely repressed beneath her incredulous expression.

"What did the Hamilton Agency think of your getting a booking through Brixner?" I asked.

"What have they got to do with it?" Her tone was a little less hostile, now that she knew I was a fan.

"I followed Murillo there this afternoon. They have a file on you. Gerda Hamilton seems to think…?"

"Oh, I quit them."

"Why?"

"Guy Hamilton was a crook. He was stealing from all of us. It was in the papers last month."

"Gerda had to take over because her brother is in jail?"

"I think the police are still looking for him," she tossed off in a voice that made a production of being noncommittal.

"How did you get mixed up with an outfit like that in the first place?"

She gave a frustrated little shrug. "Finding a decent agent is Catch 22. You need one to get good bookings, but you have to have already proved you can handle good bookings before any of them will talk to you."

It was just as well the waitress picked that moment to arrive with an armload of plates. I didn't have any snappy comebacks for hopeless dilemmas. My hot beef sandwich was about half the size of the hole in my stomach. Jean's dinner was a cake of some kind of fish, baked light brown on the outside and served with a lot of nonfattening greens.

"Is all this investigating really necessary?" she asked when the woman was gone. "Can't you just make some phone calls and check my credit and stuff? Then we could both get this over with."

"Who are your credit references?"

"If I give you some, will you stop bothering me?" she asked hopefully.

It's a little more complicated than that, Jean."

She quit paying attention to me. We ate in silence. After a while I said, "Tommy Lipton is planning to put a lot of money into backing you. He'll have to have a complete business background so his lawyers can clear all your old contracts."

"Oh. Well, that's all right, I guess."

"It's not something we can to in quickie meetings in lounges and coffee shops. When would it be convenient for you to sit down and go over it?"

"I don't know. We're changing six numbers in the routine for the weekend. I'll have to check the rehearsal schedule and call you."

"When should I call you, if you forget?"

She put her knife and fork together on the plate and gave an exasperated, "Honest to God! You haven't one scrap of faith in people."

She insisted on paying for her own meal when the check came. The sidewalk outside was a mob of homebound office workers and shoppers. I walked along with her toward the Crown Colony.

"Where are you going?" she wanted to know.

"I have a little contract business with Lipton."

"He won't be in tonight."

We went a block in silence.

"Can I ask you a question?" she inquired.

"Sure."

"There was a Porsche parked outside that lounge last night. Kind of shiny, like it was all kept up."

"It was mine."

"Where did you get it? Those things cost a ton of money. I priced all the ones I could find before I bought that junker of mine."

"I did a lot of that myself," I remembered. "I finally just bit the bullet and paid too much of my own money and too much interest on the bank's money and cut corners to make it work."

"Mid-life crisis?"

It wasn't an original idea. Two days after I'd bought the car I'd tracked a wandering husband to a seedy trailer court. He sat for an hour on an unmade bed with his arm around a sixteen year old dropout, explaining in soporific detail how his entire life had been nothing more than a series of knee jerk reactions to the situations in which he found himself. This time he was going to do it his way. The thing that really scared me was that even after hearing him out, buying the Porsche still seemed like a perfectly normal and reasonable thing for a man in my position to have done.

"Probably," was all I conceded to Jean.

I opened the door with the dragons and we went downstairs into a hum of vacuum cleaner noise. The tiered club was lit up like a set at Universal, just before the second unit director yelled for the cameras to roll. Efficient waiters raced the clock setting up while the straight-backed maitre'd did a slow prowl, checking everything down to the alignment of the silverware with the unforgiving eye of a regimental Sergeant Major. Jean went down across the dining floor without saying good-bye.

She had been right about Tommy Lipton not being in. He had left a message, in case I came by. He was entertaining at home. I was invited to stop out and see him. Any time before seven thirty. All very proper and correct.

Chapter 12

The house wasn't overly large by Pasadena standards, which meant it probably didn't have more than one indoor swimming pool. The architecture was as formal as King Edward's coronation. Attendant roses were every shade of red, from virgin pink to the crimson of freshly spilled blood. The half-acre lawn was as fine as silk thread from the China concession and as green as Guyana emerald. It had been cut to laser precision within the hour and sharply edged along a wide sidewalk shaded by a magnificent oak.

I parked at the end of the sun-dappled drive and hoofed past a line of gleaming luxury cars. Scattered among current models were a six window Cadillac that had carried its owners to celebrate Eisenhower's second inauguration, a glossy black Lincoln from the Kennedy era and a forty year old Rolls Royce that looked like it had been bought new last week.

An elderly oriental houseman answered the self-conscious noise I made with the lion's head knocker. If he had been expecting something a little better dressed, his features didn't show it.

"May I help you, sir?"

"Henry Spain to see Mr. Stafford." I sounded like the butler announcing myself.

"Please come in, Mr. Spain."

A two-story hallway ran the depth of the house between framed oils of a peaceful, verdant Los Angeles that once had been and never would be again. At the back, evening sunlight slanted in through the French doors and made elongated diamond patterns on the rich old parquetry. Shadows drifted back and forth on the leaded glass and sedate cocktail hour sounds filtered in from the patio beyond. We didn't go to the party. The houseman opened a door under a walnut staircase and held it for me.

"Will you wait in the den, Mr. Spain?"

The room Tommy Lipton used for a den was big enough to swallow a tract house. It had a remote ceiling and heavy old drapery drawn back at tall windows. The carpet would have needed all of Ali Baba's forty thieves to roll it up and carry it off. A massive antique billiard table under a stained glass fixture gave the room the jaded atmosphere of one of those upper crust London clubs where a couple of genteel hard cases decided the fate of the world over a game of snooker. Spaced at precise intervals around the walls, standing like sculpture on varnished pedestals, with a small bronze museum plaque to explain each, was a collection of slot machines. I moved from one to the next with my hands in my pockets so I wouldn't put fingerprints on anything. There was a primitive liberty model from the century before last; staid shapes from the years before World War I; pre-depression chrome; plastic and furbelow from the thirties and forties, all burnished to a sheen they hadn't seen since they left factories scattered in space and time.

"They all work," Tommy Lipton said sociably, "if you're feeling lucky."

He pressed the door closed behind him. A smooth stride brought him across the carpet. There was nothing casual about his appearance this trip. He was decked out in a midnight blue tuxedo. His shoes shone like black glass and the studs in his starched shirtfront were as straight as a paratrooper's gig line. At a glance he was done up for one of the umpteen dollar a plate political feeds that would be happening about this time of year. I supposed the cocktail hour out back was a redeemable favor for a candidate who needed a suitable atmosphere for some warm-up handshaking and polite buttonholing.

"I thought working slot machines were illegal in California. Even as souvenirs."

"I've always been a bit of a scofflaw," Lipton confessed. "You've brought a contract for me to sign?"

I told him I had and we shook hands and sat in a pair of leather armchairs drawn up to a vast, cold fireplace. He was finished reading and reaching for my pen by the time I had it out and uncapped. My business seemed to be getting short shrift in favor of people who had more money than I.

"How well do you know Walter Brixner?" I asked before he had a chance to shoo me out.

"Why do you ask?"

"He arranged Jean LaBostrie's booking at the Crown Colony. She claims he isn't her agent."

"Walt is a consulting accountant. He recommended the girl because he thought she would be good for business. As usual, he was right."

"My information is that he cooks the books for a charity bingo racket."

If that was a shock, Lipton took it calmly. "I never inquired about his other clients. I understand charity bingo is pretty tightly regulated to be a racket. Government regulation is Walt's specialty, though."

"I thought it might be extortion. I also heard he served time for that."

Lipton nodded confirmation. He handed the paperwork back and raided his pockets for a smoke. He regarded me cordially, as if to inquire whether I had any more trivial details bothering me.

"I guess I don't understand this situation," I confessed. "You're worried about running into a crooked agent in a singer's background, but you keep a convicted extortionist on as your own consulting accountant."

"Walt is one of the brightest people in the business," he explained through the rich blue haze of a freshly fired cigar; long, slim and green dappled. "The brightest people in any business are always a little unusual. You see, they know they're the brightest right from the start, but it can be a long, frustrating wait for a chance to prove it to the rest of the world. Sometimes they get discouraged and try something foolish."

"Brixner could get discouraged again, if he decides you short changed him on the singer."

"The fees Walt charges me work out to about five percent of what he saves me in Government levies. If he wants to hold me up for a little more, I guess I can afford it."

Romeo and Juliet had nothing on a rich man and his tax accountant. The only thing I had gotten for my revelations was the impression Lipton didn't know Brixner was dead. Or if he did, it was worth an Academy Award performance to keep anyone from knowing he knew.

"All right," I agreed, and inked my name in the appropriate blanks. "As long as you're satisfied, I won't spend any more of your money checking up on him." I wasn't about to stop checking.

"Don't think I don't appreciate your diligence, Spain," Lipton said pleasantly while he folded his copy of the contract, "but my idea in hiring you was to head off surprises. If you could concentrate on people I don't know?"

He was ready to stand up when I asked, "Do you know a talent agent named Guy Hamilton?"

His polite impatience vanished. It happened instantly, with no more than a millimeter of change in any muscle or facial feature. I had his undivided attention.

"Does he represent the LaBostrie girl?"

"He used to, before he did a fast fade ahead of some kind of police trouble. She says she dropped the agency, but they still have a folder on her."

"Find him."

There was nothing abrupt in Lipton's tone, but a two word sentence from a man who didn't speak in two word sentences carried the sting of a lash.

"I can probably check her contract without the expense of a skip trace that the police will do anyway," I advised.

Lipton leaned forward and put a forearm across one knee. His eyes held mine tight and hard. There was cigar smoke leaking out his nostrils when he said, "This Hamilton is in a jam. If he's got anything on the girl, in or out of his contract, he'll expose it now if he's given the idea

I can help him out. Once the police get hold of him, it will be too late. They've had too much experience handling people whose schemes are bigger than their brains."

I had debated when to tell Lipton that he himself was liable to be dragged into a couple of police investigations because I had stumbled into two fatal shootings. I had decided to wait until I had a signed contract to prove I was engaged in legitimate work at the time of my discoveries locked in my safe deposit box. Lipton's eagerness to put the squeeze on Guy Hamilton made that decision seem more like self-defense than disloyalty.

"Hamilton goes to the top of my list," I promised.

"Are you going to need any more front money to get a line on him?"

"It doesn't cost anything to put the word out, but there is bound to be a delivery charge. How much depends on the circumstances."

"I'll stand anything reasonable. Don't turn down any offers until you've talked to me."

"All right." I wondered what the limit really was. There had to be a pretty tight lid on what he could expect to make backing Jean.

"Did you turn up anything following the singer last night?" he inquired. The garage man had sharp eyes to go along with his sense of responsibility.

"I got to talk to her. I got enough to make a good start on her background. And a few tidbits of other information. Tell me, how much goes on in the Crown Colony that you don't find out about until it's too late?"

"Owning a supper club requires what the management science types refer to as a high tolerance for ambiguity."

On Lipton it looked more like boss gambler's nerve, riding a fast current of adrenaline and cold blood.

He stood up. "Well, if you'll excuse me, I'd better get back and see if I have any guests left."

I stood up and we shook hands as solemnly as two mourners at a Hollywood funeral. Lipton went silently across the thick carpet and out the door. His slot machines hung back in the shadows and watched me hungrily through their three vacant eyes. The houseman returned before they had a chance to close in.

I drove back downtown to my office. Voice mail had a return call from Tod Grayson. I was getting weary of that particular game. I dug the skip trace directory out of the bottom drawer. There was an agency in Stockton I owed some work to from last year. The partner I pulled away from his dinner recognized the name LaBostrie in connection with a pharmacy there, and with local civic affairs. He thought a background on Jean would take about two days. He thanked me for the job and hung up.

The phone rang almost immediately. I picked it up wondering what I had forgotten to tell him.

"Henry Spain, Investigations," I said from habit.

"Mr. Spain, please." It wasn't Stockton. The voice was young and assertive. It reminded me vaguely of a green lieutenant introducing himself to a platoon of combat veterans.

"Speaking," I told him.

"This is Tod Grayson, Mr. Spain. I'm terribly sorry I missed your call earlier. How long will it take you to reach my office?"

"What's it about, Mr. Grayson?"

"I thought I made it clear in my note that it was highly confidential."

"You didn't make it clear what it was, Mr. Grayson. Mortgage companies and supermarkets have strict rules about not accepting pie in the sky as legal tender. Those rules force me to spend my time on work I know to be productive, no matter how intriguing other possibilities might sound."

I had refrained from calling him 'Sonny'. While I was patting myself on the back, he said, "One moment," and put me on hold. He was back before I gathered the presence of mind to hang up.

"We will call at your office, Mr. Spain. Please wait for us."

Chapter 13

Tod Patrick Grayson lived up to his schoolgirl note and his telephone personality. He marched through the door like the landlord's favorite nephew. He was dressed for success. Wire frame spectacles and a skinny leather briefcase rounded out his uniform. His expression couldn't have been graver if the fate of western civilization rested on his shoulders.

The other half of the 'we' Grayson had mentioned was a managerial fifty. He stood perfectly still in twelve hundred dollars worth of tailored flannel, surveying his surroundings with pale blue eyes that could go from simpering accommodation to chill a Manhattan cocktail in nothing flat. They were slightly flabbergasted at having reached my sanctum sanctorum without encountering a reception room.

My work habits probably contributed a little, too. My jacket was thrown over the file cabinet, my tie pulled loose and my shirt cuffs rolled back. The desktop clone was logged onto the skip trace network and the entry screen was up. I was making good headway on Guy Hamilton and chewing on a bite of the Snickers that was filling in for the second half of my supper.

I said something meant to sound like, "Have a seat, gentlemen," and pecked out the rest of the entries.

The standard phone calls had told me Hamilton was six one by two hundred, brown and brown, sixty-three. His hobby seemed to be collecting complaints at the Better Business Bureau. His religious beliefs probably forbade the paying of bills. His credit was so bad they had run out of alphabet before they could give him a rating. A finance company had a hundred dollar bounty outstanding for information leading to the repossession of a 1960 Mercedes 190 SL, so I assumed that was what he was driving.

I logged off as soon as the confirmation screen came up. "What can I do for you, gentlemen?"

Grayson had done his duty as junior partner and closed the door. His companion hadn't taken advantage of the leatherette divan or the chair beside the desk, so he hadn't either.

"Mr. Spain," he announced, "this is Arthur Drew, Executive Vice President of Osborne Associates."

The older man said, "Good evening, Spain," accompanied by a nod that indicated I wasn't scoring too well so far, but that he was striving mightily to reserve final judgement in the interest of total fairness. I put it down on my list of things to worry about on slack days.

"Good evening, Mr. Drew. Help yourselves to a seat."

They sat together on the divan. They looked at me sternly. As if I were four years old, and I had been caught doing something naughty out behind the all-metal Sears storage shed.

"Mr. Spain," Grayson said, "we know you are working for Tommy Lipton, and we know what you have been hired to do."

"So do I," I said, removing any possibility that they could enlighten me on that score.

They didn't like my attitude. They glanced at each other and reached immediate agreement on the point. They didn't even have to say anything. There was nothing quite like watching a well-coordinated team in action.

Drew took a minute to inspect the remainder office and its refinished furniture again. As theater it hadn't been very original the first time around.

"Been having a rough go of it, Spain? Financially?"

"Down at the heels private detectives went out with boat tailed Packards. I don't need to take my mittens off to count the number of weeks I haven't worked since I started nine years ago. Gold doorknobs wouldn't do me any good. Most of my business is referral from out of town agencies who never know anything but my address."

"I suppose there is a certain logic in that," Drew conceded. "But you must have had some reason to accept an assignment from a man of Lipton's reputation."

"I suppose there is a certain logic in that," I conceded.

Drew didn't like being mimicked. I didn't seem to be making a very good impression on him.

"Do you think we came here to be frivolous?" he inquired.

"I think you came here fronting a political boss named C. Benton Osborne. That's frivolous enough for me."

"I would scarcely characterize a man of Mr. Osborne's integrity as a political boss."

"That's not the point."

"Precisely what is the point, then, Mr. Spain?"

"Your man Osborne is on one side of the political fence and Lipton is on the other. This happens to be one of those times when you political types get very interested in what each other is doing. I wouldn't last long in this business if I gave away secrets to a couple of amateurs with a lot of pompous eyewash about urgent, confidential matters."

"Mr. Osborne has spent forty years of his life campaigning against just that sort of tactic," Drew informed me. "It has cost him a good share of his personal fortune and his health. I wonder if you are aware that he has spent the last six weeks in the cardiac care unit at Cedars Sinai?"

"I wonder if he's aware of the kind of juvenile nonsense his staff is pulling while he's laid up?"

"You seem less willing to give us the benefit of the doubt than we are to offer it to you, Mr. Spain," Drew remarked in a voice that wondered why.

"What doubt are we talking about?"

Tod Patrick Grayson could no longer contain himself. "Mr. Drew is offering you a chance to clear yourself," he said in a voice taut with disapproval.

I didn't think they knew a hell of a lot more about my situation than they were letting on, but neither seemed quite dense enough to be pushing an obviously unworkable bluff. Which left the possibility they were serious about something I hadn't heard about yet.

"What am I supposed to clear myself of?"

"Do you deny that Tommy Lipton hired you to trace a young woman passing herself off as the illegitimate daughter of Mr. Osborne?" Grayson asked.

"Absolutely." I made a face. "That wouldn't even make a good television plot."

They hadn't expected that. Grayson stared at me. Drew had more experience. He regarded me narrowly, covering his surprise with an unspoken demand that I bare my soul to satisfy him of my innocence.

I had something else on my mind. "Is Osborne far enough gone that you need to worry about his heirs?"

The suggestion made Drew nervous. "Is it not possible, Mr. Spain, that Lipton might have misrepresented the facts of his assignment to make it look legitimate, so that you would take it in good faith as honest work?"

"What am I supposed to do? Tell you why I was hired and let you decide?"

"If you want."

"I don't."

"But you are a skip tracer, a professional manhunter. Lipton must have hired you for something along those lines."

"What are we doing now, Mr. Drew? Playing animal, vegetable or mineral until you eliminate everything but the right answer?"

"How familiar are you with Lipton's background?"

"I know he was a boss gambler. He may even be a killer, though that was never proven. None of which alters the fact that I took a job from him and I have an obligation to finish it without double crossing him in the process."

"Why do you feel that merely clearing the air in this matter is double crossing him, as you put it?"

"I don't see that there is a matter. You two have imposed on my time with a couple of sentences of vague melodrama and waved a little second year forensic interview technique at me. You've provided no substantial narrative, no corroboration, no evidence of crime or tort."

"Very well," Drew allowed in an egalitarian voice that was prepared to descend to my level to insure no stone had gone unturned in his effort to enlighten me. "C. Benton Osborne is a man of the highest principles. Many years ago he became acquainted with a young woman who tried to take advantage of those high principles by accusing him of paternity. The fact that the matter never went to court is ample evidence of its lack of merit. But the event left a deep impression on Mr. Osborne, and heightened his natural concern for the innocent child, a girl named Mandy.

"Six weeks ago, after a highly stressful campaign, Mr. Osborne suffered a severe cardiac seizure. At the time he was discovered, in a service corridor of the Hollywood Roosevelt Hotel, a valuable property in his possession had vanished. All he could tell us was that he had given it to Mandy. Clearly, someone posing as his illegitimate daughter…alleged illegitimate daughter…had confronted him, perhaps with extortion in mind, and that confrontation precipitated his heart attack. The girl then took advantage of the opportunity to steal Mr. Osborne's property."

"The girl's play is the sort of thing they think up in tabloid news rooms," I told Drew. "No one with Lipton's experience and resources would waste his time commissioning soap opera."

"I don't suggest Lipton originated the scheme. Merely that he might try to exploit the confusion created when it went awry."

"To the best of my knowledge, he hasn't."

"And there is nothing further you are willing to tell us?"

"I'm sorry, Mr. Drew. Nothing you've told me connects even remotely with what I'm doing for Tommy Lipton."

Drew thanked me coldly. He emitted a crisp, "Tod," and stood up. Grayson was on his feet immediately. They left like a pair of trained penguins making a vaudeville exit.

It had been quite an act. Casting by the California Bar Association and Executive Headhunters Anonymous. Story from graffiti in the Triple-X Theater men's room. Additional dialogue from the Standard Manual of Business English. Set decorations by Auction Liquidators, Inc. Mr. Spain's wardrobe by Goodwill Industries. The preceding comedy has been tape recorded for release to our fighting men in South Central.

It wasn't hard to reconstruct the background for 'The Bobbsey Twins Meet Sam Spade.' Osborne had keeled over at a political rally. Any property he had with him probably had political value. When it disappeared, his staff started keeping a nervous eye on the opposition. As soon as Lipton hired me, the executive task force drew the obvious conclusion and swung into action.

I watched for a tail when I left the building. Drew had called me a skip tracer and a manhunter. Those words weren't part of the normal executive vocabulary. They were a distinction only another private investigator would make. Whoever was doing Drew's legwork might want to know how far the flannel suits had spooked me.

I didn't expect anything as obvious as the black Trans Am that pulled away from the curb when I came out of the garage. Six blocks later I really began to wonder. The driver got too far back, lost me in traffic and burned rubber through a red light to catch up. Then he hid behind a Subaru so I wouldn't notice him.

Chapter 14

Fifth Street from Central Avenue west to Pershing Square was a grimy remainder of old Los Angeles, and the last stop for countless failed lives. When your luck ran out, when your habits took over, when your attitude used up the last of society's patience, when you heard voices no one else could hear, this was where you came and this was where you stayed. Merchants didn't linger after business hours. They locked iron pantograph grilles across the narrow fronts of hockshops and surplus stores, put on dim security lights far back in the crowded catacomb interiors and left for luxury homes in the suburbs. By dusk the neighborhood had all the charm of a San Quentin broom closet. It seemed a strange place to put something called a Temple of Cosmic Awareness.

That was the only listing in any of my directories that combined the words cosmic and temple in the name. A phone call got me a serene masculine invitation to leave my message at the sound of the chimes, which indicated they were still doing business. I wasn't making much progress toward the address. A fire department medical truck was parked in the next block with its emergency lights flashing. A white utility ambulance was backed in to the curb with its blunt nose out far enough to close off two lanes. A motorcycle cop wasn't having much luck moving gawking drivers through the other two. It looked like walking might be faster.

I squeezed the Volvo in at an empty meter and trotted across the intersection to beat the signal. A small knot of people pressed around a doorway in the quivering aura of the emergency lights. A stocky Indian woman clung to her impassive husband's sleeve and tried to peer over the shoulders of a pair of doddering pensioners, arm in arm for mutual support. Stubble-faced slovenly winos stared vacantly in at a narrow flight of bare linoleum stairs. A couple of hostile street people haunted the fringes of the group, devouring the scene with scary eyes. A green neon sign hissed malignantly above and lit up random letters of the words 'Weekly Rates.'

A big black cycle cop waded out of the doorway, ordering, "Clear back, now. Give it room," and spread the little crowd across the sidewalk just in time to block my path.

Necks craned and someone asked, "Is he dead?"

"There's a sheet on him," a reedy voice said. "They got a sheet all over him."

Two sweating attendants wrestled a gurney out onto the sidewalk, sprung it up and wheeled it across. The body under the white cover was so frail it scarcely disturbed the lay of the cloth. The crowd reformed in the pulsing red glow around the back of the ambulance, trading rumors on who it had been. Before I could slip past, two fire department medics came out and dumped enough equipment on the rest of the sidewalk to start a medium sized hospital. One of them unbuttoned a shirt pocket and took out a notebook.

"Did you find anything that shows how to spell that name the manager gave us?" he asked the cycle cop.

"Naw. We've got all we'll get."

"You must've found something," the medic insisted. "Social security card or pension papers or something. I mean, he had money for room rent and a toaster oven."

An indulgent smile spread over the cop's moon face. "Social Security card is worth ten bucks to anyone who needs a spare name. This part of town, they don't stay on bodies long enough to get found."

The medic didn't like that, and said so. I didn't know what he expected the cop to do about it. The Egyptians hadn't been able to stop corpse robbing with millions of tons of pyramid. Neither they nor anyone since had been able to confine it to any particular part of town. I forced some friendly grinning and mumbling, stepped over two impact cases and an oxygen bottle and went on down the block trying not to think about the night that I would be wheeled out under a sheet, with only a knot of casual gawkers to wonder who I was and what I had been. Maybe that was just as well. Most of what I had done with my life was better forgotten. Including my plans for this evening.

The Temple of Cosmic Awareness didn't seem to have an advertising budget. The address was a narrow brick front, with Schaeffer-Pilon Hotel carved into an old granite lintel. But it wasn't just another run-down rat trap owned by a another syndicate of scheming shysters and sharp-eyed CPAs angling for a rich investor to cash them out while the residents waited around to collect on their funeral insurance. There was no sign of light anywhere inside. The street level glass was heavily draped, behind the standard iron grille-work. The lock was a high security model with a pickproof reputation that begged for a little action.

Pulling a bag job with no bag and no police monitor wasn't exactly professional technique, but the police in the area were still busy down the street and the black Trans Am was nowhere in sight.

There turned out to be some light inside after all. Just enough for me to make out that I was flanked by a couple of tall urns that looked as if they might have been picked up at a garage sale at Forest Lawn. There was a distinct impression underfoot that the carpet was a lot better padded than the neighborhood warranted. A crisp aroma of newness and a vague impression of remote walls and a high ceiling completed my immediate sensations.

My eyes began to adjust, and a lobby emerged out of the shadows. A multi-faceted glint resolved itself into a chandelier as menacing as an attack helicopter. A marble-faced pillar took form and grew a circular divan at its base. Rubber plants sprouted in the corners like they were screen testing for a fertilizer commercial. I didn't see anything that had been in style later than 1910, and I didn't smell anything older than last month. Paying back that kind of outlay could easily call for a network of shills in the right places. Ricky Calland and the Crown Colony came to mind, followed immediately by my baser instincts.

Management had a well-known affinity for top floor corners, so I padded across and pressed a luminous button beside the single elevator. The door opened promptly. I stepped into some better light. The car gave me a lift in more ways than one. The walls were done in some very explicit and still somewhat tasteful erotica. I got off on the fifth floor and explored a dim angular hallway. Between the carpet padding and the solid old construction of the place, I couldn't have made noise if I had wanted to.

There was noise on the floor...a voice that sounded like it had a bad long distance connection. It drew me along to a door that was not quite closed. Behind that was a closet lit by a 25 watt ruby bulb. The voice came from a small diameter speaker mounted on the wall, turned way down.

The voice originated in the next room, which I could see through a good quality piece of one way glass. There was also a camera looking through the glass. The camera was bigger than I was. It was a state of the art 35-millimeter motion picture job mounted on a motorized tracking dolly, with enough dials and knobs for a missile launcher. It looked like it might have gotten lost on the way to work at Paramount, but I wasn't sure why it had wandered in here. Even stolen, it would have cost too much to be a simple tool of blackmail. After the elevator, though, I wasn't surprised to find a group of people sitting around in their birthday suits.

The group was doing its sitting on big brocaded pillows on a mosaic floor. The walls were intricate frescoes that gave the room the look of a made-for-television Byzantine harem. I wouldn't have known a real Byzantine harem from a Babylonian bathhouse. I doubted that any of the group would either. The hairstyles were strictly modern and the tanned and tuned bodies hadn't come from any library. Women outnumbered men about two to one…they usually did at these gatherings…and there were a few pruriently tightened nipples.

The speaker had the muscle tone of a screen idol and that rare angelic facial structure that always managed to look a poetic eighteen, no matter what had happened to it on the way to sixty. His eyes sparkled mysteriously while he spoke, like sunlight catching the dew in some hidden forest glade. He had a huge folio open on a heavy pedestal, but I didn't think he was really reading from it. The flow of his fingers across the text was left to right, and I seemed to remember that Arabic was written right to left. He moved away from the pedestal without missing a syllable and padded lithely among his flock while he went on with his monologue.

I reached for the volume switch to try to get the gist of what he was reciting.

"Sir Richard Burton's translation of *The Perfumed Garden*," a woman said in my ear.

I climbed back down from the ceiling and stared at her. The ruby light bled any color out of her tightly pulled back hair and made a ghastly white slash of her mouth. Her eyes worked on the same principle as a microwave oven, cooking interlopers in their own juices without wasting any energy trying to singe clothing and other incidentals. The arid fragrance of sandalwood filled that little room as thick as mustard gas.

All right, so maybe I should have caught a warning whiff. I never claimed Walter Brixner had been the only voyeur in town.

"Isn't *The Perfumed Garden* a little out of period for the decor?" I asked, mostly to see if I still had a voice.

"Not at all. The *Garden* is a sixteenth century compilation of works written much earlier. In fact, the absence of reference to gunpowder indicates that all of the original text predates the delivery of Constantinople to Mahomet II by the siege cannon of Urban the

Magyar in 1453. It may have been preserved orally in just such a setting as you see. But then, you didn't come to discuss the classics, did you?"

"Didn't I?" I asked in a supercilious wheeze that was as close as I could come to ivy-covered walls and evening lecture groups.

"Our focus may be on the cultural aspects of life," she said in a consciously patient tone, "but we are not without the benefits of technology."

That probably translated to an ultrasonic anti-intrusion package. It definitely suggested they had something to hide.

"I'm a private investigator," I said, dropping the act and feeling a lot more comfortable. My heart was beating again, and I felt sure I could expect blood pressure by the weekend. "I'm here about a former employee. Midas Turner."

She let out an enlightened, "Ahhh," that put me in the category of bearable crosses and confirmed half my suspicions about the place. "One of the fathers heard about Mr. Turner's death and thinks he can use the circumstances as leverage to extort a settlement he couldn't obtain otherwise without unpleasant publicity."

"I'm not working for anyone's father, dear. I'm the poor sap who found Turner's body this morning. And unless I get some straight answers, I may have to persuade the police you people did the job." Maybe if I sounded tough enough, I could even forget this broad had scared me out of my Florsheims.

She opened her ghastly mouth to say something emphatic, then snapped it shut before anything came out. She was through talking. She went out without a word and marched straight down the hall. I trailed along behind the half a foot of rear overhang that would save her from the empty life of a sex symbol. She led me through a door at the end of the hallway, straight into the nineteen thirties.

The illusion couldn't have been more real if I had just stepped off a DC-3 and had my chauffeur whisk me down here in a Chrysler Airflow. The room was a posh private office furnished in streamline curves and deep upholstery and lots of silver and gray edging. The muted strains of a society band drifted from a polished radio cabinet. The only light came from a small copper lamp that put a brilliant rectangle on a couple of square feet of sheenless desktop and diffused a hazy glow toward the ceiling.

The woman marched around behind the desk, and confronted me through the glow. The light didn't do anything for her. She had solid Nordic cheekbones and full red lips and the general bearing of someone who would favor cavalry boots and a whip for informal entertaining at home. She probably came in handy when the girls got into a hair pull over one of the resident hunkies. She curled a set of violent red fingertips under the lip of the desk and smiled. The smile was a withered smirk that went nicely with the dry whisper of a pocket door sliding open in the wall behind her. Lamplight focussed itself as a sadistic glitter in her eyes. I was really going to get it now. I was going to gulp down my terror and go through that door and when I came out I was going to be a changed man.

I winked at her and went through the door. It whispered shut behind me.

Chapter 15

The room was a library that someone had transplanted from the windowless depths of a nineteen twenties art deco mansion. Bronze sconces spread clouds of light as obscure as celestial nebulae up three azure walls, just enough of it to show that I had the place to myself. One wall was an ultramarine fireplace against which a Lucite clock lacking any visible works turned a bronze second hand with an eerie electric silence. Inset bookshelves of polished ebony made hexagons between the deep cobalt of the carpet and the indigo shadows in the cove of the ceiling.

The books in the shelves weren't bought by the lineal foot for decoration. No two bindings matched, and some of them were very old leather. Not all the titles were in English, and a lot of those that were looked like pretty heavy going. Taken together, they represented a major investment. If they had been acquired legally. I turned on a bronze torchere lamp to preserve my eyesight and pulled a likely candidate to check the flyleaf. What I found set me to work pulling more books and scribbling at the insurance bounty tab of my notebook. Thirty minutes of it gave me writer's cramp.

I didn't bother trying to describe the fanciful bits of sculpture that looked like Rube Goldberg creations and probably qualified as museum pieces. There was a display case in one corner. It was locked. The contents were probably valuable also, although they didn't look it. They consisted of two strips of a dozen frames of thirty five millimeter film sealed in transparent plastic brick and surrounded by five faded still photographs. Outdoor shots of men in whipcord jodhpurs and campaign hats and women in ankle length shapeless dresses posed around a big square wooden crank camera on a spindly tripod, with endless rows of orange trees in the background.

"The sole remaining artifacts of what is arguably the first motion picture filmed in California."

I hadn't heard him come in. He had simply appeared. Not with any juvenile intent to surprise. It had just happened. From the timbre of his voice, he was the lecturer from the harem down the hall. To look at, he was a different man entirely. He had put on a business suit. The fit was perfect, the press was perfect, the collar of his white shirt was starched to perfection over a perfectly knotted silk tie. Wire rimmed spectacles added just the right touch of respectability. He was a pillar of the community.

"I am Jeffrey Haven," he said.

The name didn't do anything for me, but at closer range the face was Deja Vu. I had seen him somewhere before...a very long time ago...and couldn't put my finger on when or where.

Haven pivoted a section of blue wall panel and pressed gently with the tips of his fingers until a latch clicked. He was in no hurry about it. Nothing of any moment was going to happen until it suited his purposes to make it happen. He knew it and I could feel it. His aura of command was palpable, like a sex therapist getting ready to debrief a client's latest orgasm. He drifted across the cobalt carpet as silently as smoke and settled into a turquoise gondola chair. He considered me with the sort of impassive fixity I remembered using when I spotted a unique bug moving across my desk while I was listening to hold button music.

"Do you have any concept of the significance of the artifacts in that case?"

"No, aside from the fact that there is probably a museum or a film studio somewhere that wouldn't mind having them back."

"Neither museums nor studios care in the least about the history they possess. Only a tiny fraction of their inventory is ever exhibited. The rest molders unrestored and unappreciated. Warehouses of volatile nitrate film that could ignite at a spark and vaporize decades of cultural heritage. Those particular fragments were discovered during demolition of an old building in Alaska. In the silent film era, Alaska was the end of the exhibitor circuit. Studios did not consider prints worth the postage to reclaim them, so they were thrown in a basement to rot. The recent resurgence of ownership claims by the successors of those studios is solely the result of the videocassette and DVD phenomena, which raise the possibility of mass-market distribution. Hardly practical with those pathetic remnants. Do sit down, Mr. Spain."

I sat in a matching gondola chair. "If nobody wants it, why bother to lock it up?"

"Value transcends commercial exploitation. The significance of that film lies in its history. Where it was made, and why. Filmmaking was, in its earliest days, a legally airtight monopoly. Airtight because it was based upon patents...primarily those of Thomas Edison. Monopoly permitted extortionate pricing. Extortionate pricing bred exhibitor resentment. Resentment opened the door for infringement. Infringement drew retaliation. The infringers moved their production facilities west to avoid the thugs of the monopoly. The early companies settled north of Los Angeles for the ideal filming weather, and the distance from process servers. It was a lawless business in those days. Directors routinely wore revolvers when filming in remote locations. But in time the eastern monopoly was broken and the pirates became the power. A new monopoly that choked on its own arrogance when the sound patents arrived in the late twenties. Those crowned yet another generation of princelings to grow fat until television came. It is a cycle. Innovation brings power. Power corrupts. Corruption breeds resentment. Resentment fuels innovation. Within that case is the beginning. I wonder, Mr. Spain, if you or I would have endured the privation those men and women faced?"

"I've always been a big fan of indoor plumbing," I confessed.

"You did not come here to be insolent, Mr. Spain. You are stupid, but not that stupid. What is it you want?"

"You know my name, so I assume you've been following the news items on Midas Turner, and that I've been mentioned."

A smile touched the corners of Haven's mouth. "Midas was clearly shot for reasons having to do with activities outside the scope of his work for the Temple. I am in no way connected with those. I have already told the police as much."

"You're not dumb enough to think they believed you."

"There would have been no point in my asking Midas about his personal activities. Our corruptive society has forced such men to lie so often they do so out of habit."

"What was the point in your hiring him at all?"

"You would scoff at anything involving sympathy or social responsibility, would you not, Mr. Spain?"

"Absolutely. No one shrewd enough to put together the asset base you've got here would give an inner-city talent scout the run of the premises for humanitarian reasons. Turner wouldn't have gotten in the door unless he brought something of solid economic value to the party. Even then, you would have sounded him out pretty thoroughly to learn what risk he might represent to you. As you are doing with me now."

"Midas' police trouble admits only two possibilities," Haven said serenely. "Either I failed to question him or I bungled what questioning I did do. Believe whichever you chose. Both lead to the same conclusion. I am ignorant of his activities."

"The police are still going to wonder why Turner wasn't back standing on street corners when you canned him. He was at loose ends when he came here, or he wouldn't have let himself get sucked into a flaky operation like this. Any contacts he made, he had to make while he was working for you."

"During the time he worked for me," Haven emphasized. "Not necessarily as a result of working for me."

"You have a lot of glib answers. Maybe the police already tried this line of questioning on you?"

"They expressed an interest in doing so. I declined. No amount of candor would change their attitude toward me."

"All right, let's get back to money. You've got a lot invested here. Did you borrow any of it from Tommy Lipton?"

"Certainly not." The idea seemed to amuse him.

"You've got a boy named Calland who picks up customers for you at the Crown Colony. Ricky Calland."

"The Temple cannot function in a vacuum. Troubled people are referred to me from many sources."

"How well did Calland know Midas Turner?"

"I presume they got on well enough. They are, or were, approximate intellectual equals."

"Can you be a little more specific? Did they have business dealings? Compare penises in the halls? What?"

"I really wouldn't know."

"What do you know about charity bingo?"

"Jeffrey Haven's smile was as faint as last year's Christmas. "Don't you think this is turning into rather an obvious fishing expedition, Mr. Spain?"

"You've played this pretty smart up until now. You've sat back and parried each of my questions, knowing the more you could goad me into asking, the more you'd learn about what I did and didn't know. Why stop here?"

"The game has grown tiresome, Mr. Spain."

"Maybe I can spice it up a little. Turner was shot because he murdered the chief numbers cruncher for the bingo rackets. The only connection I know of between Turner and the accountant is Ricky Calland. Your roper at the Crown Colony."

If Haven had been any less perturbed he would have fallen asleep. A faint click attracted my attention while he was saying, "I shall ask Ricky about all this when I see him next. I shall ask you, Mr. Spain, to leave the

Temple and not to return. In future, I shall not hesitate to prosecute you for illegal entry."

"Why don't I stick around," I suggested. "It looks like you'll get a chance to ask Ricky right now."

Haven's features were stupid in their complacency. When he did stir, it was condescension to my childish devices. He turned his head to follow my eyes.

Chapter 16

Calland looked like something wild out of the woods. He hadn't shaved. His Prince Valiant hairdo had the frizzies. The purple suit with the nifty touches hung limp on his tensed muscles, like he had lived in it all week. He straight-armed the panel closed, advanced stiff-legged and gave me a close look into the business end of an automatic. The gun was a bushed down military Browning left over from the Russian revolution. Firing one required about the same pressure as strangling a weasel. Any less and it would have gone off in Calland's clenched hand.

"Get up!" he ordered. "Get on your feet! Turn around!"

I kept my hands where he could see them and stood up and turned around. I felt as self-conscious as a novice ballerina trying out for *Swan Lake.* Calland pawed my torso.

"I'm not carrying a gun."

"Yeah. You ditched it after you whacked Midas. You made the evening news."

"I didn't shoot Turner. I found the body. I wouldn't be running around loose if I had pulled the trigger. The police aren't fools."

"Sit down," Calland snarled. "Sit down where I can watch you."

He prodded my ribs with the muzzle of his gun to emphasize the point. I didn't like it, but anything I said was liable to goad him to worse. Haven didn't share my inhibitions. Confronting a cruiser weight flip-top with a hand full of sudden death didn't ruffle him in the least.

"Ricky," he lectured from the comfort of his chair, "you know I have forbidden firearms in the Temple."

"Shut up, you lousy fairy!" Calland said in a strangled voice.

He stood with his feet in a belligerent spread and glared down at each of us in turn. I got the worst of it. Whatever grudges he was harboring against Haven, his beef with me seemed to take precedence.

"All right," he finally demanded. "Where the fuck is it?"

"I told you, I'm not carrying…"

"The fucking Doomsday Book!" he spat at me.

Surprised probably wasn't the word for my expression. I stared at him like a kid who'd just run ten blocks for his catcher's mitt and got back to find everyone playing basketball. Evidently I should have paid more attention to the late Walter O. Brixner's last telephone message. There was no time like the present to find out what I had missed.

"What exactly is this Doomsday Book?" I asked.

I had pulled dumb stunts in my life. I had two Purple Hearts to prove it. But that was Vietnam, and this was now. Calland's self control popped loose like the safety spoon on a grenade. Rage bloated his features. A spasmodic step brought him forward. The automatic was in my face again, twitching madly.

"Don't jive me! Lipton hired you to find it! Where the fuck is it?"

"Look," I said as soothingly as I could manage, "there is a limit to how much righteous anger that gun will take before it goes off. Why don't you relax a bit, so you don't accidentally blow my head off before I can tell you everything I know."

"Where the fuck is it?"

All I had to give him was a big cooperative smile. "You're the second party who has had the idea Lipton hired me to do something he didn't. The other consisted of a couple of executives from Osborne Associates, the advertising company."

Calland knew both Grayson and Drew by name. He fanned a gentle rain of spittle down on me expressing an opinion of them in very agitated and not very coherent profanity. I got the impression he was accusing them of treachery.

"What was your deal with them?" I asked sympathetically.

"I was supposed to be the one to handle Lipton," he railed indignantly.

His nostrils flared with angry breathing while he waited for me to offer some lame excuse.

"I was supposed to handle everything to do with Lipton," he spat at me when I didn't.

Haven wasn't happy with me either, in his quiet unruffled way. "You should have told me you represented Tommy Lipton, Mr. Spain. Out of common politeness, if nothing else."

"Any business I have with Lipton is between him and me."

"I am entitled to candor, Mr. Spain. I have a right to know what Ricky may have involved the Temple in."

"That depends on exactly how he was involved in the murder of Walter Brixner," I replied, mostly to see if I'd get a rise out of Calland. What I got was another harsh string of not very specific profanity.

"Oh, really," I said, as if it all made perfect sense to me.

"That little square nuts Brixner…him with his briefcase and his geek shoes…he's the bastard that put me down behind my back. Trying to get that nothing singer of his promoted. I tried to get both of them straight, but they wouldn't get with it. Man, I had ideas. Real ideas. Fucking Brixner just wouldn't let Lipton hear them."

I winked at Haven. "Get the picture? With Brixner dead, Ricky thought he'd have the inside track with Lipton. So he suckered Turner into doing the job."

Haven wasn't losing any serenity over it. "I know Lipton, of course, in a casual way. I will accept his telephone call or meet with him at his convenience to assure him I am in no way involved. You will tell him as much."

"No."

Haven arched his eyebrows.

"So far as I know, Lipton isn't remotely interested in either of you. I make a point of not annoying my clientele with things that don't interest them."

Calland kicked me in the shin. "Don't do that. Don't talk like I wasn't in the room. People are always doing that. Talking like I wasn't in the room."

I gave him a dirty look while I rubbed my leg. "As long as you are here, do you have anything to add to the conversation?"

"I was the one who told Lipton about the Doomsday Book. He never knew old man Osborne lost it until I clued him. That book could get him in solid with some sharp political dudes, instead of those out of it stiffs he's backing now. I told him I could find it, make the connections, set things up. Brixner must have talked him into hiring you and shafting me out of the picture."

"This Doomsday Book must be hot stuff, the way you people are double crossing each other to get it."

"Come off it! Lipton clued you. Or else how would you know when you found it?"

"It was just two words on Brixner's answering machine until now."

Our eyes met like two cats across a property line. Too many new ideas had overloaded Calland's limited mental capacity. It was a minute before something that resembled thinking began to percolate behind the blood tracks.

"You were Brixner's guy," he remembered from his earlier theory. "Lipton was too smart to trust you. That's why you disappeared Brixner's body and cleaned out his crib. You did it so Lipton wouldn't find out and trash your deal before you knew enough to push in."

"Not even close," I said.

"Fuck you. I was just up at Brixner's. There's a real estate sign in the yard. The old bag doing her garden next door said the movers were there all day cleaning the place out. Brixner was transferred to Chicago real sudden, they told her."

That was news to me, but not a surprise. Charity bingo worked with the quiet thoroughness of nerve gas. "You should have checked on Brixner a little closer before you had him killed. He had some tough friends."

"You ain't so goddamn hard."

"Not me, Sonny. Brixner was the accounting brains for a bingo racket. He had to disappear. Discovery of his murder would've meant an investigation. The house was cleaned out to make sure no records were missed. The killing must've smelled like the opening move in a takeover play. Brixner's friends shot Turner to head it off. They took the trouble to talk to him before they killed him. With a gun at his throat, it's not likely he left you out of his story."

"You can forget that crap," Calland told me. "I was down at that Scheherazade place after the cops split. The shit bum loading the videos didn't try to get tough until I asked about the Doomsday Book. That's what it's about. If it ain't, why is the sucker that owns the place hiding out?"

I didn't have any answer for that. I hadn't talked to any people at Scheherazade's. It might be interesting to know what they had said. Before I could think of any appropriate questions, a red light came on brightly over the door. It had the impact of a police cruiser in the rear view mirror.

"The emergency light," Haven realized. "There is a problem in the Temple."

Calland wasn't impressed. "Your problem is the four bills back commission you owe me."

"The checkbook is time locked in the safe," Haven reminded him.

"Cash, Peter Pan! You ain't hanging no more paper on me. That bread has to hold me until I get the Doomsday Book."

"Ricky, the Doomsday Book is beyond your reach. The moment you told Lipton it was available, you had outlived all but the most temporary usefulness. Come to your senses. Hitchhike to Guatemala. Vanish and be grateful for whatever years you have left to you."

I wondered if I shouldn't tag along. As familiar as Haven seemed to be with the Doomsday Book, it was probably on the best seller list. He also seemed to have some rather definite ideas about Tommy Lipton. And he was about as far from stammering hysteria as he could get.

My wondering was cut short by an emphatic noise that penetrated the heavy sound deadening between the outer office and us. Calland stared at the wall. He was built like Superman. Maybe he thought he had X-ray vision as well. Haven came to his feet. Calland whirled and shoved the gun against his stomach.

"Sit down, Fairy!"

Haven didn't move. He spoke without raising his voice. "Ricky, there is a situation in the Temple. It must be attended to."

Calland forgot he was armed. He forgot he was big enough to fold Haven up and stuff him into a bookshelf. He took a hesitant step back, like a schoolboy with a water pistol, and gave Haven room to pass. A second later he had no more idea than I did why he had done it.

"All right," he snarled at me. "We're going out there so daddy can spank the rich bitches on the bummy. Get up, you bastard."

"That's not the spoiled rich acting up," I warned him. "You better get out the way you came in while Haven and I get some police down here."

"Crapola!"

Calland collared me and hauled me up and pushed me after Haven. It was the wrong move. I was telling Calland that and trying to hang to one side when Haven slid the door open.

Chapter 17

There was more light than I remembered in the outer office, and not much nineteen thirties' atmosphere left. The people from the Hollywood harem were lined up with their backs to one wall, not wearing anything but goose bumps. They had the uncomfortable look of Army recruits about to be checked for hernias. The doctor was wearing a black ski mask with red accents around the eyes and mouth. It clashed rather badly with the paisley shirt hanging out over his baggy camouflage trousers. Coffee colored skin showed in the knuckle slits of leather driving gloves wrapped around the handle of a blue steel .22 automatic.

Behind the heels of his Nikes a plastic shopping bag from an exclusive boutique had tipped sideways under a clumsy load. Tooled leather and a Rolex watch peeked out. A nearby section of carpet had been thrown back to reveal the circular door of a compact floor safe sunk in a shallow well of polished hardwood. Another ski mask in a chartreuse jogging suit was down on one knee pointing a Kalashnikov assault rifle at the dial of the combination lock. Standing over him and jitterbugging at the hopelessness of the idea was a third ski mask in skintight leather. His delicate white gloves belonged on a hotel doorman. He held a stubby .38 revolver, with the gray residue of recent firing staining the muzzle.

Haven's assistant was sprawled cross-legged, her skirt bunched up to expose obscene rolls of pasty fat on her thighs. Her full red mouth hung open in the middle of a blank expression, as if she had started to say something and forgot what it was. The small hole in the shock white of her temple looked almost insignificant. She was the only one in the room who didn't stare at us like we had just landed from the second moon of Neptune.

I think I yelled, "Shut the door!" The words were rolling thunder inside my head, but no else seemed to hear them.

Calland panicked. He tried to drop the whole ski team at once, firing as fast as his automatic would cycle. He scattered terrified people all over and missed everything but the walls.

The ski mask in the jogging suit jumped like a galvanic current had gone through his legs. His Kalashnikov stuttered wildly. Calland's grip on my collar evaporated. He collapsed before the shock of the wound had time to show on his face. I back-pedaled out of the line of fire. A gondola chair blind-sided me and I came in for a one-point landing. Haven was hit solidly. I saw two bullets lift the back of his coat as they exited. I heard them punch into book bindings across the library. The impact rocked him only slightly and fazed him no more than the warm wind from a building lobby. He went on through the door. Pistols played a minor accompaniment to the concerted savagery of the assault rifle.

Wailing voices welled up in the outer office; some of it the terrified screaming of terrified people; some the ecstasies of warped minds near orgasm from the sudden vicarious jolt of mortal combat…from the stench and ear punishing reverberation of confined gunfire. The fragments that riveted my attention were animated keening street gibberish.

"You get them, Man?"

"They come right out the mufuckin' wall!"

"We gotta know, Man."

"I ain't goin' in there, Man. They got they shit on them. I ain't goin' in on nobody when they got they shit on them."

"Do it, Man! Do that thing!"

I rolled flat on the carpet as the automatic rifleman opened up again, spraying the rest of the magazine through the intervening wall. Wood chips flew. Books exploded out of the shelves, bringing those packed in tightly against them cascading down on my back. Glass popped quietly and finally in the display case. Silence. A new magazine was worked into the assault rifle. I squirmed flush against the wall. The first go round had just been suppressive fire. This time the ski masks meant to kill. The bullets came in low, about knee level and angled down to catch anyone hugging the floor. I hugged the floor and waited to be cut to rags. More books fell on my back. They kept falling after the automatic rifle had moved to work the other end of the room. It came back. Bullets gouged the carpet inches from my face. My whole mind was one silent shameless horrible scream for the inevitable end to come.

The shooting stopped with an abruptness that could only mean another empty magazine. Cold-blooded survival instinct seized me in the same instant. I heaved up out of the books and wood chips like some dripping monstrosity out of a slime-covered swamp. Books and pieces of books were strewn over everything. Bullet craters made random patterns everywhere. Lifeless entrails of stuffing bulged out of shredded chair coverings. Electricity sizzled in a shattered wall fixture. A torchere lamp was tipped against the opposite bookcase. By some miracle the delicate glass shade hadn't broken. I didn't see Calland where he had fallen. He was gone and his gun was gone. He must have rolled clear of the doorway before the barrage started. He had reached the panel and gotten out. The wall had resealed itself with a mocking tightness that defied me even to remember which was the moveable section. My only remaining hope was to surprise the ski masks before they finished reloading and came in to check the body count. Maybe I could grab a gun. More likely I'd get shot to pieces trying.

I charged through the door like a drunken cape buffalo and stopped short, teetering on rubbery legs. The office was as empty as a tomb. It was a tomb. Jeffrey Haven sat erect in a corner made by one wall and a silver edged gray file cabinet, staring at nothing. His legs were thrust straight out in front of him. Death had deflated him. He looked like the decaying remains of some ancient ruler set out in full regalia to sit sentinel over long forgotten mysteries. Burned nitrocellulose was a hazy garrote. The scene reminded me vaguely of a panel in the Classic Comics' version of *King Solomon's Mines*.

The ski team, with visions of police SWAT teams dancing in their heads, had beat it before anyone could use a telephone. The naked people probably had scattered when the shooting started in earnest. I found a woman out in the hall. She had jumped into white denim pants and jacket and a pair of peasant clogs. Either the pants didn't fit too well, or she had them on backwards. She was trying to stuff a wad of underclothes into a bulky shoulder bag and pull a door open at the same time. She saw me coming and jumped back against the wall.

"Where did they go?" I demanded.

Her eyes were as moist as oysters. Her mouth moved furiously and couldn't make a sound. Her legs kept moving, is if she thought she could back right through the plasterboard. I wrenched the door open and stepped through onto the top landing of a dingy stairwell. The chill of night penetrated a filthy casement window and left condensation on a concrete wall. Light from a broken fixture showed dribbles of damp blood going down the aggregate steps and puddling against peeling traction tape. There was no particular reason for it to be Ricky Calland's. Anyone could have been hit. But it was still worth a try. If I could deliver Calland to the police alive, I could step out from under both Brixner and Midas Turner.

I followed the blood down to a basement full of bright fluorescent light shimmering in the sheet metal of low hanging ductwork. The floor was scrubbed cleaner than some office buildings I'd been in. Irregular teardrops of blood angled across, as if someone had gone quickly and unsteadily. I stayed close to a wall of shelves full of cartons and gallon bottles. They seemed to be arranged to feed a gray machine that took up most of another wall. It might have been a film-processing machine. Dramatic images flickered without continuity across the twenty-inch monitor of a digital editing computer, like a runaway dream sustained only by sheer velocity. Whoever had been using the apparatus had knocked over his high stool clearing out.

The dribbles of damp blood led me up four concrete stairs. A door stood ajar at the top. I felt cold air beyond it. I slipped out and shut the door immediately to keep from being silhouetted. The rough brick of a wall against my back was my first and most reassuring sensation. An exhaust whispered nearby in the darkness while I waited for my eyes to adjust. I was in an alley. There was a narrow rectangle of feeble sodium light down at the end. Flashes of passing headlights outlined a dark shape creeping away from me. It would be a black Trans-Am. The driver draped over the steering wheel would be Ricky Calland. I had a ridiculous idea. I thought he was out of it. All I had to do was chase the car down and shut it off. A lifetime of having to do everything the hard way should've told me better.

The running lights came on bright as my lope brought me even with the rear fender. The Pontiac lurched ahead at twenty miles an hour. It wiped out a wooden frame, scattering galvanized cans and trash. I hurdled one can and banged my shin against another. I wasn't out of the race yet. The alley emptied near where I had parked my Volvo. Calland weaved out into traffic. The last horn blast wasn't dead when I reached my slot. I piled in, fired the engine and screeched around the corner two blocks behind him. Calland drove badly, and I drove badly in his wake. I had the windows closed tight, the heater full on. Emotional aftershock from the attempt on my life had caught up with me. It had me shivering like a nudist in Nome. I needed to pull over and put myself together again. I didn't need to follow Calland up an access ramp.

The Santa Monica Freeway was running seventy-five miles an hour in the slow lane. When Calland turned north, things got worse. The Coast Highway had more bends than a six-mile string of pneumonia virus. I was aging fast listening to my tires scream and trying to remember how many miles ago I had bought them. Calland's muscle building courses must have done him some good. Or else the demands of his profession made for a lot of endurance. Shot up as he was, he still managed the curves and the traffic well enough to pull away from my ninety odd miles an hour. My last glimpse of him was a pair of low taillights braking to turn up one of the roads that curved into the hills above Malibu. He was long gone when I made the turn. The only lights came from widely spaced houses. The closest were just below the road, clinging to the edge of a steep bluff on the ocean side. It occurred to me that any one of them would have a phone. A phone meant I could turn the search over to the County Police. I was slowing with that in mind when I spotted Calland's lights in a ditch ahead.

The Trans-Am hadn't left the road at any hundred miles an hour. It hadn't hit at even ten miles an hour. Both headlights still functioned, shining into a dirt bank. The car was hung up midway on the frame. The rear wheels were still turning slowly under power, not going anywhere in the air. I pulled off the road and stopped just short of an asphalt drive that curved down to a bluff house. My high beams shone full on the low Pontiac. Calland was jackknifed forward; half turned and half wedged with a rag doll limpness between the wheel and door by the weight of his torso. On the evidence he was finished, but I had already made that mistake once tonight.

I shut off my engine and killed my lights. I felt a tang of salt air in my nostrils and rough gravel under my feet as I catfooted the fifty yards to the Trans Am. Brilliant headlights passed in a rush going the other way. Calland didn't move. I came up behind his left ear, just in case. It was all a waste of time and effort.

I hadn't ever gotten used to stomach wounds, to the trail of intestines and the blood and the smell. This was one Trans Am the repo artists weren't going to enjoy picking up. It was all I could do to reach in the open window and shut off the ignition. I didn't try for the lights. The car was liable to be hit if I left it dark.

Calland's neck offered the only artery I could reach without opening the door and spilling him out. I steeled myself and tried to find a pulse. I didn't stay at it long. The situation called for immediate police attention.

Chapter 18

I could see light leaking out on the ocean side of the house immediately below, spilling down the bluff toward an endless run of deserted beach where rollers came in smooth off the Pacific and dissolved into foam on the moonlit sand. A gull gliding low over the gentle vee of the roof beat its wings twice and sailed off toward the water as I started down the steep drive. I had to go down with short, careful steps to keep my wobbly legs from being forced into a run. I went along the windowless fieldstone front of the house and leaned on the door button. Musical chimes made faint noise somewhere inside. Below on the Coast Highway cars went by in a furious rush. The sound reminded me of cold wind. Perspiration from the heat in my car hadn't completely evaporated and my teeth had to work at not chattering. What was left of my morale could have been run down by a fast moving snake. I was getting ready to try the button again when the door opened a crack.

The face that peered out was long and lean, with lots of masculine good looks. It had probably made the sports and fraternity pages of a college yearbook about ten years ago. Its owner had cultivated a professional hairstyle in the meantime, but he was still using the furtive hostile curiosity he had developed for bookworms who made the mistake of knocking on the door during loft parties.

"Yes? What is it?"

"There's been some trouble on the road," I was able to tell him without stuttering. "I'll need to use your phone to call the police."

"Sorry. No phone here. Try down the road."

I had my shoe in the crack before he could shut the door. I glanced at the phone line leading in under the soffits. I was too beat to get mad. The smile I gave him felt as heavy as a lead sinker.

"Look, friend, there's a dead man at the top of your drive. You're going to see some police whether I call them from here or somewhere else. I promise I won't peek if you want to tidy up in there while I'm using the phone you haven't got."

The house was too far below grade for him to see much, but he could see the headlights and he knew they weren't supposed to be where they were. He drew the door back a foot. I slid past, close enough to smell expensive scotch on his breath, and found myself in an entry done in the quarry slate and blond wood trim that had been all the rage in the nineteen fifties. A gap between the tops of the walls and the low vee of the ceiling gave the illusion of openness popular then, and let the noise of television news circulate from the back of the house. My gracious host closed the door and turned the deadbolt. He was a few inches taller than I was, and he stood close enough to make it obvious.

"I didn't hear the wreck," he said suspiciously.

"There was no collision. The car is still intact."

"The driver have a stroke?"

"He was gut shot. With a .30 caliber Kalashnikov."

Mr. Altitude didn't quite jump out of his country club tan. He scrutinized my impatient expression to see if I thought I was being funny. He got very worried when he saw I didn't.

"This way," he ordered.

At the rear of the house was a living room straight out of *Better Homes and Gardens* featured homes of 1959. The wide picture window was an endless expanse of dark ocean, dotted by the tiny lights of a ship that might be halfway to China. The room itself had a wall length sandstone fireplace and more blond woodwork, and copper spotlights fastened up under the main ceiling beam. The sandstone needed cleaning and the wood needed varnish and the spotlight housings were going green. For a pricey piece of real estate, it hadn't seen much maintenance.

A man about sixty ignored the view and the deterioration to watch a console television from a threadbare armchair. A flaming red short-sleeved shirt with fleur-de-lis designs hung out over his thick belly. Gray hair fringed a head the shape of a full moon. Coarser gray hair grew in the neck vee of the shirt, under a choker of rawhide and shells, and more of the same matted on his thick forearms. He held a highball glass in his thick fist. He looked like a man who drank partly because it gave him an excuse to make a fist.

My escort addressed him uncertainly.

"Charlie?"

Charlie turned to glower at the interruption. Then he glowered at me.

"Who the hell is that?"

His voice had the volume turned up to rattle dishes in Santa Barbara. The volume wasn't what made me stare. It was the same voice I had heard hiding its bad nerves on Walter Brixner's tape machine. Calland had said the man who owned Scheherazade's was in hiding. He just hadn't lived long enough to introduce us.

"He says there's a dead man up on the highway," my escort tattled. "There's a car up in the ditch. I saw the lights."

Charlie used the revelation as an excuse for more glowering. Something in my mousy smile may have tipped him things weren't exactly right.

"What the hell's your name?"

"Elmo Slotmachine," I said.

"Is that supposed to be funny?"

"I'll bet the police get a real rush out of it. Why don't we call them and find out?"

"Don't police me!" Charlie came to his feet. He was as big as a firehouse in his red shirt. He poked a thumb into his chest. "I'm Charlie Watrous, Attorney at Law. Come up the hard way. Night school and all that crap. Thirty-seven years in the business. Cops I can handle.

Harv here is a lawyer, too. Fair haired boy of my firm. Real bright, ain't you, Harv?"

Harv half closed his eyes. "I guess so, Charlie. That's what you keep telling people."

I was in poor shape. It was all I could do to keep from coming down with a roaring case of the giggles. "Let me get this straight. You're a couple of hot dog shysters? School trained and all? And you've got yourself in so much trouble over a few naughty movies you've got to lie low out here with the artistes?"

Harv measured me for a long, ominous minute before he said, "Maybe you don't know who you're talking to?"

"Sure I do. He just told me. He's Charlie Watrous, Attorney at Law. Came up the hard way. Night…"

"Shut up!" Watrous ordered. He finished his drink in a fast gulp and brought the glass away in a three fingered fist. He put a thick forefinger in my face. "You got an angle. What is it?"

"Elmo Slotmachine has no angles," I said solemnly. "You could wind up with three lemons, though, if you don't have the right answers when the time comes."

Watrous scowled indecisively. I knew something, and it looked like I wasn't going to be scared into giving it up. He took the thick forefinger out of my face and chuckled. He sounded like an asthmatic steamroller.

"Hey, look, old Charlie ain't a bad guy. Somebody does a turn for me, I always pay off. Don't I Harv?"

"Sure, Charlie."

"Harv knows. He saved me some grief. Married my oldest daughter before she could get herself knocked up. Or was it after? Anyway, I took him in right out of college. Hey, Harv, how much dough you ever make that I didn't show you how?"

Harv didn't have anything to say about that.

"Not one Goddamn cent," Charlie Watrous chortled. He waved his glass in Harv's direction, clinking ice cubes in the bottom. "While you're remembering that, you can get me a refill. What are you drinking, uh...?"

"Slotmachine. Elmo Slotmachine. I'll have a Coke, Harv. I don't like talking to the police with liquor on my breath."

Watrous did some more chuckling. "Hey, come on, let's leave the cops out of this. Let's sit down and talk awhile. Just you and me. I bet we can work something out. Come on, pick yourself a seat."

I moved scattered newspapers and sat on the sandstone hearth. I took my time about it. The more comfortable I looked, the less comfortable Watrous could afford to feel. And Ricky Calland had all the time in the world.

"Forgetting the police won't make the dead man up the drive go away, Charlie,"

Watrous turned off the television. Harv came back and put a highball glass of Coke beside me. He looked worried when he handed Watrous his refill.

"There's a car up there, Charlie. I saw it when I let him in. The lights are still on."

"Well why the hell don't you go turn them out?" Watrous bellowed.

Harv closed his mouth. His teeth clicked lightly. The tiny muscles of his lean face were tense, prominent. He padded silently out of the room.

"Kids these days," Watrous complained when we had heard the front door open and close. "You gotta tell them when to blow their nose."

"The cadaver was a kid named Ricky Calland. I think he was on his way here to see you about something called a Doomsday Book."

"That piece of shit again?" Watrous exploded irritably.

"You phoned a man named Walter Brixner about it last night," I reminded him.

He put a number twelve loafer on the hearth, rested a forearm on his knee and swirled his fresh drink in front of my face. His eyes twinkled shrewdly.

"You seem to know a hell of a lot about my business."

The problem was that I didn't, and I needed to. "I got your name from Brixner," I lied. "He said you might be able to find a certain type of merchandise. For a special client."

"What kind of bucks we talking?" Watrous wanted to know.

I hadn't expected Brixner's name to carry an immediate stamp of approval. "Five figures," I threw out casually, hoping that was vague enough to be in the ballpark. When Watrous looked dissatisfied, I added, "For starters."

"This client shy or something?"

"Chicago is a long way off. He'll catch a plane when the deal is roughed out."

Watrous jerked his head. He was half way out of the room before it dawned on me that I was supposed to follow him. We went downstairs to a recreation room as long as a bowling alley. The far wall was a theater screen, complete with layers of curtains. Framed movie posters and publicity stills covered two more walls, with track lamps strategically aimed to show off the highlights. There were a lot of famous and not so famous faces, but only one kept repeating. One I had seen pictures of just that afternoon.

I let out an enthusiastic, "Hey, that's Guy Hamilton," just to be sure.

Watrous didn't hear me. He was busy wrestling a portable projector up on the built-in bar. It took him a couple of false starts to insert the film in the right pattern.

"Siddown," he blurred at me.

It was another striptease film, about the same intellectual level that I'd seen in Walter Brixner's play room, filmed a little earlier. There was a well screened swimming pool and a well built young woman in a two piece bathing suit that would have drawn wolf whistles from the boys coming back from the Berlin Airlift. She put a 78 rpm record on a portable machine and started to dance. After a while she got tired of wearing her bathing suit. For a minute she danced a little more coyly.

Then someone off camera coaxed her around to show off a healthy mat of pubic hair.

"Whatta you think?" Charlie Watrous asked over a bop music track.

"It's not what I think," I said, not having the foggiest idea what made the film worth five figures, for starters. "It's what the client thinks. Just give me the particulars and I'll pass them on."

"Didn't you watch teevee back in the fifties? And don't give me no bull about you weren't old enough."

"We didn't have one." Actually we had once had a seventeen-inch Admiral, but it was repossessed before I got used to it.

Watrous clicked off the projector. He turned up the lights up to the level you'd find in a police interrogation room.

"What did this client of yours tell you to look for?" he asked suspiciously.

"Striptease," I tossed off, and knew instantly it wasn't enough. My surroundings probably explained why I chose that particular moment to remember where I'd seen Jeffrey Haven before. It had been on a movie poster in Hollenbeck, coming attractions of too many years ago. A lot of gladiators and slave girls in as little clothing as the censors of the day would allow. "Actresses," I added, guessing: "Late forties to early sixties. No look alikes. Real Hollywood."

"You just saw it, pal," Watrous said, and mentioned the name of a female character and a very old TV show.

I was surprised and curious and skeptical, all at the same time.

"Why?"

"Why what?"

"An actress has it made. Good television part. Why take her clothes off in a piece of garbage like this?"

"To get the part in the first place." Watrous fired a fat brown cigar and rasped at it. "A finicky broad could screw up the shooting schedule, cost a company millions. So part of the contract, not written, was the stripper. The broad don't make the schedule, she's pumping her humps in smokers all over the country, which finishes her in Hollywood."

"Or playing strip poker?" I offered.

"If she can't dance," Watrous allowed. "Or they get some stud to jiggle her jugs. What does she care? Them days, a broad hadda make with the nookie up front anyway. What's a little stripper?"

"Jeffrey Haven must have been a big help tracking this old stuff down for you. Is he shooting newer versions at the Temple?"

Watrous coughed out smoke. He fortified himself with a stiff belt. "You talk to Haven?"

"Briefly."

"He try to undercut me?"

"Haven is dead. He was machine gunned by the same men who killed the kid at the top of the drive."

A sick, incredulous expression spread over Watrous' moon face with the definition of melting gelatin.

"Studio job?" he wheezed.

"The shooting?"

"Yeah, the shooting. What the hell are we talking about?"

"Why would a film studio have Haven shot?"

"Why did they have him chucked in a private snake pit? They shot him full of more dope in there than he ever took on his own. Why lay out legal fees to get a guardian named so they could get in his safe deposit boxes? He knew things. He was on the inside, and he knew things."

"They sell Hollywood scandal at the check-out counter at Safeway," I said sourly.

"That crap? You think a fast head like Haven gave a shit who was fucking who? He knew where the money wound up. He knew who gave the orders and who was just window dressing. He knew the dangerous stuff."

"How much of the money Haven spent on the Temple was yours?"

"Two hundred grand. Two hundred lousy grand. He finish the film? You know if he finished it?"

"The stripper?"

"Stripper, my ass. That history of Hollywood he needed all those crazy sets at the Temple for. All the dirty deals and the rip offs and the suicides that weren't suicides except some poor slob got too close to something he wasn't supposed to."

"You ponied up two hundred thousand for a piece of an independent film?" I asked skeptically.

"So?"

"So not even neurosurgeons are that naive anymore. With studios buying up theater chains again, Haven would be distributing into the teeth of a vertical monopoly."

"Internet," Watrous coughed. "DVD. You shoot a film that never hits a theater. It goes straight to the web. It's out on DVD. It's a phenomenon waiting to happen. Suppose Haven scores? I'm sitting on my butt watching somebody else rake in two mill because I didn't have the guts to front two hundred large. I ain't getting any younger."

It was too much explaining and too little bluster for a man of Watrous' temperament. "Come on, Charlie. I told you I'd met Haven. He told you to lend him two hundred thousand and that was that. You wrote the check and thought up the reasons for it later."

"If you know, why ask?"

"I need to know how the Doomsday Book fits into all this. And I need it without the alibis."

It was Charlie's turn to hear alarm bells. "I think maybe I should have checked you out with old Walt," he decided. He fumbled a phone up onto the bar. "I think I'll just do that little thing right now," he said, and pressed out a number.

He had a lot of ringing to listen to. I got up to stretch my legs. I opened a door and found a linen closet. I opened another and found a Lincoln the size of a Pharaoh's barge in a garage stall. The other stall held a 190 SL Mercedes coupe. The paint, under a few weeks of dust, was at least as old as 1960.

"Where's Guy Hamilton keeping himself these days?" I asked casually.

Watrous put the phone carefully back on the cradle, without taking his eyes from me. Maybe the lack of an answering machine told him something was wrong.

"There was a private snoop found the body this morning. That smoke I hadda hire off Haven to keep his mouth shut. Snoop was named Spanish, no, uh...?"

"Slotmachine. Elmo Slotmachine."

"Yeah," he growled. "Do it."

It had been a long, nasty day. My mind had faded from the effects. I had forgotten Harv as soon as he went out, and hadn't heard him come back. All I saw was his shadow flash across the worn out carpet. I think he hit me with a fireplace poker. A pit as deep as a coal mine opened under me and I started to fall. The shaft lights glowed whorehouse red. Women danced naked in living black and white. I don't remember ever hitting bottom.

Chapter 19

A whoop-whoop of insane laughter welled up in the darkness and died away into a low wail. I groped toward the memory of the last notes. The floor rose and fell like a Cessna over the San Gabriels and made each step an adventure. I saw light ahead. I recognized it. It was the light at the end of the tunnel. I was the last GI out of Vietnam. I was supposed to turn it out.

I yelled, "Clear, Sergeant! Airborne!" and charged.

I ran full tilt into a door. Glass tinkled on concrete. I got a grip on the knob and managed to keep from toppling over. The latch gave way. I swung through and hung on to the knob to stay on my feet.

A chilly fog wrapped itself around me. I could see more lights now. Vague mysterious lights at the top of a steep hill. Druid lights, circled by faceless figures in hooded robes, chanting to call up the Devil so they could barter away their souls. Come on, Spain. Why just dream of money, power, women and fast cars? Dial this 800 number and make it all come true tonight. Remember, it's a free call, and fallen angels are standing by.

I took a step toward the lights and went three steps backward before I could stop myself. I tried again, with the same effect. There was only one thing to do. I got down on my hands and knees and began to crawl. It was hard work, crawling. I was out of practice. I kept at it anyway. I had to reach the lights.

I met some other people on the way up the hill. They picked me up. We hung on to each other and kept climbing while the world tilted and swayed like the platform on a carnival ride. We didn't seem to be having much fun. That bothered me. When you went to the carnival, you were supposed to have fun. I told the people that. They didn't seem to appreciate it. They let me go. I sat down hard. I felt it all the way up my spine.

The lights hurt furiously. Brilliant white headlights fenced in by a line of sputtering red highway flares. Multicolored domes flashing rhythmically on police cruisers and ambulances. Syncopated orange blinking from a tow truck that was trying to separate the steaming wreckage of a big old Mercury from the buckled remains of a Trans Am I seemed to remember from a past life. A pair of high beams flashed past and set the whole scene tumbling like a kaleidoscope. The contents of my stomach tried a surging run at my esophagus. I clenched my teeth and put my head between my knees.

After a while a hand shook my shoulder. I tried to shrug it away, but it wouldn't leave. A voice was saying something, but the band was playing *Wipeout*, and I was sitting right next to the drums. Finally the voice gave up.

It was a police voice, of course. Harv had clobbered me to buy Charlie and himself a little getaway time. They had left the Trans Am dark, and it had been hit. Sirens responding to the accident had rattled me out of slumberland a little early. Everything since had been the last nightmare before morning. The one that was supposed to be crammed full of subconscious insights into your life.

A man in white probed my scalp and brought my head up screaming inside. He made comforting noises while he wrapped the head to keep it from disintegrating. A superficially bandaged girl rode the ambulance with me. She was sobbing uncontrollably, with her face buried in her hands. A middle-aged attendant was consoling her with the moral gravity of a Baptist elder.

"Sixteen," he clucked at me. "Six in one car. All drunk and not one over sixteen. This one was lucky. She was in the back seat. The…" He noticed the effect the movement and the odor of antiseptic were about to have on my stomach. He muttered, "Oh, shit!" and scrambled to find a bag.

The hospital emergency room was backed up like a fogged in airport terminal on Christmas Eve. A harried nursing supervisor was telling everyone who could walk to take a chair and wait. I spotted an empty one, with skinny wooden arms clinging precariously to the stainless steel frame and swatches of green tape where the yellow foam rubber cushions had been slashed. A pregnant woman with her face bruised and discolored from a beating got there first. I sat on the floor against the wall and tried to think whether I should be sorry the last capital improvement bond hadn't passed, or mad because it had. Pretty soon it didn't seem important and I quit trying to remember. My stomach was too empty for further violence, but a fluorescent tube in the ceiling kept flickering on and off and made my headache worse.

People came and went and waited. Mostly they waited. Hurt people and friends of hurt people, talking quietly or lost mute in their own concerns. Young children fitfully asleep and older ones cranky and fidgeting and not seeing any reason for it all. I thought about going to the reception desk to ask for an aspirin. I thought about it off and on for half an hour without mustering the energy. Finally a nurse called my name. She was a bone tired young sourpuss with acne scars and a body that deserved better. I went with her and didn't bother to stare. I was as empty of life as a hamper of outgoing laundry.

A studious black resident sat me on an examining table. Once my slightly fuzzy answers had satisfied him that I knew my name, what day it was and which planet I was on, he unwrapped my bandage and went to work on the remains of my skull. The nurse took an arm out of my coat to see if I still had any blood pressure left. She was looking in the wrong place. It was all throbbing around in my head, where the doctor was working.

"Any dizziness? Nausea? Disorientation?" the resident asked in a professional patter.

"All those," I said.

"How is he, Doctor?" a voice asked.

"If you will allow me sufficient time to make a proper diagnosis, we might all find out," the black said in a voice that didn't expect any results. It didn't get any.

"Mr. Spain," the voice said, "I'm Detective Oliver, with the Los Angeles Police Department."

Oliver was a compactly built man with rounded shoulders. He had short bristly hair like a small animal's coat. His face had a jutting formation to it, with the nose and mouth out further than the forehead. His cheeks were pouched, like he carried nuts around in them. I squinted and angled my head, but couldn't put him in any different focus. He looked like a Griffith Park squirrel. One who affected dark rimmed glasses so he would be taken seriously.

"We have information that you were present during a multiple homicide at the Temple of Cosmic Awareness on East Fifth this evening," he advised me.

I wasn't surprised. Haven's assistant would have written me up in whatever day book the Temple kept directly she had me locked away. With all the bloodshed, a hospital check would be routine for any name not logged out. But unless I had been out longer than I thought, they were moving the investigation along rather smartly. Maybe Jeffrey Haven qualified as a high profile victim. Whatever the reason, the pressure seemed to be on to clear his murder. The overbearing plodders and streetwise sharpies had been sent to the showers on this one.

"Mr. Spain?" Oliver asked.

"I was there, I was there."

"One sixteen over seventy eight," the nurse announced.

"Can you describe the assailants, Mr. Spain?"

"No. Yes. Somewhat."

I spent a minute dragging rambling recollections of their clothing and general builds out of the fog of my memory. Oliver wrote it all into a leatherette folder with precise, unhurried strokes. He interrupted with a couple of the usual questions to be sure I wasn't making it all up as I went along. I wasn't sure if I was matching all the characteristics up properly, but the first guess was generally the best and I was going to sound like a liar or a crackpot if I tried to correct myself.

"No evidence of retrograde amnesia," the doctor remarked to no one in particular.

"Will you certify him as competent to make a statement, Doctor?" Oliver asked.

"Been smoking the evidence?"

"It was a reasonable question, Doctor."

"It was a pretty stupid question to ask a man who works a seventy hour weekly schedule, not counting emergency overtime. If there's anything I don't need, it's to spend another six hours on call for two questions in somebody's court trial."

Oliver copied addresses and phone numbers for my home and office. The doctor taped on a bandage. He didn't write prescriptions for head injuries. Instead he gave lectures on something called postular hypotension. The upshot was that if I stood up too fast, the blood would drain out of my head and I would keel over. I thanked him for the cheery news, left my insurance number at the desk and went out to do battle with the off hours bus schedule. I didn't get home until after midnight. My head reverberated like a B-52 strike. I took more aspirin than I was supposed to and collapsed into bed.

Jeffrey Haven pushed two columns of political mudslinging off the front page of next morning's paper. His biography (complete film credits on page F8) ran ten paragraphs. In it he rose to and fell from fame, overcame personal problems brought on by the crass materialism of Hollywood and found inner peace operating a counseling center in a rundown neighborhood. He didn't sound much like the Jeffrey Haven I'd met, but this was L.A. and life was a fantasy. As an afterthought, the article mentioned that the police weren't releasing any details on the actual shooting or their investigation. The Malibu crash was on the blood, guts and gossip page. It consisted mostly of stunned families and sob stuff from a woman who had witnessed the collision. Wild youth careening into a disabled car and learning in an instant the sobering tragedy of life. The old values remained intact. Ricky Calland wasn't part of the stereotype and had probably wound up in some editor's wastebasket. Skip tracers who wandered half conscious out of nearby houses also didn't rate any ink. I had to go all the way back to the local news to find the blue movie warehouse slaying. There was no connection made with the other stories. This was a terse recital colored slightly by an oblique reference to one Henry Spain, who had found the body. He sounded like a shady character. I was surprised he was still at large.

I was also surprised that I was still alive. Five people had died violently in my immediate vicinity in a space of twenty four hours. Each time the violence had crept a little closer, like some invisible vise screwing itself shut around me. I was having trouble convincing myself that the whole nightmare was just fallout from a simple background investigation on a cabaret singer.

As soon as the bus dropped me at my office, I made a call from the city directory. It was the wrong union. They didn't handle singers. They were upset with me for calling. I wouldn't call the plumbers' union if I wanted a painter, would I? They hung up when I asked whom I should call. On the next try I connected with a bossy woman who put me on hold. I spent the next five minutes feeling sorry for myself. My stomach hadn't settled enough to let me put down a decent breakfast, a fist full of aspirin had only dulled the pounding in my head and I had momentarily lost track of which key would let me into the office. The woman came back to ask what I wanted.

"I'd like the agent of record and references for a singer working in the Los Angeles area," I recalled. "The name is Jean LaBostrie."

"A vocalist, sir?" she corrected.

"Yes."

"Would this be in connection with a possible booking?" she inquired in a syrupy voice that left no doubt it damned well better be.

"I'm sorry," I said, businesslike and only slightly apologetic. "The management does not permit me to go into specifics during preliminary inquiries. There have been, well, embarrassing misunderstandings in the past."

"I see. One moment, please."

I spent it wondering whether she was going through her files, or looking for a supervisor who had some experience handling difficult types.

"I'm sorry, sir," she came back, a little puzzled. "Ms. LaBostrie's file doesn't list an agent or references, and it was updated just last month. It does show that she is on holdover engagement, however, so I'm afraid she isn't at liberty just now."

I muttered a quick, "Thank you," and put the receiver back on the cradle without taking my hand from it.

I had learned very little about Jean LaBostrie so far, and most of that had yet to be verified. I was also a little short of places to do the verifying. I had no personal references, no business references, no credit references. I wasn't even sure who had the authority to book her. An agent named Guy Hamilton might know something. I hadn't found him either, but I had run across a good number of his photographs. Most recently in the party room of a house above Malibu. Ricky Calland had driven there with a serious bullet wound, passing up any number of clinics, fire stations and hospitals on the way. His business with Charlie Watrous must have been very important. Either that, or Calland had gone where he thought something called the Doomsday Book was hidden, and Watrous just happened to be hiding there instead. I got to wondering about that house on the bluff. I tapped out another phone number, and gave a receptionist my name and an extension.

"Hello, Henry! How's crime these days?" The loud voice belonged to a fan of mine who was a lawyer with a title insurance company.

"Don't yell. I've had a bad night."

"Ah-hah! Wine and wrenches. Or is that wenches? Well, never mind. What priceless tidbit do you seek from these musty archives?"

I gave him the address of the bluff house as closely as I could remember. Can you check your microfiche cross-reference and tell me who is paying taxes on it?"

"The game's afoot, Watson!"

I sat and listened to the saccharine hold button music and remembered all the reasons I didn't like him. I didn't like anyone who got a vicarious kick out of what I was stuck doing for a living. My not liking him didn't seem to discourage him.

"Girts Hauser," he came back. "Billed to an office address on Hollywood Boulevard. What's up?"

I had never quite believed the name Guy Hamilton. It had too much tinsel town in it. "I'll also need a recent title history on something called the Schaeffer-Pilon Hotel. The place in the Jeffrey Haven article in this morning's paper."

"You're kidding!" He sounded ecstatic.

"Not in my present condition," I assured him and hung up.

Chapter 20

Acting Captain Snyder sat behind an executive desk in the downtown police high rise in his business suit. I sat on the other side with my sport coat buttoned and a plastic visitor's tag growing like a cowlick out of the lapel. I felt like a Presto-Log with a tie on.

Snyder rippled his fingers on the leather corner of the blotter and studied my head with one of those civil service expressions that looked ready to treat your personal hangnail like an outbreak of plague. The man at the County impound lot had studied my head for twenty minutes while I filled out the paperwork to buy my car back. A couple of traffic investigators had studied it for an hour while they grilled me about the Trans Am. I was getting tired of it.

"Charlie Watrous' son-in-law was cleaning a fireplace poker and it went off," I reported.

Nothing changed in the angles and planes of Snyder's face. It was cool and quiet in the office. Thin slatted exterior blinds were angled to deflect the late morning sun. On the other side of the interior blinds his investigators sat at rows of smaller desks and worked thick case files with the dispassionate silence of mortgage processors. It didn't seem to be the sort of place where conversations started easily or lasted long.

"Maybe it's none of my business, Captain, but I got the impression you had more than a routine interest in Scheherazade's. And the man who owns it."

Snyder's, "Oh?" practically fell over itself apologizing for giving me the wrong idea. It didn't cure me.

"It was the timing, mostly. You showed up within ten minutes of the division detectives, who were there within fifteen minutes of the call. An unverified homicide report wouldn't have gone straight downtown

unless there was some kind of flag on Scheherazade's. And I'd be surprised if your driver could have gotten you there that promptly without
burning the blue lights."

"You haven't told me what I can do for you, Mr. Spain."

"I have a license to protect. I don't want any police captains upset
with me for withholding information on their pet projects. Since I have
no way of knowing what you already know about Charlie Watrous, I
thought I'd stop in and tell you what I ran across. If you're interested."

"I'm a sworn officer, Mr. Spain. It's my duty to be interested."

"If it's just a question of duty, I can talk to one of your staff rather
than take up your time."

Snyder left the idea to drift on the vague currents from the air conditioning.

"I stumbled over Charlie Watrous following a man who was wounded
in last night's shooting at the Temple of Cosmic Awareness," I said.

"You were doing what there?"

"You sent me, Captain."

"Not that I recall."

"You mentioned Turner and the Temple in front of me," I reminded
him. "Policemen don't discuss police business in front of citizens, except
as a calculated probe."

A chilly look and a quick ripple of Snyder's fingers did a better job of
letting me know I was on thin ice than any words could have.

"I'm not suggesting you could have known the Turner killing would
precipitate three homicides while I was there."

"Do you have any evidence that it did?"

"The killers needed one or more keys to defeat the Temple's security
system. Turner must've had a set when he worked there. He needed
money for legal fees. He likely wanted to get even for being canned. He
probably did some duplicating before he turned his set in and passed
the word that there were rich pickings in the Temple."

"Turner was canned weeks ago."

"The high bidders wouldn't be in any hurry. They had exclusive access to the property. They'd want to watch comings and goings and pick the best time. Drive the getaway routes. Find a truck that wouldn't be missed when they borrowed it. Line up a self storage locker to cool the loot while they dickered with fences."

"That sounds like everything last night's perpetrators neglected to do."

"The Turner killing changed things. Even if Turner wasn't done by a rival gang trying to muscle in, they couldn't be sure the police wouldn't stumble over the plan during their investigation. They had to hustle down to the Temple as soon as it was dark and grab what they could. As soon as the police left a dead body call down the street, they moved in."

"Speculation," Snyder concluded. "There is no justification for focussing on Turner as the source of the keys, if indeed any were used. Haven employed other staff, and cultivated a disturbed clientele. And the fact of robbery does not establish robbery as the only motive. Or even the primary motive, for that matter."

My agency supervisors had never been impressed by my theories either.

"The timing was right, and it had the look of a target of opportunity job," I said. "For whatever reason, it did blow up in gunplay. And I did follow one of the victims to a house north of Malibu where Charlie Watrous was staying. The house is in the name of Girts Hauser. Guy Hamilton to the entertainment industry. You probably know more about him than I do."

"Nothing beyond paperback trivia. He had a short run of luck as a B-movie lead when brooding good looks were in vogue. He currently operates a talent agency. He has had no police contact as a procurer of talent for pornography, if that is what you are suggesting."

"Hamilton is the subject of at least one open police investigation. Fraud, I think. And Watrous was using his basement to hawk striptease films of television and film actresses shot during Hamilton's years in the industry. The prices were high enough to make me wonder if Watrous and/or Hamilton might not have come by the films illegally."

Snyder lifted the phone without bothering to shoo me out. "Lieutenant Ingraham, please. Captain Snyder...Hello, Don. Earl Snyder up at Ad Vice. Say, I...Hell, Don, nobody treats me. I have to work for a living. Say, do you have a Guy Hamilton in your actives?...No, just a tip he might be tied to a smut peddler. Like to talk to him, if you've got him on recognizance...Really? Well, maybe they're sitting on him and not telling you...They haven't, huh? Well, I guess that's out, then...Yes, Don, I'd appreciate it if you would. And you know, any time I can return the favor...Yes, thanks, Don. You too. Good bye."

Snyder hung up. He hadn't taken his eyes off me all the time he spoke, and didn't now that he was silent again.

"They haven't found him?" I asked.

"The IRS hasn't found him, either."

"I didn't know they were looking for him."

"According to Fraud, he was deducting Income Tax and Social Security from the checks he paid his talent, then forgetting to pay it into the quarterly impound. It's a common trick. Not too bright, but it can be worked for a while. The Treasury Department would like to chat with him about it."

Jean LaBostrie had lied to me about not remembering the imprint on her checks. The fact that her lying bothered me didn't make it important. It just meant that I was a dirty old man with a case on a dynamite chick. That didn't take the edge off my yen to talk to nice Mr. Hamilton.

"That's pretty unusual, isn't it?" I asked Snyder. "Ducking that much high powered law enforcement for any length of time?"

"Higher profile fugitives have been outstanding considerably longer than the six weeks or so Hamilton has been posted. Police departments tend to concentrate on the so-called 'at risk population', which is single men aged 18 to 30. Officially that's because they're the most likely sources of violent crime. As a practical matter, their higher arrest rate and vulnerability to plea bargains put a large percentage of our workable leads in that age group. An older man with connections like Hamilton's moves in circles that don't get as much attention."

"What about the IRS?"

"Probably too little potential recovery to justify much effort."

"I don't seem to have been much help," I said. "Maybe if I knew what it was that took you out to Scheherazade's?"

Snyder gave the idea some thought. "You may have noticed some film making equipment at the Temple?"

"Yes," I said, and perked up.

"It was, until recently, used by one Meyer Paul to grind out some rather unpleasant pornography. It could be used that way again. Recreational pharmaceuticals bankrupted Mr. Paul. His shylocks, necessarily chagrined, moved in to foreclose on the equipment. They were a bit late. Prime suspect, one Midas Turner, enterprising former employee of Mr. Paul, who had neglected to leave a forwarding address."

"That explains how Turner bought his way into the Temple," I said. "Not why a command level police supervisor dropped everything to hustle out to a warehouse full of dildoes."

"It doesn't occur to you that the back alley banking establishment might have shot Turner trying to extract enough information to reestablish contact with their collateral?"

"The officers at the scene didn't know it was Turner who'd been shot. You had to ID him for them. You took one look at the body and left. Based on that alone, I'd say Turner was not the interest that took you to Scheherazade's."

Snyder took an uncomfortable interest in me. "That's a little threadbare, Spain, even for your reckless brand of speculation. What have you learned about Turner's death?"

"Jeffrey Haven seemed to think Turner was taken off by enforcers for a charity bingo racket." I wasn't about to mention that I had told Haven that, and that Haven had simply declined to argue. Especially since Haven was in no position to compromise me.

Snyder said, "The churches and charities and political clubs that sponsor bingo say it's harmless. The operators say it's marginal. The State says it's properly regulated. None of them would like to hear words like 'enforcers' and 'racket'."

And Jeffrey Haven wouldn't have used words like those. I didn't know if Snyder had caught the slip and was needling me, or if he was just talking. Either way, I hadn't claimed to be quoting Haven verbatim.

"I'm not here as a salesman, Captain. The law requires that I pass on information regarding crimes to the authorities. Administrative Vice seemed like the appropriate place to drop off my tidbit on charity bingo. Whether you believe it or not is a little out of my sphere."

"This whole conversation is a little out of your sphere. You've got brass balls, Spain, walking into a Police Captain's office the way you have this morning."

I stood up and felt a flash of light-headedness. "Thank you for seeing me, Captain. Maybe I've wasted your time. If I have, I'm sorry."

I got almost to the door before Snyder said, "Spain," in a soft, significant voice. When I turned, his smile was as wide and cold as an alligator's. "Exactly how much do you know about charity bingo?"

"I know at least some of it is controlled from San Pedro."

Snyder didn't come anywhere near laughing out loud, but he was as close to relaxed amusement as I had yet seen him.

"I seem to have jumped to a wrong conclusion," I said.

"You have enough to worry about without that. When the homicide investigators do get around to you, ask them to call me before you answer any questions. And Spain, ask them politely."

I assured him I would. Being Snyder's private snitch didn't bother me, but his attitude toward my knowledge of charity bingo did. Charity bingo wasn't a subject on which the head of LAPD Vice would have incomplete or incorrect information. Which meant there were facts at large that I didn't have.

It would do me no good to ask Snyder what they were. I still didn't understand why he had bothered to see me. Let alone why he had gone to the trouble of trying to trivialize his interest in Scheherazade's. His only visible reaction had come at the mention of twenty minutes worth of juvenile celluloid. I paused with my hand on the doorknob, just long enough to try it out again.

"Oh, about those striptease movies Charlie Watrous likes to sell for so much money," I said. "He had one in his possession last night."

I gave him the name of the actress. I had the idea he would remember it.

Chapter 21

It was habit more than hope that sent me out Foothill Boulevard and up Holland Canyon Drive. 'Open House' sandwich boards pointing up into the exclusive enclaves reinforced my recollection that today was Realtors' caravan day in that area.

Half Moon Lane was a different world in the light of day. The houses were just houses, fastened to the hillside any way they could anchor them in. The yards were landscaped as primly as pictures in a multiple listing book. The residents were off overachieving somewhere, and the silence made the throaty compression whisper of my exhaust sound like a weekend outing of the Hell's Angels.

A canary yellow Mercedes sedan was parked with a sandwich board on a cloth on its roof, pointing up at the last residence of the late Walter O. Brixner. I read a San Fernando business address off the yard sign as I climbed the concrete stairs. The front door was blocked open.

A woman gave me a German accented, "Hello!" from back in the kitchen. She was forty something, tall and sleek as a thoroughbred race-horse. She approached confidently along the hall, saying, "Don't be bashful. Come on in. I'm Didi Asher."

"Hi, Didi," I said, and glanced into the living room. It had been picked cleaner than a probated estate. "I didn't know Walt was moving."

"Oh, are you a friend of Mr. Brixner's, Mr...?"

"We shared a client. Did he say where he was going?"

"Danny Rupert, who gave me the listing, said he was called to Chicago quite suddenly."

"Danny Rupert? Is he Walt's lawyer?"

"Oh, no. He's a commercial real estate broker. In San Pedro. He's just the nicest young man you could ever hope to meet. I've known his mother for years. He has power of attorney to handle the sale."

San Pedro had a familiar and disturbing ring. Mr. Rupert and his power of attorney were a new wrinkle. The tenth of a second I spent thinking about them were enough to let my end of the conversation lapse.

"Have you been through the house?" she inquired.

"Uh, yes. Yes, I have."

"Had you thought about buying it? It's quite a bargain. Only six hundred sixty five thousand. Another custom by the same builder went for eight hundred just last month, and the view wasn't nearly as good."

"It still might be a little rich for me," I said in the understatement of the half-century.

"There's fantastic financing," she confided. "I can get you in for less than a hundred thousand down. The existing loan is a private contract. All you need to assume is the holder's approval."

"Who is the holder?"

"Danny Rupert has all the information on that. All you would have to provide is your earnest money and a commercial credit report."

Another minute and she was going to have me signed up for the place. "I'll think it over," I promised, and retreated through a group of incoming Realtors.

I drove back down the canyon and thought instead about a dead accountant named Walter Brixner. Square nuts Walter Brixner, dressed up in his geek shoes, sitting in his doorway watching the world go by through his crooked glasses. He had cooked the books for a charity bingo racket. He had also done tax work for an old time boss gambler named Tommy Lipton. Maybe that had given him ideas. I didn't bother to speculate on the possibility that Lipton might control the bingo racket. It didn't look rich enough to interest him. Lipton might or might not be interested in something called a Doomsday Book. He hadn't mentioned it to me if he was. Ricky

Calland thought so, but his impressions had been notably unreliable. Walter Brixner seemed to be the man to call if you wanted to talk about the Doomsday Book. A lawyer named Charlie Watrous had called him. Watrous sold striptease movies at five figures a crack, for starters. Actresses from the late show and the rerun channel doing a little private wiggling for a handful of mild mannered voyeurs. Harmless striptease so hot the commander of the LAPD Vice Division could pull rank on two homicide investigations.

The movies were still nagging at me when I reached the office. I opened my catalog of Jeffrey Haven's library and got on the phone. Insurance companies hated bounty hunters with a black passion. Almost as much as they hated losing money. Those two hatreds collided head-on in the recovery department, where the vanguard of an invasion from Mars tried to wrap its tentacles around all the stolen property it could locate on a budget of bus tokens and grocery coupons. The first party I reached tried to convert me to Christianity with ten minutes of hell fire and brimstone. When it didn't take, he massaged his computer terminal, found two of Haven's books and consented to sign my percentage agreement in a voice that consigned my soul to eternal damnation. In subsequent calls I had my license threatened, I was lectured on my duty to help the insurance industry in these troubled times and I was told there was more to life than money by a woman who sounded like she could back up the statement. If even half of my list had survived the machine gunning, I was going to have a good month, financially. My last call was to UCLA. A bound volume of thirties' pulp adventure had their logo back in the glue. I didn't expect a cash payoff. UCLA, along with USC, was the repository of most of the organized movie lore, and I needed information. I explained the nature of that information to an associate professor named Roy Lee Exum and got an invitation to buy her a late lunch.

She looked like someone who might have gotten involved with a professor of dramatics on her way to not breaking into films, and had enough between her ears to stay on in academia after the marriage or whatever had soured. But that was speculation. Beyond her profession, all I knew was that she didn't wear a wedding ring and still projected enough sophisticated appeal to send the male half of the social register out for brisk walks around the block.

"You're not a collector," she said in a Cape Cod drawl that wondered what I might be, but wasn't getting personally involved with the question.

"The standard collector being a middle aged milquetoast who has made enough money to indulge his juvenile fantasies?"

She made a credulous, "Mm-hmm," in her throat.

"You're right," I confessed. "I don't even know how many of these particular striptease films were made."

"Probably about eighty, between 1948 and 1961," she revealed, fingering a glass of notably expensive cabernet. I was a potential paying customer, and I was springing for lunch in what she had been careful to let me know was her favorite restaurant. The lure of a seventy five dollar an hour consulting fee and a panoramic view of the Pacific Ocean probably entitled me to a tantalizing glimpse of the available information.

"How many sixteen millimeter copies were made of each?" I asked.

"Sixteen millimeter dupes were struck of no more than two dozen, and those are almost as rare as the thirty five millimeter originals."

"If they weren't copied for distribution, where did the production budgets come from?"

"Creative accounting. The cost would be buried in the budget of some feature or series as test footage. Not only were the films all studio grade, but a few actually show innovative nuances of lighting and camera work that appeared later in major films by the same directors, establishing them as a significant link in the chain of technical development."

"What did the actresses think of the gratuitous undressing?"

Roy Lee considered the question while an overdressed waiter traded limp salads and a dish of high-octane garlic bread for plates of mixed seafood with the deftness of a stage magician. His condescending manner was flawless until Roy Lee crossed her legs under the little glass table. Even then he recovered in an instant. I thought he departed in rather a hurry, though.

He left Roy Lee considering me with cool blue eyes while she nibbled delicately on a prawn. I was probably lucky there was nothing between us but a spot of business. She looked like she could do a lot of damage if she set her mind to it.

"We are talking about children, Mr. Spain. The products, the beneficiaries and ultimately the victims of the star making machinery. An actress has no word, no song, no emotion of her own. Those are all crafted for her by others. She is simply make-up to cover the blemishes of life, charisma to draw attention to the insights of her character. She must mold her delivery to the satisfaction of a director before it is ever committed to film. She is powerless to control the editors who piece together her disjointed rushes. Or to influence the executives who pass judgement on the finished whole that may determine whether she becomes immortal or never works again. The frustration and insecurity were greatly amplified in the nineteen fifties. The growth medium of the time was television, of course, which was broadcast directly into the viewer's home, and which, consequently, had to reach the lowest common denominator of innocence to be acceptable. It must have been terribly confining for actresses who were acutely aware that their fragile sexuality was being frittered away in saccharine Pollyanna roles. For some, striptease films were an emotionally painless way of immortalizing that sexuality."

"That's the second answer I've had to that question," I said. "The other one also said more about the person doing the answering than the films or the women who made them."

"The second answer?"

"I want a list of all the films you've researched for Charlie Watrous. I want the names of the backers, the staff, the casts and the crews. I want to know where and when they were shot and to whom they were delivered. I want all the information you've got on subsequent owners, including heirs, bankruptcies, judgements, thefts, everything. And I want it tomorrow morning. I'll pay your consulting fee up to five hours for your work."

Her eyes sliced me up like cucumber in a Cuisinart. "I don't pretend to understand frustrated little men who can spend fortunes for the sole purpose of indulging their vices by proxy, but I can have some compassion for their sickness. But you...what is your problem?"

"Earl Snyder," I said.

"Who is Earl Snyder?" in a slow drawl dripping icicles.

"He's an Acting Captain who commands the Vice Division of the Los Angeles Police Department."

There was pity in her smile. "Those films are not vice, Mr. Spain. Not by today's standards. If you had seen any of them, you would know that."

"If this were a routine vice investigation, it would be handled by staff investigators. The command structure wouldn't get involved unless there was considerably more to it. Maybe you'd like to tell me what it is?"

"A thin bluff, Mr. Spain. An errand boy's bluff. Is that it? Did you sneak a peek in an envelope? Get a glimpse of something interesting? Decide to dress up in last year's sport coat and see what you could make of it?"

I showed her the wallet copy of my investigator's license to buy whatever credibility I could. "My calling you was no accident, Roy Lee. Asking up to six figures a copy, Watrous has to be able to prove his material is authentic. Only a professional researcher with unlimited access to primary source materials could provide conclusive evidence. I got your name when I returned an overdue library book."

The pity was gone but her smile stayed on, like a party guest who has forgotten the way home. "Mr. Spain, the men and women who made those films are not only still alive, but wealthy, influential and far too respectable to want to read about themselves anywhere but a history book. Yesterday's children have children and grandchildren of their own now. They have the same impossible expectations for them as all parents. They would spend any money, exert any influence to protect those children from the corrupting examples of their own youth. I don't want to compromise those intentions. And you don't want to expose your license to that influence. Believe me, you don't."

"I'm buying insurance, not blackmail. You came here knowing what I wanted and ready to sell. You didn't choke until I mentioned Charlie Watrous. Are you afraid of what could happen to your reputation if it gets out that you deal regularly with a pornographer? Or what could happen to your income if Charlie finds out you dealt with me?"

She uncrossed her legs and pulled the hem of her skirt down to her knees. "I'm trying to raise two boys of my own on a State salary, Mr. Spain. They are not an excuse, and I am not using them as a shield. But they are a fact I have to face every morning when I wake up."

Kids were a dangerous subject for a man who had spent too much time recently wondering why he had never had any. I was liable to give Roy Lee more slack than would be good for either of us. I poured a double shot of Simon Legree into my voice.

"Do you want a formal introduction to Snyder? Or should I just give him your name?"

"Why, Mr. Spain?" in a low drawl savage with the resentment of defeat. "What's so damned important about these films?"

"Was Jeffrey Haven ever connected with them?"

She shook her head instantly. "Right era, wrong man. Jeffrey Haven was a major talent. Very cerebral. Striptease was well below his threshold of boredom."

"Guy Hamilton?"

Something clicked in her memory. "I'd have to check to be sure."

"All right."

Roy Lee went back to her lunch. She ate without haste, savoring the meal and the view. We spent the time discussing old movies. It turned out that most of my favorites belonged to a genre called Film Noir. It was, according to her, a uniquely American form in which an obsessed hero was progressively alienated from an unstable and indifferent society by a succession of often random and sometimes innocent events with results that were always explosive and seldom satisfactory. I liked them better when they were just movies.

I drove back downtown to my office and dialed the Crown Colony. "I'm going to need some more of your money," I said when they had found Tommy Lipton for me. "And the services of one of your lawyers."

"Would I be prying if I asked what for?"

"I found Guy Hamilton's car. A finance company has a valid lien. I need the title cleared to get the car into a private forensic laboratory. I also need to pay the laboratory."

"Details," was all Lipton said.

I gave him the name of the finance company, the location of the car and the number of the laboratory. I probably sounded surprised. I had expected an argument. I was working a pretty slim lead.

"I also need four hundred dollars to pay a professor at UCLA," I said, as long as I seemed to be on a roll. "She's their expert in Hamilton's movie and TV era."

"How close are you?"

"In forty eight hours I should have enough leverage to pry some answers out of Hamilton's closest known contact. And enough random information to ensure that the answers are true."

"Keep me informed," he said, and he was gone.

I touched the cradle and punched up Osborne Associates. "I'd like to speak to Winston Drew," I told the receptionist.

"I'm sorry, sir," she said in a maddeningly cool air-conditioned voice. "Mr. Drew is not in at the moment."

"All right, Tod Grayson, then."

"I'm sorry, sir. Neither Mr. Drew nor Mr. Grayson is in. "May I offer you voice mail?"

"No," I said in a low, strained voice. "You tell Drew that Henry Spain wants to talk to him. He wants to talk about Ricky Calland and the Doomsday Book. He wants to do it right now. Immediately."

"I'm sorry, sir. Mr. Drew really is not in the office. I will have him call you back when…"

"Do that," I growled, and hung up.

Chapter 22

I had my recovery agreement in the word processor, matching insurance companies with my notes from the library of the late Jeffrey Haven, when I heard a scratching noise outside the door. The knob made a couple of false starts, then the door exploded inward. It ricocheted off the rubber stop and swung back to collide with a man on his way in. The man was short and scrawny, what I could see of him, and he was carrying a carton that weighed almost as much as he did. He had leaned forward to get a little starting momentum, and now the weight was in control. He wasn't going to stop until he hit something bigger than he was.

He hit the desk. He dropped the carton on impact. It landed with a solid thud and didn't move. Everything on the desk jumped. The telephone handset rattled off the cradle and disappeared over the side. Free at last of his burden, the man stood trembling and swaying. He looked like a Middle Eastern terrorist from the six o-clock news. Calvin Klein jeans and a loose peasant pullover and a swarthy young face. He thrust out a limp yellow sheet with his demands scrawled on it.

"Cashonlypleasecompanypolicy," he gasped.

The yellow sheet was a cab company delivery bill. Reading around the damp finger smudges, I discovered he had brought me Walter Brixner's folder of tapes and the printout. Between the petty cash tin and my wallet, I scraped up the thirty one seventy five charge. The driver watched his tip evaporate.

"Thankyouverymuchsir," he said, but his eyes called the wrath of Allah down on my head. The fleas of a thousand camels would infest my armpits forever.

I put the phone back on the cradle and locked the door after him. I wanted privacy to size up my ill-gotten gains. There was no copyright legend or other indication of who might have written the code, when or for what purpose. The printout was page after page of real estate holdings; names, legal descriptions, assessment information, financial summaries and miscellaneous Sanskrit. I unfolded perforated paper over half the office before I found anything that rang a bell. What I found was the Schaeffer-Pilon Hotel, aka the Temple of Cosmic Awareness. It seemed to be owned by Hannah Hilliard, Stefan Rakubian and Barragon J. Camacho, an unlikely partnership if ever there was one. Jeffrey Haven had been their sole tenant. On paper they were losing money even when he was alive. That suggested tax shelter. Tommy Lipton had suggested Brixner wasn't above turning an honest dollar. Which raised the possibility that I had filched his legitimate client list. Legitimate or not, a connection between Walter Brixner and Jeffrey Haven was the last thing I could afford to have lying around the office when Brixner's murder entered the public domain.

The phone rang while I was trying to fold the mess back into something I could run through the steamship company's shredder. It was the receptionist from Osborne Associates. She gave me an address on Rexford Drive. Mr. Drew would be expecting me as soon as I could get there. I bundled the printout into the nearest corner.

Rexford Drive curved up into a veddy, veddy exclusive section of Beverly Hills. Splotches of afternoon sun lay on the black asphalt like they had been painted from an artist's palette. Behind high walls of manicured shrubbery lay the great estates built back at the far reaches of living memory, when stranded carnival people, itinerant vaudeville troupers and unemployed stage actors who had hoped only to eke out a meager existence in a flash in the pan called moving pictures suddenly found themselves the idols of millions. Perhaps one or two of them still resided there. Jeffrey Haven might've known, but only the tax assessor cared any more.

The number I wanted was woven into an eight foot gate and framed by wrought iron cupids. The cop on duty was the real item. LAPD uniform and all. Umpteen dollars an hour, including fringe benefits. He brought the Volvo to a stop with a palm down motion of his hand and looked in the window.

The skepticism I couldn't see behind his sunglasses came out in his voice. "May I see your invitation, sir?"

"Invitation? What's going on? A party?"

"Yes, sir. Private and by invitation only."

"I was told a Mr. Drew would be expecting me here. Henry Spain."

There was probably a reaction behind the sunglasses. "Could I see some identification, Mr. Spain?"

I handed him some. He let me inspect my reflection for a minute before he gave it back. "Park at the right of the house. You'll be guided from there."

The house was three stories of Spanish stucco roofed by overlapping red tiles. It stood aloof on a broad knoll, flanked by ranks of eucalyptus and pierced by lancet windows decorated with bits of wrought iron railing. Wide rivers of green lawn meandered down among islands of flowers surrounding limestone statues and stone pools.

The line of parked cars started just inside the gate. Sports cars with swooping avant garde shapes, boxy oriental jeeps, a mixed fleet of German and Swedish high tech, shiny old Studebakers and a pink Nash Metropolitan. Anything to let the bourgeoisie know you weren't stamped from the same cookie cutter they were. Up close to the hacienda there were enough Colorado plates to suggest that a few stahs had dropped in from Aspen.

A perky young brunette in a straw boater hat and a red, white and blue crepe sash reading 'Walker for Congress' waited under the porte cochere. She peered in the window to see if my old coupe were really a Ferrari in clever disguise. Anyone who rated a guide around here ought to be driving at least that much car.

"Mr. Spain?" she wondered aloud.

"I'm afraid so." I climbed out reading 'Hi, I'm Kelly' off a quickie cal-ligraphic nametag stuck to the lapel of her navy blazer. "What's going on? Some kind of election rally?"

She smiled apologetically. "I don't know much about politics. I'm only hired for the day as a hostess."

"I've never bothered with it myself. My district has voted the same ticket since Ivan the Terrible."

Her laugh was a couple of notes of nervous confusion. "Would you come this way, Mr. Spain?"

If the door was any clue, bill collectors in this neighborhood favored medieval siege engines. She got it open and led me along a wide hall-way. Gilt framed oils full of Iberian color and boldness adorned the walls. Massive exposed beams and rough plaster and wooden benches gave the corridor an early Warner Brothers' flavor. It looked like a shooting set for *Rose of the Rancho*.

"Interesting place," I remarked.

"It belongs to Tony Fidalgo," she confided in an awed hush. The name conjured up an image of dark wavy hair and a bedroom baritone stirring romantic cravings eight shows a week, including matinees. Blow in his ear and he'd thank you for the refill.

"Did he loan the house to the campaign while he's in Vegas?"

"Oh, he's here today. He's chairman of the celebrity committee for Mr. Walker. They're organizing a canvass for the weekend. I guess a lot of show business people are really into politics."

"Anything for another minute in the spotlight."

She gave me a nervous glance and decided to confine herself to guid-ing. She stopped at another heavy door. A demure knock got her nowhere. She cracked the door and spoke timidly without looking in.

"It's Kelly, Mr. Drew. Mr. Spain is here."

"Show him in, please, Kelly."

The room wasn't much. The Great Hall in Castile probably had a higher ceiling. There had to be at least a dozen museums with more suits of armor. Some of the furniture looked to be less than five hundred years old, and had probably never belonged to anyone loftier than a baron. Winston Drew was holding court behind a carved desk that couldn't quite double as a full bed if too many shirt-tail relatives turned up for the social season.

Tod Grayson stood dutifully at his elbow. The two men smiled attentively at a woman drawn up regally on a straight back antique chair. I didn't recognize her, except as a native. Designer wardrobe by Kiki. Hairstyle by Mr. Paul. Body by Hostess Bakeries. The carefully groomed man trying not to fidget at her shoulder was familiar. I had seen his picture in full-page newspaper ads, striding purposefully toward an official looking building over the caption 'Glenn Walker. Decisive Leadership.' I had expected him to be taller.

Drew cleared his throat and spoke in a firm, fatherly voice, "I am sure Glenn will do very well next Tuesday, Trudy. The newspaper articles are simply the result of hysteria surrounding Mr. Osborne's illness. The polls they cite lack statistical validity. Our own surveys reveal no abnormal slippage. Now, if you and Glenn could possibly excuse us?"

Trudy Walker didn't like being displaced by an obvious cluck in a corduroy sport coat. She clicked her heels across the shiny hardwood. Decisive leadership had a foot race to get the patio door open before she went through and took out several thousand dollars worth of leaded glass romance. A distant hum of conversation drifted in while he closed the door delicately. Kelly closed the hall door and left me alone with Drew and Grayson.

Drew didn't seem to know he was supposed to be worried. He had a hard time keeping triumph out of his managerial expression.

"Well, now, Mr. Spain, the receptionist indicated you were most anxious to speak with Mr. Grayson or myself."

"I didn't mean to snap at your staff. I was saving that for you two dingbats. If I could catch up with you before the police caught up with all of us."

"I beg your pardon?"

"Your boy Calland had a man killed trying to get the Doomsday Book. Didn't he tell you?"

Drew gave me the same level of tolerant bluff you would get if you spotted a Miss America Contestant as a first stringer from the cat house down the street. Grayson also looked as if he found me tedious. He was getting to know what to think even before Drew thought it. Maybe that was the way the breed reproduced.

I helped myself to the antique chair Trudy Walker had warmed up. It took a little creative slouching to get comfortable. I hoped the glue had been replaced along with the upholstery.

"Hiring the club gigolo at the Crown Colony to watch Tommy Lipton wasn't too bright," I told Drew. "He sold you out to Lipton, then sicced you on me when he thought Lipton had double crossed him by hiring me to find the Book."

Drew let out his words as carefully as he would pour nitric acid. "As a practical matter, only a certain character of individual could ingratiate himself with Tommy Lipton. I believe the cliche is 'set a thief to catch a thief.'"

"The reality is that you set a homicidal flip-top to watch the kind of man he would do anything to become. Calland had the accountant for a gambling ring killed chasing that dream. Last night he was shot dead himself."

"I am aware that Ricky is dead," Drew said solemnly, "but I have heard nothing about his killing anyone."

"The victim's associates concealed the killing for their own purposes. They also traced Calland's trigger man to a mail order pornography outlet. The police did find out about that killing. They'll be a little longer putting the pieces together than they would've been if they'd known about both killings from the start, but don't think they won't do it."

"All of this rather anonymous scenario relates to Mr. Osborne's file in what way?"

"The Doomsday Book was mentioned in a telephone message to Calland's victim from the owner of the porno outlet."

Drew and Grayson exchanged significant glances. Drew said, "Please continue, Mr. Spain."

"The Book was mentioned in connection with a problem Mr. Porno Merchant shared with Mr. Victim last month. The only common denominator I've found is a talent agent named Guy Hamilton."

Drew slapped both hands down flat on the desk. The smile he directed at Grayson was ecstatic. I seemed to have struck a responsive chord.

"I assume you are the ones offering Hamilton any price for the Doomsday Book."

"Yes," Drew said.

"How do you know he has it?"

"He was quite candid about it. He called and offered to sell it back to us."

"Called? When?"

"The night following the theft. His reference to a Doomsday Book was quite incomprehensible at first. Apparently it was the invention of his own syphilis-ravaged mind. However he was able to offer a lucid description of Mr. Osborne's property."

"You seem to know a little about him," I remarked. "What exactly did your investigators turn up?"

"Am I correct in assuming, Mr. Spain, that your coming to see Mr. Grayson and myself is an indication that you are no longer satisfied with Tommy Lipton as an employer? Perhaps even that he is one of the gamblers you referred to?"

"I doubt that. Lipton was making more money than these jokers seem to be back when a dollar was a dollar."

"You must have some reason for sharing your findings with us rather than him?"

"Lipton hasn't shown a shred of interest in the Doomsday Book. He may know even less about it than I do. I'm here because I need answers and you've got them."

"The only answer that really matters," Drew said, dancing his knuckles on the desktop like castanets, "is the whereabouts of the file."

"What's the big secret? What did you do? Copy some names off tombstones and register them to vote? Are you afraid the talking heads on Eyewitness News may get wind of it?"

Drew's face turned to granite. "Understand this, Spain. If one whisper of such irresponsible slander surfaces, your license will come under the most hostile scrutiny imaginable. I hardly need mention you would be calling into question the election of high state officials."

"You're not getting the point," I said irritably. "Five people are dead by violence. A lot of very capable policemen are poking around the edges of this thing. Police investigations break the way dams do. A lot of little cracks that don't amount to anything at first, then, before you know it, you've got a twenty foot wall of city detectives bearing down on you. If we don't put our heads together and find some safe ground to stand on, we're all going to be swept into the State correctional system."

"You present a colorful metaphor," Drew told me, "but..."

"Shove it," I snarled.

"Where is the file, Spain?"

"I don't know."

"Liar."

I had been called worse, by better people, but Drew's single word brought me to my feet. "I don't know where it is, and I don't give a damn. I only care what it is. And when I find out, everyone from San Diego to Seattle is going to know."

I went out through the patio door and didn't look back to see if I'd cracked the glass slamming it behind me.

Chapter 23

Stone stairs took me down through manicured shrubbery and brought me out below the house, at the edge of half an acre terraced flat for a huge swimming pool. The view beyond the windscreen of tall eucalyptus trees was spectacular. Century City and the financial district were reduced to a shimmering high rise cluster; a coven of Aztec priests ruling over a supine sprawl of enslaved suburbs stretching all the way to the colorfast blue of the Pacific. It was a heady place for a party. It had attracted a lot of people. Just then the only things about them that interested me were the drinks they were holding. I queued up at a plush portable bar.

While I was waiting, a voice from the past said, "The police are not going to solve Jeffrey Haven's murder."

The voice belonged to Connie Moore. The actress. She went back farther than I did. She had started as an ingenue in half an hour of family fluff on television and graduated to a couple of decades of 'serious work' in pompous message films. Now she was back on television as the obligatory rich and troubled woman in overwrought miniseries. According to *TV Guide* she didn't do talk shows. Probably out of fear that she'd wind up competing with herself on three other networks.

"The police didn't solve Marilyn Monroe's murder," she reminded a small audience, "except to say she OD'ed on barbiturates that were never found in her stomach. And George Reeves, who played Superman on TV. Shot dead a week before his wedding. And they called that suicide. I mean, my God, not even Superman is safe in L.A."

There were murmurs of indignation. Someone recalled that Sharon Tate had been murdered a few miles away in Benedict Canyon. The conversation drifted to even more recent happenings. Connie lost interest.

She noticed me watching her. She remembered. She came over, drawn like a zombie.

"My God," she said, hushed and incredulous, "the man who murdered Jesus."

Jesus had been coal black hair and shining white teeth. He had happened in my agency days. I spent a week lugging sound gear around one of the big studios to locate the pusher of the month. Jesus was dealing out of the pockets of his security guard's uniform. The night he was canned he came after me with his six-inch .38. It was over almost before I was aware it had started. I was sitting in the back of a squad car, handcuffed and shaking, and Jesus was on his way to White Memorial in the back of an ambulance. He survived surgery, but he didn't have enough left to make it through hepatitis and heroin withdrawal.

Before I could remind Connie of any of that, someone blew into the microphone of a public address system. After a minute of amplified breathing, a man remembered how to talk.

"Could I have your attention, please. I wonder if we could all gather around here?"

The voice was familiar from nights when there was nothing good on television. It went along with silly skits and a lot of intricate choreography, impressive sets and songs that no one would remember in another week. The songs faded, but the voice droned on. It attracted attention. The crowd began to coagulate under red, white and blue letters spelling out the name WALKER.

"Yes, that's it," Tony Fidalgo encouraged them. "If we could all just gather around here."

"Yes, sir?" the bartender asked me.

"Cuba Libre."

"You'll rot your teeth," Connie warned.

"They'll match my morals," I said, mostly to beat her to it. "It's unusual that you mentioned Jeffrey Haven."

"What's unusual about that? I haven't been anywhere today where poor Jeffrey wasn't the premier topic of conversation."

"Twist of lime, sir?" the bartender asked.

"Please."

We left the bar and wandered toward the crowd. I was walking with the dream girl of millions. The eucalyptus trees were the painted backdrop in a Marx Brothers farce. Beyond them lay paradise in gridlock, where root bound palm trees swayed in the EPA rated smog and the natives smoked powerful weeds and fought pitched battles over turf and tribal honor. I took a slug of my drink to reestablish contact with reality. Connie sipped a daiquiri.

"Have you been hired to do something about Jeffrey?"

"How well did you know him?"

"Nobody knew Jeffrey well. Jeffrey was the one who did the knowing. He was always there when you were confused and never in the way when you knew what you wanted. You could expect anything of him; he never expected anything of you. He was the perfect father that none of us ever had. It was partly sham, of course. Nobody is that good. But I guess he enjoyed the role."

It was also a good way to turn up lucrative secrets. Connie had probably accumulated a few of those in her years in Hollywood. Roy Lee Exum's remark about actresses wanting to immortalize a sexuality they knew wouldn't last forever came back to me.

"Jeffrey offered to sell me my choice of several strip tease films," I lied. "Your name was mentioned in connection with one of them."

"The man who called me wanted a hundred thousand dollars. What was Jeffrey asking?"

I shrugged as if that was close enough. "What did you say?"

"I told him where to stuff his film, of course. Heavens, after what they're doing in family theaters nowadays, I don't know how the poor dear could expect anyone to pay for that silly old thing."

I mumbled something about there being no shortage of strange habits in the world.

"Jesus really was a nice boy," she said.

"I didn't go after him. And I didn't put the needle in his arm."

"I know."

Her face was as wooden as it had been the day she sat through the inquest. Jesus was the only thing we had in common. When we were through talking about him, we were through talking. She smiled good-bye and wandered off.

I attached myself to the rear of the crowd. Glenn Walker was telling everyone how the creative community was admirably suited to influence lesser mortals to do the right thing politically. It was lip service to something everyone took on faith, and nobody was listening particularly hard. It struck me as a waste of a well-oiled audience. I sidled close to a man who looked a self-conscious forty dressing twenty-five.

"This is all very nice," I told him sotto voce, "but what I want to know is who is this private investigator that's supposed to be skulking around here?"

He peered and decided he didn't know me. "Beg pardon?"

"Investigator," I repeated, and got a little attention from the immediate vicinity. "Some questionable character named Spain. Haven't you heard?"

"No. What about him?"

"Skulking around asking a lot of questions, so I'm told. I'd like to know why. And I'd like to know what this so-called Doomsday Book is, and why it's so secret."

That was as far as I got. Glenn Walker had kept it short and sweet. Tony Fidalgo had the mike again, telling everyone how wonderful it would be if they would all join their respective groups. I lost my audience faster than a Republican with measles. You were liable to be talked about if you were late reaching one of the little card tables done up in bunting. I drifted over to the fringe of the nearest group so I could finish my drink without being conspicuous. A hostess in a sash and a boater passed among us with pamphlets of handy hints for getting along with the common folk. The members could have used some hints on getting along with each other. A stylish gray beard was trying to assert himself as leader and having trouble with just about everyone who could get a splashy word in edgewise. I took advantage of a side argument to catch his arm and speak into his ear.

"Don't forget," I told him in an official voice, "to warn your group that there is a suspicious person named Spain making inquiries about a Doomsday Book. No one should talk to him under any circumstances."

Armed with my endorsement, he charged back into the fray. I wondered if the idea would play as well at the other tables.

I was mumbling my way into the adjoining group with that in mind when I found myself face to face with Frank Murillo's bingo blonde. The crepe sash and straw boater made her a political hostess today, but there was no mistake. It took an insistent tapping on my shoulder to make me aware that I was staring.

The fingers belonged to a smooth paunchy number with a walrus mustache. Judging from his pained smile, I had stepped into the middle of his best pick-up line. I put on my nastiest bodyguard look.

"Does Mr. Grayson know you hang out with losers like this?" I asked the blonde in a voice full of dire consequences.

It was the walrus who got the message. He had no way to know that Grayson wasn't nine million dollars tall, with six more of me on his staff.

"I, uh, just remembered I've got to make a phone call. Excuse me, huh?"

There was no particular reason for the blonde to know who Tod Grayson was, either. But the light in her face said she did, and suggested more. "Thank you, Mr."...her eyes searched my lapels for a nametag. "I'm terribly sorry, I don't remember your name."

"Henry Spain," I supplied, and snuck a glance at her calligraphic stick-on. "You're Sarah uh...?" I wiggled my fingers, fishing for a name as if I had just that second forgotten it.

"Trapnell. Yes." My face still wasn't familiar. Her smile began to waver. "How long have you worked for Tod?"

"Actually I don't. I'm a big fan of charity bingo. I was out at the church on Monday."

She didn't remember. She didn't bother to try. "Look, Mr. Spain, my agency gets me this work. It's a bingo game one time and a political rally the next. It's not something I get emotionally involved with."

If you believed her eyes, I was boring her stiff. Tommy Lipton was probably right. A lot of girls fancied themselves hard cases these days. It probably never occurred to them that the cool facade wouldn't be necessary if there weren't insecure thoughts darting around behind it, like spiders behind the walls. I began wondering about those thoughts. Osborne Associates had infiltrated Lipton's organization. They might have done the same with the Hamilton Agency.

"You're booked through Guy Hamilton, aren't you, Sarah?"

"Gerda Hamilton. Guy Hamilton is in trouble with the police."

"Guy Hamilton is in trouble with a lot of people. Has Grayson asked you to keep your eyes open for him?"

"No. Why would he?"

"Hamilton is supposed to have come into possession of an Osborne Associates' political file. Grayson hasn't mentioned that to you?"

"No." I believed the surprise in her eyes.

"Did he send you out to work the bingo games?"

"No," she blurted. "He...he knows I work at other hostess assignments, of course."

"You've been keeping the bingo games quiet."

"With the election coming, he has to work every night, and I do need the money."

"But he does know that you work out of the Hamilton Agency."

"All Tod ever asked me to do at the Agency was talk to the women about who had worked as hostesses at political rallies before. He wanted to hire the most experienced girls. Like if they had ever worked for Osborne Associates' campaigns."

"Didn't he know who had worked for Osborne?"

"Why would he ask me to ask if he did? Anyway, those things are hard to keep track of. The women are only there for an afternoon, mostly."

"The Agency keeps records of work experience," I reminded her. "It's their bread and butter."

It was a fact she couldn't reconcile with Grayson's behavior. Her eyes grew wary and hostile.

"Why are you asking all these questions about Tod?"

"I'm a private investigator, Sarah. Do you mind if I call you Sarah?"

"Is Tod in trouble?" she asked uneasily, as if this weren't the first hint she'd had.

"Has he ever mentioned anything called a Doomsday Book?"

"A what?"

"Have you ever asked him what's bothering him? Not just casually. I mean pressed the point?"

"Nothing is bothering him. It's just stress. It's the campaign. That's all."

"What are you afraid of, Sarah?"

"I am not afraid." She glanced at the group she was supposed to be playing hostess for. "I don't know what you want, Mr. Spain, or why you are saying these things about Tod, but I don't think I want to talk to you any more."

"I know it's tough to put pressure on people when you're young, but sometimes it helps. Problems are like steam. They're only dangerous when they're bottled up. Tod will have to talk to somebody sometime. It might be best if he talked to you now."

"I don't want to cause a scene, Mr. Spain, but I will if that's what it takes to make you leave me alone."

She looked just desperate enough to do it.

"All right." I fished around in my pocket and found a business card. "Keep this. When what I told you has chewed on you long enough, ask Tod about it. Call me and tell me what you find out, no matter how inconsequential it may seem."

She put the card in the seam pocket of her skirt. She wasn't planning to call. It was just a convenient way to get me off her back. She melted into her group.

I looked around and didn't see anyone who wasn't part of a busy little group. I didn't see any executives rushing in my direction to pour out their souls. I also didn't see any gendarmes coming to eject me. All in all I didn't seem to have made much of an impact.

I trudged back to the Volvo and headed down toward reality again. The events on Rexford Drive were no coincidence. Charity bingo, the striptease movies and the Doomsday Book were all marching in lockstep. I was just too deaf to hear the cadence.

Chapter 24

I drove home and mowed my lawn, washed both cars and swept out the garage. It was a lot of work. It took the edge off my frustration and made me hungry. After dinner I loaded the CD player, uncovered the pool table and got a cue out of the wall rack. My first visitor was the neighbors' Seal Point Siamese cat. He meowed piteously to get me to open the slider, then rubbed against my leg until I poured him an ashtray of beer. He left when the doorbell rang at nine fifteen. I noticed the time because I wasn't expecting anyone. At least not anyone I wanted to see. The doorbell rang twice more while I was hiding two voice activated microcassette recorders.

I put on my very best indignant-citizen-minding-his-own-business look and opened the door. It wasn't the police.

Jean LaBostrie.stood an inch from the door. Her almond eyes were a couple of degrees cooler than a reactor core meltdown. Her dress would have turned heads on a department store mannequin. It was belted tight at her waist. Other than that it was free to cling lecherously or puff out in the breeze and play peek-a-boo. Just then it was doing both. I recovered from an overlong window shopping expedition and put my jaw back where it belonged.

"Hello," was all I could manage to say.

"I think I've figured out what's wrong with your love life," she said huskily. "A chick can't get beyond standing outside your doors."

"Come on in. My etchings are at the cleaners, but I'll think of something."

Jean checked out the front of my T-shirt on her way past. It had a picture of a chubby little fellow up to his chin in weeds above the caption: 'I fought the lawn, and the lawn won.' It went nicely with my grass stained khakis, but it wasn't exactly the thing to impress today's enlightened young woman. Jean taunted me with a laugh and went toward the music and the lights, leaving me to absorb a head-spinning dose of Gardenia. It took me a couple of tries to get the door properly closed. I found Jean perched decoratively on a barstool when I got to the recreation room.

"Shouldn't you be working?" I asked.

"The Club is closed tonight. Some private political dinner."

"How about some liquid consolation? Gin gimlet, wasn't it?"

"I'd love one." She sounded enthusiastic. I was getting the message now. All I needed was a little encouragement. "What happened to your head?" she asked while I ducked behind the bar.

I mumbled something about the hazards of my profession while I flipped through a 1969 *Playboy Bar Guide* to see what went into a gin gimlet besides gin. Jean went to work admiring the premises.

"That Coca Cola lamp over the billiard table is cute. There's a classy restaurant in San Francisco that did the wainscoting in carpeting just like this."

The progressive turn she was doing on the barstool tightened the fabric of her dress to the point that I was now sure she had no foundation underneath. It was an opportune time to be handling shaved ice.

"The investigating business must pay pretty well," she said. "A house like this must be worth a fortune."

"About a third of what Walter Brixner's place is on the market for."

It was her turn to stare. "Who is selling Walter's house?"

"Whoever he worked for."

"Can they do that? Don't lawyers have to do probate on dead people's stuff? I mean, Walter is dead, isn't he?"

"They seem to have had a signed power of attorney handy for emergencies. Did Brixner ever mention the name Danny Rupert?"

"Who is he supposed to be?"

"A real estate broker."

She shook her head. She accepted her drink as if I were presenting her with a diamond lavaliere. She tasted it reverently.

"Mmm. This is good."

I let my questions lapse while I measured an ounce of Bacardi over ice and added Coke. Her eyes fell on the pool table.

"Do you let your babes play?"

"I would if I had any."

She parked her drink, took a cue off the wall and chalked it while I built a tight rack. When she bent for the break shot her breasts massed and firmed under their own weight. The dress sagged from belt to shoulders. There wasn't anything above her waist I couldn't see directly. If she were aware of my gaze, it didn't put her off her stroke. The cue ball rapped the rack just behind the head ball, took the eight cleanly out of the center and came within an inch of sinking it off two banks. The twelve dropped obligingly into a corner pocket. She ran off four more balls and did interesting things to my pulse rate.

"My dad had one of these things in the garage loft," she said while she lined up the fourteen. She couldn't quite make it hug the cushion from the length of the table.

"Walter Brixner had one, too," I reminded her. "And you've had recent practice."

"Well, all right," she admitted with a musical laugh. "It's not like I'm trying to hustle you for money or anything."

"Found a new steady yet?"

"I wasn't really Walter's mistress. I just told you that because you were being snoopy."

"You also acted like you didn't know he was a voyeur. You knew enough to hang over his pool table in a loose evening dress."

She leaned on her cue and rolled her hips in slow enticement. "Are you trying to tell me all men don't like to stare?"

She had caught me with a pair of smoking eyeballs. I put my nose down near the felt, lined up an easy shot to angle the four into a side pocket and proceeded to miss. So much for Henry Spain, man of steel. I retreated to the bar and retrieved my Bacardi and Coke.

"Did Brixner ever mention a Doomsday Book?" I asked.

"No, he didn't." She tapped the fourteen into a corner pocket and left herself a tough choice to take the ten.

"And you don't have any idea what it is."

"Yes, I do. It's a kind of census William the Conqueror had made when he took over England so he would know how much stuff people owned and where they kept it. Didn't you go to high school?"

"Sure." The 101st Airborne even insisted I finish. I also took a lot of night classes at UCLA, for reasons that seemed appropriate at the time. "But this particular Doomsday Book is a lot more recent than 1069. It seems to be some kind of file, stolen from an advertising company called Osborne Associates. It was the motive for Brixner's murder."

Jean's teeth went to work on her lower lip. The smoldering eyes and seductive banter were gone. The look she gave me belonged on a lost puppy.

"If you're going to talk about Walter, I don't think I want to be stared at anymore."

"Ricky Calland had him killed," I told her gently.

She put the cue on the table felt and left the eight ball to stand. She took her glass to the sofa and sipped morosely at the translucent liquid.

"I went on break with the girls at that ship company. That's how come I knew you weren't married or living with anyone or anything so I could come here. They think you take pictures of people in bed for divorces and stuff. The chunky little redhead said you were pond scum. I think she's losing weight so you'll hit on her."

I leaned my cue against the bar and went to sit beside her. "Calland had it twisted around in his mind that this Doomsday Book was the key to everything he wanted, and that Brixner stood in the way of his getting it."

"Ricky is dead. Mr. Lipton called us all together at rehearsal and told us. In case anyone wanted to go to the service, or anything."

"The men who killed him lacked only an inch of nerve, or I'd be dead too."

I told Jean about the shooting at the Temple of Cosmic Awareness. I told her without knowing why I was telling her. Maybe I wasn't telling her at all. Maybe she just happened to be there when the dam broke and the words started coming out. I could hear myself speak, but I didn't seem to have any control over what I was saying. I had become part of my own audience. I heard myself drone on, describing the Temple and the people and then reconstructing my conversations with Jeffrey Haven and Ricky Calland in stupefying detail. In addition to sounding boring and cynical, I also needed elocution lessons.

Jean was fascinated. She didn't say a word. She watched me oddly as I told her of lying helpless on Jeffrey Haven's carpet while the automatic rifle raked the room. I realized then that my hand was trembling, slopping chilly liquid over the edge of my glass.

"It gave me a pretty good scare," I confessed.

"Wow, I guess."

I put the drink aside and got out a handkerchief, feeling foolish.

"What were you thinking?" she asked.

"My life didn't flash by. Or any of that other romantic nonsense that's supposed to be part of a close brush with death."

"You're afraid of romantic things," she realized.

"One of the requirements for good pond scum."

"Did you find out what that Doomsday Book thing was? Or what it had to do with Walter?"

I put the handkerchief away and shook my head. "I've hit a stone wall there. I don't know that Brixner had any connection with the actual book. As far as I can establish, he was the victim of Calland's fantasy."

"Poor Walter. Nothing I've touched in L.A. has turned out right. I wish I'd never come here."

The Mello-Kings smooth, sentimental rendition of *Slow Dancing* drifted from the speakers. She sang along in a forlorn contralto while I was at the bar mixing two more drinks.

"I like your dress," I said brightly.

"It's a hooker's dress. I don't know why I bought it. This is the first time I ever wore it. I feel dirty in it."

She found security in the deep corner of the sofa and curled her legs under. I brought the glasses back and sat down beside her.

"Hasn't been a very good week, has it?"

"We're putting six new numbers into the routine at the Club. Or did I already tell you that?"

I thought she had, but I didn't say so.

"Some of it is request stuff that just isn't going to work," she said, and added a chorus for demonstration:

> I asked your mother for you
> She said you were too young
> Now I wish I'd never seen your face
> Nor heard your lying tongue
> Irene, Goodni-ight
> Irene, Goodni-ight
> Goodnight Irene, Goodnight Irene
> I'll see you in my dreams

"I mean, my own mother cut an arrangement of that when she fronted Gus Romberg at the old King Edward Ballroom."

There had been a King Edward Ballroom in L.A. It was a synonym for square when I was in high school. Years later I rounded up a few runaways there, after it had deteriorated into a teen hangout. It was gone now, along with a lot of other King Edward Ballrooms in a lot of other cities Jean could have been talking about.

"I'll bet everyone at the Club thought you were great," I said.

"Little Albert Cooper was the only one who said anything nice. And that's just because he still feels bad over what happened at that stupid agency."

"The bookkeeper at Lipton's club worked for the Hamilton Agency?"

"Albert worked for a service that did the books there. They bullied him into going along with Guy Hamilton to keep the Agency as a customer. Then they denied everything when he got sick over it and told the police. Walter got him a job at the Club to help him get probation after some cheap lawyer made him plead guilty because he didn't have the money to defend himself in court. I mean, where did that crummy lawyer in the Prosecutors Office get off charging him in the first place?"

"A deputy prosecutor's conviction percentage helps determine how much salary he's offered when goes into private practice. He can't afford to pass up an easy mark."

"Do all lawyers have crummy ethics?" The possibility seemed to bother her.

"They have their own definition of ethics."

"One of them lives in my apartment building. He's just a law student, but he's already a creep. I read somewhere a law professor said he wouldn't trust even half the students he graduated to represent him in court. Isn't that awful?"

"Terrible."

She leaned against me and rested her head against my shoulder. I didn't know whether she knew what her Gardenia was doing to me, or if she was just bushed.

"Are investigators nicer than lawyers?" she asked.

I put an arm around her shoulders. "Its practically an insult to put us in the same sentence with them."

"Sorry," she cooed.

She snuggled comfortably against me. Our faces were inches apart. Her breathing was a delicate zephyr against my skin.

"I really came here to seduce you," she confessed. "So you would tell Mr. Lipton everything was all right."

"No, you came here to give me the idea you were seducible. To get me to fall in line until you had what you wanted and could stiff me."

"You'll screw everything up for me. You've got no more heart than a lizard."

I kissed her once, experimentally. Then I kissed her again, a lingering kiss that opened her mouth under mine. We adjusted to more comfortable positions. I didn't stop kissing her. Her fingertips played exotic music on the nape of my neck. I was eighteen again.

Chapter 25

Jean didn't want any breakfast. She backed her Honda out of the drive and accelerated away into a heavy morning overcast. I drove to the office. There was nothing on voice mail and more of the same in the paper. There were probably some other reasons I had come in, but just then I couldn't think what they might be. I let my chair turn slowly on its worn bearings until I could put my feet up on the sheet metal over the radiator. Rain dribbled down the window. The airshaft dissolved gradually into a fog, and my contact with reality went with it. Not even a succulent raspberry from the phone buzzer broke the spell completely.

"Henry Spain Investigations."

"Earl Snyder, Spain." His voice was sharp, not pleased. "You sound spaced."

"Sorry, Captain." I shook a couple of the cobwebs loose. I didn't tell him I had been on something a little stronger than controlled substances. "What can I do for you?"

"We located Charlie Watrous. I expect you already know the circumstances."

I put the ominous silence that followed down to police theater. Guaranteed to make the purest citizen blurt out his entire litany of misdemeanors.

When it didn't work, Snyder said, "You knew about the boat, of course."

"No."

"The old Chris Craft, registered to Girts Hauser?"

"News to me, Captain." I curled my fingers over the mouthpiece to keep my expectant breathing to myself.

"The Coast Guard found it for us on Catalina. Watrous and his son-in-law were aboard. The supply of scotch would have held out for a week, even at the rate they were going."

"That's what you call boating in California. You motor out and drink a little and fish a little and you don't catch anything so you motor a little more and drink a little more then you get tired of motoring so you tie up at Catalina and you just drink until it's time to go back and lord it over the peons, letting them in on what a high old time you had."

"As a matter of public record," Snyder said crisply, "Hauser has owned both the house and the boat since his days in films. Both are now mortgaged to Charlie Watrous for more than their market value."

"Mr. Watrous must be a very trusting soul, to leave his capital at large with inadequate security."

"Financial arrangements like that are what the Department calls investigative leads," Snyder advised me. "Your theory about Hauser having a business relationship with Watrous is now police property. Which means when your lab reports on Hauser's car, I hear about it straight away. Verbally on the important points. Follow-up copy on the paperwork within twenty-four hours. Understood?"

"I didn't know I was being watched that closely."

"Just so you remember," he said.

I couldn't see him, but I knew he was smiling his alligator smile when he hung up. I also knew from the fact that he wanted to talk to Guy Hamilton that he hadn't had enough on Watrous to hold him. The only number Watrous kept in the phone book was his law office. He wasn't in. His receptionist was ever so sorry she couldn't give me his home number. I had her take a message for him to call Elmo Slotmachine. I had to spell it for her.

The laboratory had a preliminary report on Hamilton's 190 SL. Analysis of the gasoline told them the same thing a film of dust had told me. It hadn't been started in some weeks. Residue from the ashtray told them Hamilton smoked a custom cigar blend, in case I was breaking in a new pair of shoes and wanted to cart his picture around to the couple of hundred shops that dealt in such things. They were also excited about a charred scrap of paper that had probably once been a list of female names. Until I told them Hamilton had made what passed for a living brokering talent. They assured me they would keep working. They probably liked the size of Lipton's deposit. I couldn't find either Lipton or Snyder to give them the bad news.

It was getting to be noon and my stomach was getting emphatic about missing breakfast. A trip down to the close combat of the building deli put me in a sharp elbowed frame of mind. Up in my office again, I called the Crown Colony. Albert Cooper wasn't there. I left a message and tried the home number they gave me. He wasn't there either. I called the title insurance company. My army of admirers was in court. I left a message for him to dig up the contract holder on Walter Brixner's house, in addition to the other things he hadn't called me back on yet. I got the rest of the insurance recovery contracts ready and sent them down the mail chute. That left me staring out at the rain again. Some time before mid-afternoon I stirred myself enough to build a pot of coffee. There was a dusty pint bottle in the bottom drawer with enough Jamaican rum left in it to put me partway out of my misery.

I was lacing my third cup when a small, careful shadow appeared on the marbled glass of my door. It hesitated, fidgeting for a minute. Then the door opened a foot and Albert Cooper slipped in and closed it quickly behind him. He hadn't expected to step directly into my private office. The surprise ruined whatever front he had ready to put up. His little mouth twitched wordlessly.

"Good afternoon," I said gravely.

I sounded like I had been drinking. With a pint of rum in my hand, I probably looked like I was still drinking. I put it away to try for some professional composure. I could have passed out cold for all the difference it made to Cooper.

He was as stiff as the new tan raincoat he was wearing. His Adams apple bobbed uncertainly above a fresh white collar that fit properly this time. His crimson tie looked to be silk. Whatever bit of money he had come into had done more for his wardrobe than his nerves. It was a moment before he stopped blinking and his bright, bulging eyes found the chair beside the desk.

"You mind?"

"Go ahead. You're invited."

He slouched down uncomfortably, like a high school toughie with an appointment in the principal's office.

"Okay," he said. "You called, so I guess you heard about my police record."

"I heard you may have had an attack of the stupids. The local law enforcement community may hold that against you, but nobody gets along with them anyway."

"I guess you think I'm pretty naive," he said. The solemn tone of his voice said more. His police record was important to him. It may have been the only thing of consequence that had ever happened to him.

"Maybe we both are," I said.

"Maybe Miss LaBostrie is too." His cheeks reddened painfully as soon as he made the suggestion. "I mean, she wants a singing career and…well, you know, maybe she doesn't always know what she's getting herself into."

"We're all concerned about Miss LaBostrie," I told him, sounding a good deal more sober than I was. "There ought to be a law against women looking as good as she does. But there's only so much you or anyone else can do. People can't be caged for their own protection, like animals in a zoo."

"Suppose she was going to get into trouble?" he asked uncertainly.

"Just as an example, Albert, this is the beginning of November. Before the month is out, that phone is going to ring and I'm going to be asked to trace a runaway for a worried parent. I've traced at least one a month since I opened my door. When I find them, it's always the same story. They ran because they felt trapped. Caged by their parents' expectations and fears for them. Caged by me when I found them. Last August a fourteen-year-old girl ripped my arm from wrist to elbow with a razor blade. She wanted the freedom to make her own mistakes. Miss LaBostrie does, too."

It was a good little speech. Even if it was mostly for my own benefit. Cooper made some noncommittal movements with a jittery hand and brought a cigarette out from inside the raincoat. He poked it into an ingratiating smile that looked like it wanted to run for the nearest fall-out shelter.

"You...uh, well I suppose you do a lot of work for Mr. Lipton. Off and on. I guess."

"Lipton wasn't even an occasional name in the news until this week."

The little man blinked through smoke. "Then maybe you don't know."

"Why don't you tell me?" I suggested brightly.

Cooper was leery of my attitude. He kept it brief, speaking quickly and tonelessly. "Lipton runs this city. Politics, real estate, rackets; he's into everything. He runs it all."

The little man was absolutely serious about it. He watched deadpan while I drank some more of my loaded coffee. His bright eyes got feisty as soon as they were sure I hadn't taken him seriously.

"Okay," he snapped. "If you're not going to believe it, you're not going to believe it."

"Nobody runs this city, Albert. Between urban sprawl and urban decay, it's gotten too big and too tough. Corporations can own fifty story skyscrapers, but they have to borrow most of the money to do it. Gangs can control bits of turf and pieces of the action, but the Hell's Angels make damn sure they're out of South Central by sundown, and not even the Syndicate has more than a race wire franchise in East L.A. The city administration is doing well if it can keep a lid on things from one day to the next. Lipton may be a big player compared to you or I, but overall he's about a one point two on the Richter Scale."

None of it registered. "She could already know," he speculated for my benefit. "Somebody could have told her. I mean, if they were trying to impress her how much they knew, and like that."

"Miss LaBostrie has the power to cloud men's minds," I said dramatically. A couple of more Jamaican coffees and I was going to be in a bad way.

"Mr. Brixner wouldn't have told her," he said. "He told me I'd be dead if I ever told anyone. Someone else might have, though. There's an operator named Murillo that's always passing remarks about her."

"You know Frank Murillo, do you?"

"I know all the operators. Mr. Brixner brought me in to do the merchandise accounts for Mr. Lipton. The merchandise is prizes in a bingo racket. Except you aren't believing any of it."

"Did you actually report to Lipton? Or did Brixner just tell you that's who you were working for?"

The little man stared at me.

"That's the way it goes sometimes, Albert. A good way to keep an organization in line and discourage competition is to use a name with a tough past for cover. The work and risk involved in small time bingo wouldn't interest Tommy Lipton."

"The gross receipts are over seven million dollars a year. Nobody told me that. I've seen the cash control sheets, the hard and soft count, the imprest makeups and the bank reconciliation."

"That's fine, Albert, but you can't run a business without expenses. Even at lottery percentages, over half of that seven million goes back to the players as prizes. Or they don't come back to the games. Another sizeable percentage goes to charity. Payroll and overhead are going to eat up most of the rest. I don't see Lipton's end of that arrangement doing much damage to his mortgage payments. And a real estate owner of Lipton's standing has to structure his time and risk with those little goodies very high on his priority list."

Cooper stabbed his cigarette contemptuously into the desk ashtray. "Lipton doesn't buy the merchandise prizes. He has them stolen. Trucks leaving San Pedro harbor are hijacked with whole cargoes of small appliances. The cash prizes are money from robberies. He buys traceable bills a dime on the dollar and holds them until they cool."

"That's not bingo you're talking about, Albert. That's a large, economy size fencing operation."

"So what? Four million dollars profit is four million dollars profit, isn't it?"

I had reasoned myself into a corner. Four million Cooper's way would make all the mortgage payments any other four million would.

"Have you actually seen the income statement?"

"I've seen everything. Close up and personal, like they say on TV. I had to do the trial balance at the end of the month."

"Sure, you would have had to," I realized. "Brixner was dead by then."

His mouth made a couple of false starts before any words came out. "Do you know how Mr. Brixner died...was killed?"

"Miss LaBostrie knows too," I told him.

The little man fell somber. "I think Mr. Brixner helped her somehow. He was kind of an odd man, so it was hard to know. I don't think he was really bad."

"Hell, no. What's a little gambling and hijacking and extortion among us All American Boys?"

"Everyone who knew him liked him. Even the bingo hostesses. He came to the Agency to hire them. He used to stare at them like he wanted to undress them. I guess he really did, from the things I heard later, when I went to work for him. Some of the operators said he had arrangements to watch women being undressed by men who were going to...well, you know, fuck them."

"Yes, I can imagine," I said thinly. The liquor was at work again on what few brains I had left.

"Mr. Brixner was the only one who came to see me in jail. He was in trouble once himself. He didn't like police or judges or lawyers because of it. He thought I was getting a raw deal."

"Are you sure he didn't set things up with your lawyer to get some cheap bookkeeping help?"

"At least he took me seriously. It gets old after a while. People treating you like a joke because you don't look like the ads in the *Wall Street Journal*. You got something to prove to the world, and pretty soon you don't care so much what you have to do to get a chance to prove it."

"Did Brixner have anyone else proving something? A real estate broker named Danny Rupert, for instance?"

The name did something to him. He sat up as stiff as a recruit on his first visit to the mess hall. "Danny Rupert works for Mr. Lipton," he informed me in a brittle voice.

"Doing what?"

Cooper stared at me with his little mouth pressed so tight that his insignificant jaw almost disappeared.

"Doing what?" I repeated.

"He buys the money and arranges the hijacking. He's the boss in San Pedro, like Mr. Brixner was here. Mr. Lipton called him here the night Mr. Brixner was killed. To find out who was trying to take over."

"What caliber gun does Rupert carry?"

The bulging eyes blinked vacantly. "I don't know. I never saw him with a gun. I guess he must have one. Even the gangs that do the hijacking are supposed to be scared of him."

"What does he look like?"

"He dresses kind of formal. I've never seen him without a suit and tie, and he always wears a white shirt. His face is kind of sensitive. He looks pretty young, unless you look close. He always smiles, and he's friendly and polite when he talks, but he never seems to relax. The tension is what's scary. It's like you hear what he's saying, but you know it's not what he's thinking."

I had met men like that. Men who bottled up normal emotions behind the veneer of conformity that protected them from the criticism of family and society, until hostility started boiling out under the lid in dark places and secret ways. I always had the same reaction to them. They scared hell out of me.

Cooper seemed relieved to have me looking like I finally took him seriously. "I have to meet him at eight tonight at the Discount Appliance Warehouse to go over the unallocated overhead and bulk sales vouchers, if you wanted to get a look at him."

"You might want to call in sick for that one, Albert. I'm pretty sure Rupert killed a man recently. The trigger man in the Brixner shooting was found dead. Shot without an inch of mercy."

"I've got protection," the little man said.

His hand came out of the raincoat with a small black automatic. My reaction was instinctive. I caught his bony wrist, twisted hard and used my free hand to pry the pistol loose from his fingers. A stifled cry tore itself from his throat. I had him bent sideways across the desk. Startled eyes full of pain swore he only meant to show me the compact Colt.

I had done myself proud. I had sat there listening to him tell me what a jerk I had been, getting madder and madder at myself, until I finally took my frustrations out on a little man who had swallowed a big lump of fear to come in and set me straight. I let him go with a vague, apologetic shrug.

I dumped a full magazine on the desk, jacked a .380 cartridge out of the chamber and dropped the gun on top of the ammunition.

"Albert, do you know you could go to prison for carrying this thing? You've been convicted of a felony."

"One of the bingo operators sold it to me. It's just for protection."

"And you don't particularly care if I show up at the Warehouse tonight or not?" I asked dubiously.

"I just came to tell you what Miss LaBostrie was getting herself into. I've done that now, so…"

The phone buzzer went off. Cooper jumped a foot. I grabbed the receiver.

"Henry Spain Investigations," I said testily.

It was my title attorney. "Ah! My dear Sheerluck. I…"

"Just a minute," I growled and stood up.

I wasn't fast enough. Cooper had already scooped the little black Colt off the desk and got the shells up in his other hand. He bumped past the chair backing away from the desk. He stuffed the pistol into one coat pocket, the ammunition into the other. He backed out the door, smiling nervously through an overdose of bad breaks.

I hadn't even got around to asking him about Guy Hamilton. An elevator shut down the hall and told me I wouldn't get the chance. I was left standing at my desk, holding a phone with an idiot babbling in my ear from the other end.

Chapter 26

"I say, Sheerluck? Henry? Are you there?"

I subsided into my chair. "No. I fell overboard."

"Well, excuse me. I'm only calling with the decisive link in the chain of evidence."

"Spare me the melodrama." Fat chance.

"The contract holder you called me on?" he dangled in front of me in a tantalizing voice. "16854 Half Moon Lane. Legally described as Lot 6 Block 2 of Zimbleman's Second Addition to Holland Canyon View Estates?"

"Terrence Llewelyn Stafford. Aka Tough Tommy Lipton."

"It's not nice to ask people to spend their valuable time looking up things you already know."

"I didn't know when I asked. What did you get on the Schaeffer-Pilon Hotel?"

"That's a partnership. De facto if not declared. Probably an absentee ownership situation."

"Why absentee?"

"The taxes are billed to a property management company that specializes in those things. Also, the only Hannah Lucille Hilliard in the Los Angeles County Records died destitute in 1977. It's not likely that either she or the Julio D'Aguilar Barragon-Camacho buried at county expense in 1981 got together with any of the fourteen Stefan Rakubians in the greater Los Angeles area phone directories to buy a hotel in 1983."

"Hold on," I said, and put the phone down. It had just occurred to me what I had stolen from the late Walter O. Brixner. I heaved the wadded mass of computer printout up on the desk and started scrambling through it.

"Listen, if I give you a couple of legal descriptions and sets of own-ers' names, can you check the death records to see if any of the owners died before they bought the property?"

"I was kidding about that, Henry."

"I'm not." I read him two sets of foreign names that weren't likely to belong to more than one person.

"Where did you get these names, Henry?"

"From the Doomsday Book. Ever hear of it?"

"Henry, have you been drinking?"

I wished I hadn't. "What would you say to several hundred proper-ties owned and recorded under cover names?"

"Be your age, Henry. This is the land of Looney Tunes. Anyone who puts himself on the public record is begging to be pestered by the crack-pots and pilloried by the media. Not even the straight arrows use their right names any more."

"You're telling me neither you nor anyone else knows for sure who owns Los Angeles?"

"Speaking of not knowing," he said uneasily, "I may have short-changed you with that thumbnail sketch of Tommy Lipton. I mentioned his name to a colleague in the Prosecutor's office and wound up on the business end of a third degree. This was over lunch, mind you, and the lady was in diapers when Lipton was last arrested. I sense something very current and very ominous."

"I know about Lipton. What can you tell me about a commercial real estate broker named Danny Rupert?"

"Mother's little helper? He took over the family brokerage in San Pedro. End of story. What about Lipton?"

"Rupert is his enforcer."

"Henry, I know the man. He drinks creme soda from a champagne cocktail glass."

"Rupert is a psycho. Stay away from him. Don't ask around about him. Or any more about Lipton. Understood?"

The ecstasy was back in his voice when he said, "You're serious, aren't you, Henry?"

I hung up. The useful conversation was over, and I didn't have time to vent my spleen at him. I had to find someplace to stash the Doomsday Book, fast. I gathered the printout into a bundle, rooted the binder of diskettes out of the corner and climbed into my coat. The phone ambushed me halfway to the door.

"Henry Spain Investigations."

"Spain?" It was a blustery voice with an undercurrent of nasty schemes.

"Welcome back, Mr. Watrous. How is the blue movie business this afternoon?"

"Just listen, Spain. And don't give me none of that Elmo Slotmachine crap. You're looking to find Guy Hamilton. You get your butt out here and be real sweet and maybe, just maybe, we'll talk trade."

Watrous' directions took me east of the city and the maze of suburbs to where old farms had been parceled out to weekend squires. There was a mailbox every couple of acres along the worn composition road. Most of them had a sonorous combination of syllables from two first names followed by words like 'ranch' and 'stables'. Watrous' mailbox had its own little house on a post next to the road. It was a preview of the showy white colonial that emerged out of the drizzle as I curved up the gravel drive. Out there in the flat brown country it looked like the FHA version of *Gone With The Wind*.

Small dogs set up a yipping racket inside before I had my car locked. Charlie opened the front door as I came up on the porch. He was slightly more immense than I remembered, in a tan shooting jacket with rough leather patches at both elbows and one shoulder. He held a double-barreled shotgun in the crook of one arm. A small animated white poodle with purple ribbons accenting its grooming made noise at his feet. He cursed and kicked the animal aside.

"Goddamn whining mutts. My old lady can't get along with one. She's gotta have three."

"But they're so cute," I cooed.

Charlie's face went florid. He put a thick forefinger in my face. "Hey, I don't have to take that crap!"

His breath was fragrant, about the strength of a distillery main drain. I stepped back and wrinkled my nose.

"Just being sweet, Charlie. Just like you said."

He motioned me inside with a jerk of his round head, closed the door and led me down a hallway, rolling along like a sea captain in heavy weather. His shotgun was an open country piece with thirty-inch barrels. He had a little trouble maneuvering it around to get himself aimed through a doorway at the end. He made it without nicking any woodwork and pushed the shotgun aside on a couple of yards of roll top desk. A bottle of four star Martell teetered and an empty glass went rolling. He dragged a heavy wooden chair back out of the kneehole and plopped his bulk down. The impact elicited a hiccough. He waved a hand to tell me to find a seat.

The room looked like the outcome of a screaming match between Mervyn of Beverly Hills and a registered representative from Williamsburg Antiques. The furniture was stodgy maple, the carpet a prissy white shag, the wainscoting painted robin's egg blue. The walls above were papered in decorator pastels behind oil paintings of the sort of big-eyed darling horsie-worsies that women went mushy over. Ionizers sucked relentless at a thin haze of cigar smoke. Perfume hung as heavy as naphthalene. I wondered if Charlie was ducking more than the police when he camped out in Malibu and Catalina. I winked at him and made myself to home on a floral settee.

"I was looking forward to seeing Harv again. Couldn't he make it?"

"Chickened out," Watrous said thickly. "Big mouth. Always telling me to put the movies on videotape. Sell a thousand for a grand each instead of one for sixty grand. Pirates, I tell him. Get a copy. Steal us blind. No sweat, he says. We can handle them. Then he chickens out on some snitch private cop."

"Yeah," I sympathized. "Kids these days."

"Kids!" Watrous growled. "Lousy high school brats. Got drunk and hit that Pontiac out at Malibu. Cops wanna fuck me over for it. They took my movie, and they wanna fuck me over."

"You should have reported the Trans Am, Charlie. Kids don't always know how to keep themselves out of grief."

"You're the fucker that snitched me off. You think old Charlie is too shit-faced to know what's going down? Well, Charlie got this phone call, see? Now he knows a certain snitch private shoe is looking for a certain Guy Hamilton. And old Charlie, he knows you're working for Tough Tommy Lipton."

The source of the phone call wasn't hard to guess. Drew was making up in persistence what he lacked in brains. "Hardly anyone calls him Tough Tommy any more," I said.

He puffed out his chest and poked a thumb into it. "Charlie was around after Korea, when Lipton was still doing his work out where you could see it, if you knew where to look. Operators like him don't change 'cause they get older. They get smoother maybe, and smarter and meaner, but they don't change."

"Worried, Charlie?"

His chuckle leaked out of him like the steam out of a broken radiator. "Charlie can look after himself," he said, and patted the shotgun clumsily.

Harv had remembered a pressing engagement. Charlie had needed a bottle of ninety proof nerve and the shotgun to stick around on his own. It had to be more than our run-in two nights ago. I hadn't scared anyone that badly even when I was young and reckless.

"What's it all about, Charlie?"

He wagged a finger at me. "Uh-uh, snitchy-boy. Not one word about old Guy until Charlie gets clear with them creep-ass County shoes. You can tell Mr. Tough Tommy Lipton that."

"Why don't you tell him yourself, Charlie? Don't you have a phone out here?"

He focussed his little red eyes on me with difficulty. This wasn't the way it was supposed to be. He was a lawyer. Lawyers laid down the law and people quaked in their shoes and wet themselves. Lawyers were God. Lawyers knew things nobody else knew.

"I could tell Lipton plenty," Watrous said mysteriously.

"Sure, Charlie."

"About crap his boys been pulling behind his ass."

"Sure, Charlie."

"How 'bout them three bullets in Guy Hamilton?" Watrous asked significantly.

I stopped breathing. "Either you tell me or I guess. I don't know."

"Smallbores, from the look of the holes, like professional. That's what made me think Lipton had it done. That, and it was Walt Brixner called me to get rid of the body. But old Tough Tommy wouldn't be looking for Guy now if he knew he was dead then. So it looks like his boys pulled a swiftie of their own and didn't tell him. Don't it, snitchy-boy?"

"You must have been pretty tight with Brixner. I doubt he was in the habit of calling just anyone to dispose of his excess bodies."

"He called old Charlie because he knew I held the paper on Guy's place. Lemme tell you, I got a real case of the hips at that four-eyed motherfucker. I mean, putting my buns in a sling like that, calling me down there so I gotta do the dirty work. But Walt, he's cool. He lets me steam awhile, then he tells me to get rid of the body where it won't ever be found."

"Just like that? No questions from you? No: 'Hey, Walt, what happened to poor old Guy?' and like that?"

Charlie's little red eyes went shrewd. "Hey, I knew he had Lipton behind him. So yeah, no questions from me."

"Did Brixner kill Hamilton?"

"No way. Walt was no pistol. He just paid Guy to use the peekhole. Old Walt, he wasn't even a bad sort, as creeps go."

"Did he say who did the shooting?"

"Nobody talks about that fucker!" Charlie assured me with alcoholic vehemence. "I got Harv and we took Guy down to the boat before dawn. Talk about kids being gutless these days. I thought sure Harv was going to blow his cookies."

"What did you do with Hamilton?"

"I read somewhere it takes four hundred pounds to keep a body down. The dinghy went that at least. We towed it out in the Channel, chained Guy in and chopped holes in the bottom. He may come up again, but it won't be in this lifetime."

"Lifetimes haven't been lasting too long, Charlie. First Hamilton, then Brixner. How many days between them, Charlie? What date did you dump Hamilton?"

Charlie peered at me vacantly. I didn't know if he didn't know Brixner was dead, hadn't understood the question or was just thinking.

"We'n'sday," he said abruptly. "Last month. No, September ain't last month no more. Day after my old lady worked the polls for the primary 'lection. Night after. She was crapped out when the call came. It was Thursday when we got poor old Guy in the Channel. Poor ol' Guy. Got me my best broads. Had some times out in that house of his. Some real times."

Guy Hamilton had called Osborne Associates to peddle the Doomsday Book the night after the primary election. The same night Walter Brixner turned Hamilton over to Watrous with three neat little holes in him. I had taken the Book from Brixner's house seven weeks later. But Brixner hadn't shot Hamilton for it.

"Find any shell casings, Charlie?"

"Musta policed 'em," he slurred. "Uses an automatic. A .22. Old Charlie knows about him, about that automatic, a long time. Musta p'liced up the shells."

"This is Danny Rupert we're talking about?"

"Lookin' for me today," Charlie said thickly. "Says Lipton wants to know where Guy Hamilton is. Real nice and polite. Like he didn't know all along."

"You actually saw Danny Rupert the night Hamilton was shot?"

"Poison." Charlie hiccoughed. "Never seen him. Never wanna see him again. Poison."

Charlie had more things to say. He made some slurred noises, but wasn't able to manage words. I had all I was going to get out of him. Charlie Watrous, attorney at law. Thirty-seven years in the business. Came up the hard way. Night school and all that crap. But Horatio Alger never had to sink one of his indestructible cronies in the Catalina Channel. Or spend the next seven weeks wondering whether he would be murdered by Tough Tommy Lipton for what he had done or by renegade members of Lipton's gang for what he knew. The disappearance of Walter Brixner had probably tipped the scales for him. He had to talk to someone. His survival instinct had picked me. At best I would clear his skirts with Lipton. At worst I would put my face into the Malibu Substation with hearsay naming him as accessory to an unprovable homicide. I was in no position to do either.

I drove back downtown with my window open. The misty rain wasn't enough to make me feel cleaner. I got off the elevator just before five. The receptionist at the shipping company flagged me down and handed me two express envelopes.

I locked myself in the office and slit the envelope from Stockton. I was as nervous as a fraternity president on a 3 AM visit to the Dean's office to size up his chances for graduation. The caption beside the picture of a pert young Jean LaBostrie on a Xeroxed page of a high school annual confirmed what I had been afraid to guess.

Amanda Jean LaBostrie. Nickname: Mandy.

Song Queen. Homecoming Princess.

Secretary-Treasurer, Pep Club. Chorus.

Senior Girls' Nonette. Ambition: Thrush.

Probable fate: Sales Clerk. Advice from
the Senior Class: Quit asking why all
those boys hang around the drug store on
Saturday. Pet Peeve: The nickname Mandy.

I had found C. Benton Osborne's illegitimate daughter. I assumed Osborne had known all along. It was the kind of knowledge that would let him sleep nights. An established pharmacist could provide his girl a comfortable life without the emotional baggage that went with living under a controversial man's shadow. Then, seven weeks ago, she showed up at his primary election rally with a load of Hamilton Agency hostesses and jolted his conscience out of twenty some years hibernation.

The second envelope no longer mattered. It contained a fat sheaf of hasty photocopies I had extorted from Roy Lee Exum in the hope of extorting the whereabouts of Guy Hamilton from Charlie Watrous. What I needed now was a patsy for Hamilton's murder. Watrous had liked Danny Rupert for the part. The idea had nagged at me ever since. Rupert was a psychopath with a .22. The Turner killing fit him like a noose. If Turner and Hamilton were mentioned in the same breath, an eager deputy prosecutor might jump to the same conclusion as Watrous. But first I had to know a good deal more about Danny Rupert, so I could keep as much of the nonconforming evidence as possible covered up until a plea bargain had been sealed and nobody could afford a second look.

Chapter 27

Traffic made me late getting home. I tried Albert Cooper twice at the Crown Colony while my dinner cooked and once at his home while I wolfed it down. The fact that I couldn't locate him might or might not mean something. I copied his address out of my directory and shoved a microcassette recorder in my pocket. Then I dug the .45 Colt automatic out of its hiding place, oiled and loaded it. It was after seven when I stowed the pistol in the glove box and backed the Volvo out of the garage.

Cooper's neighborhood had better acoustics than the Hollywood Bowl. There wasn't anyplace that didn't get at least seventy decibels of freeway noise. The stores and apartments had a seedy look of slim profits and a square, soulless architecture that suggested most of the zoning variance bribes had changed hands between 1946 and 1964. Sodium lights made phosphorescence of the drizzle and shimmered along tight rows of older model cars hemming in the damp pavement on either side. I sandwiched the Volvo into three-quarters of a parking space and went down a steep walk to a stucco apartment building.

The lobby was silence and shadow. Mechanism creaked and moaned and the elevator deposited me in the muggy vacuum of a third floor hallway. Between the rush of passing cars I caught the muted noises of television and conversation. I knocked at Cooper's number, with my ear close to the wood. Light flickered under the door and gave the illusion of movement to the faded patterns on the threadbare carpet. I imagined a terrified little man, frozen inside, clutching his automatic. I finished with the lock and stood aside before I eased the door inward. A succession of headlight beams from the nearby freeway stabbed through an unshaded window and lit up a narrow studio arrangement.

There didn't seem to be anyone home. I slipped in, shut the door and found a light switch. After that I found a bathroom full of chipped porcelain and a tiny kitchenette.

Everywhere was an obsessive, Spartan neatness. As if Cooper saw himself as a trespasser in the world, tolerated only as long as he left no sign of his presence. Only a well fingered publicity still of Jean LaBostrie on a small scarred desk gave any clue to his dreams or longings. None of the drawers held any hint that he kept books for a major gambling syndicate. The only corroboration I had was the smell of fear when he said he was meeting Danny Rupert at eight, somewhere in three acres of discount appliances.

It was Friday night, and Aserinsky's was jumping. Starry-eyed wives steered reluctant couch potatoes down aisles of shiny new refrigerators with neat prices lined out and lower ones scrawled below in black grease pencil. Husbands just out of their teens stood petrified among the washing machines and tried to hide their terror while the sales staff rattled off payment terms. There was an overflow in ovens. The microwaves were mobbed. Children squalled and squabbled in a dozen languages and chased each other everywhere. I recognized the scene immediately. It was the American dream. For this we had stormed ashore at Normandy, fought our way to the Thirty Eighth Parallel and died in a thousand jungle ambushes. I felt like turning in my Combat Infantryman's Badge.

I made my way back through the crowd, looking for some clue to a meeting that didn't want to be found and a man I didn't want to meet. Cute cartoons plastered on the back wall suggested the escalators only led to another mob scene upstairs. A set of double doors with 'Employees Only' lettered across them bumped open and a squat, dark-complected man in white shirtsleeves backed out with a heavily loaded hand truck in tow. He was coming from a storage area where stacks of crates and wood framed cartons formed aisles that ran as high and as far as I could see in the brief glance I got. The man muscled his hand truck along to a display of small appliances in one corner. The display was a carelessly done job on wire racks, tucked away where it was all but invisible. They didn't seem to care whether they sold any or not.

A young woman held a sleeping baby on her hip and watched the man stack merchandise from open cartons. "What's the monthly note on one of them blenders?" she asked nasally.

He looked around at her. He was irked at the interruption. "The monthly payments? Have you an Aserinsky's charge card, Madam?"

She stared at him without comprehension.

"You must have an Aserinsky's charge card to buy small appliances on time," he explained impatiently. "We only sell small appliances to people with approved credit." It was too easy to make the small stuff disappear.

"I can't pay no fifty nine ninety five all at one time. I can pay like fifteen dollars down and five dollars on the monthly note."

He should have taken her up on it. The blender had replaced a cheap toaster oven that I recognized as one of last week's bingo prizes.

"I'm sorry, Madam," he said. "You might try coming back in a week. Any of these blenders left over then will be marked way down." After that the State auditors wouldn't be spot checking retail pricing on that particular item.

The woman wasn't interested. After a time she discovered that pouting at the man's back wasn't working, and she wandered off. I did some innocent ambling and filched a couple of computer-printed inventory forms from the hand truck. I marched through the double doors like I had business to do.

The activity in back was frantic. Voices yelled, crates bumped and there was a constant ding-ding from prowling forklifts. I would have been safer jaywalking on the Harbor Freeway, but the late movie was in no danger. Aserinsky was moving the merch. I found an earnest looking college boy directing traffic.

"Where's the office?" I yelled.

He took off his OSHA approved ear protectors. "Sir, customers aren't allowed in this area. Insurance."

"Forget it, Sonny. I had the runaround already. They told me to take the paperwork to the office. So where's the office?"

"Customer service and credit is on the third sales floor, sir."

"I ain't takin' any more trips through the sucker mill. Miz Stinebaugh down at Consumer Protection tells me she's about had it with this sleazy operation. Either you point me to the office or I call her up and tell her the orders of an Administrative Law Judge don't mean diddly to you people."

He glanced nervously up the wall I had come in through. It was solid for two stories. The third floor was office space, tucked up under stark iron roof trusses and reached by a single flight of exposed stairs. The glass was dark, all but one pane. Across that a shadow moved with agitated gestures.

I growled, "Okay, Kid, back to work," and strode off before he could recover from his blunder.

I climbed the stairs as silently as the creaky old planks would allow. From the catwalk at the top I had a bird's-eye view of everything out to the mass of shifting lights at the open loading dock. I didn't see anyone pointing up at me, or any huskies headed my way. I soft footed along to the door next to the lighted office. It wasn't locked. I slipped in and eased it shut. I crouched behind a desk with my ear to the fiberboard paneling that separated me from the adjoining room.

"I'm the one with my ass out front, taking all the risks," an animated voice complained. I had heard the voice before, selling slick credit schemes on television. "You gonoffs, all you do is sit back and count the profits."

His answer was the fast rattle of a printing calculator. The next words were a matter-of-fact announcement from Albert Cooper. "The trial recapitulation is sixty three cents off crossfoot."

"Sixty three cents!" Aserinsky exploded. "You bastards are going to rag my ass for sixty three lousy cents? The fuck you are."

A third voice said, "Accurate reports are the cornerstone of trust, wouldn't you agree, Mr. Aserinsky?"

It was a nice quiet voice. The kind of voice every mother hoped her daughter would bring around to introduce to the family. I had connected with Danny Rupert. I fished the recorder out of my pocket and got it running. All right, gentlemen, confession time. Let's discuss a few of our juicier felonies. It won't be evidence, of course, but the police will like nice Mr. Spain's fairy tale a lot better if it clears a few open cases for them.

The silence was deafening.

I wondered in a second of panic if they had heard me thinking. Then I heard footsteps on the stairs. I scrunched into the kneehole of the desk. The steps went past on the catwalk and a trailing shadow passed through the office. There was a tentative knock next door and the door opened. It was Danny Rupert who spoke.

"Why, hello, Frank. This is a surprise. I was sure you'd be setting up by now."

The name caught my attention. Frank Murillo's nervous Latin lilt confirmed the identification. "This was the only time I knew where to find you, Mr. Rupert. A little something happened. Maybe it's nothing, but I figured you ought to know."

"I appreciate that, Frank," the warm quiet voice said. "Why don't you come in and close the door and tell me about it?" To listen to him, Mr. Rupert was all charm and consideration. Just the nicest young man you could ever hope to meet.

Frank Murillo must have heard something else. It took him two tries to get the door latched. Shoe leather made restless noises on the linoleum floor. The dry Latin lilt fidgeted.

"Well, it's this broad I got hostessing for me, you know. I mean, she asked to see Brixner tonight."

Rupert's voice was full of reassurance. "You did the right thing to tell me, Frank. What does she want to see him about?"

"I don't know exactly. It's about some kind of book he might know about."

"What kind of book, Frank. Did she tell you?"

"I don't know, Mr. Rupert. Some friends of hers want to see Brixner about it. I didn't want to ask too many questions and maybe tip her off."

"That was wise, Frank. Very good thinking. I'd appreciate your opinion. You know her best. Do you trust her?"

"Well, she's a good kid, you know. I mean, I was kind of thinking of giving her a chance myself."

"That speaks highly of her, Frank. I mean that sincerely. I'd like to meet her. Could you bring her here when you come after the game?"

"Sure, Mr. Rupert, only she don't know Brixner's dead. I mean, like, what do I tell her?"

"You might indicate Walt often stops by. That should make her feel more comfortable. I'm sure she'll be satisfied as long as she gets to talk to someone in authority."

Aserinsky put in his two cents' worth. It consisted of, "I don't want no rough stuff here," in a fast, edgy voice that was already backpedaling before he finished.

It didn't qualify as an argument, and Rupert paid no attention. "Will you be good enough to do that for me, Frank?"

"Sure, Mr. Rupert. If that's what you want."

He would do it all right, but his jittery Latin voice didn't like the idea either. I liked it even less, particularly since I was the nitwit who'd talked Sarah Trapnell into bracing Tod Grayson on the subject of the Doomsday Book. But I was a little short of options. Rupert was certainly armed. Murillo was probable. My automatic was cooling its cartridges out in the parking lot.

I listened to Murillo's footsteps go by on the catwalk and slipped out the door as they receded down the stairs. I was able to get a glimpse of him starting for the loading dock. I took the stairs trying for speed and silence and not really achieving either. I was satisfied when nobody shot me. By the time I threaded my way to the loading dock, Murillo's van was nowhere in sight. The only bingo location I knew was the frame church where I had followed Jean. It was the wrong night for Murillo to take Sarah there. I stood in a steady soaking rain, staring helplessly at the lights moving in the parking lot and generally getting in the way of commerce. It took a while to dawn on me that if Jean knew one of Murillo's locations, she likely knew them all. I got my car out of the lot. I didn't want the call traced back to my cellular, so I found a service station with a pay phone.

"Crown Colony. May I help you?"

"Jean LaBostrie, please. Henry Spain calling."

"One moment, Mr. Spain."

Drumming my fingers on the cold glass didn't hurry her, so I tried tap dancing. Fred Astaire never had to contend with chewing gum. After an eon, Jean came on.

"I can't see you," she said firmly. "I'm sorry, I just can't."

"Jean, where is Frank Murillo's bingo game tonight?"

"Well, thanks," she huffed. "I'm hopelessly in love with you, too."

"I'm sorry, Jean. This is important. Where would he be tonight?"

"I don't know. God, what night is it, even? You've got my week all turned around."

"Friday, Jean. It's Friday night. Would they be at a church?"

"No, not on Friday night. That's Legion Hall night. You know, that one out on the old highway."

"No, Jean, I don't know. Which highway?"

"The Imperial Highway. Past Yorba Linda."

"How far past?"

"How would I know? Frank always drove. I never even lived in L.A. until this year."

"Thanks, Jean. Will you be at the Club all night?"

"I can't see you," she repeated.

"Look, Jean, there may be some trouble tonight. Stay at the Club until your last show, then go straight home. And for God's sake, leave that automatic in your purse unless you absolutely need it. All right?"

"What trouble?"

"I'll tell you when I get a chance. What you don't read in the paper."

"I really did sort of like you," she said.

She hung up before I had an opportunity to say anything. It was just as well. I had a knack for saying the wrong thing at times like that. And I was already far enough behind.

I filled the gas tank and set off in the rain to follow some vague directions to a place I might not even recognize in broad daylight so I could tell a woman who didn't trust me that she had to believe what I said because the last thing I'd told her was about to get her killed.

Chapter 28

Lights came out of the night, flashing past like the news camera strobes outside a Grand Jury room. They made me think about Tough Tommy Lipton. He had sown his wild oats in an age of bathtub Hudsons and howling jukeboxes. When the era ended he settled down to a quiet business life and spent his spare minutes cultivating influential friends. He wasn't a racketeer any more. Racketeers took meetings in back rooms and talked about action and juice. Lipton had lunch with accountants and discussed bulk sales vouchers and unallocated overhead. At worst he knew some people involved in charity bingo. Charity bingo was sponsored by the Church and the Legion. God and the Flag. Testify against Lipton and you spoke against the cornerstones of America.

Roadside signs with logos for Kiwanis, Rotary and the Lions marked the beginning and end of Yorba Linda. Except for those it was no different from the rain-blurred lights, low buildings and parking asphalt that preceded it and followed it. Traffic and the lights thinned out and I found myself in an area of one-street residential developments separated by closed up fruit stands on the remainders of what had once been sizeable farms. A six-tiered signal stopped me at a main intersection. The four segments boasted a self-serve gas station, a generic shopping mall of mom and pop franchises closed up for the night, a windowless stone frontage under a red neon scrawl that said 'Hickey's Hoe-down' and a dilapidated building with a gravel lot full of cars and light trucks that made me wonder if it might be doing weekend duty as a Legion Hall. I parked there and trotted a rat maze of wet vehicles to reach the doors.

The foyer was shallow and bare and had a wide traffic groove worn in the floor. A burly man of sixty in a string tie and a purple garrison cap stood guard over a table of Legion literature and a long rack crammed with damp coats. He wasn't favorably impressed by my appearance.

"Private hall, private meeting," he said in a quiet, level rumble.

A second Legionnaire stepped out into the foyer. He was bigger than the first, dressed up for the evening in a plaid sport coat cut from last year's horse blanket. He closed double doors on a dry Latin lilt announcing a bingo number and folded his arms across his chest to show me a pair of callused hands the size of shovel blades. For once I wasn't worried. If you wanted to do business in middle America you kept up your dues in groups like the Legion, even if you never went to the meetings. I dug out my wallet and showed the first Legionnaire my membership card.

"Sorry, friend," he rumbled more easily. "It's just we've had some trouble with those punks over to that Hickey's Hoe-down. There's a brand new ordinance that says nobody can do bare-naked dancing hereabouts. All they done over there was took down the sign. Got almighty mad at us when somebody called the cops on them."

"Izzat a fack?" I asked in a voice that had just climbed down from the rutabaga truck.

I bought a bingo card at a rickety table immediately inside the double doors, took a folding metal chair from a stack against the back wall and assumed a low profile at the rear of the hall. Murillo and Sarah had the layout arranged up on a Little Theater stage; complete with pulled back curtains. The game was playing to its accustomed packed house. There were a lot more men than I had seen previously, most of whom looked like they had built the local Church of the Nazarene with their own hands. If Sarah kicked up any fuss, I could wind up on my backside in the parking lot in two seconds flat. The more I thought about it, the more it seemed that a discreet word in Murillo's ear might be a better bet. I wasted half an hour and a dollar fifty trying to think of something would scare him worse than Danny Rupert. I was still working on it when a woman peeked around the curtain at one edge of the stage.

She didn't look like part of the bingo game. Her face was a coquettish thirty, framed in a Grand Old Opry bouffant. She put out a bare arm and waved. That got her a little attention from the audience. She put a slow bare leg all the way out and attracted enough eyes to make Sarah glance in her direction. Sarah forgot about standing and walking and smiling and just stared. A loud electronic squeal erupted from the speaker Frank Murillo had been using to call a bingo number. After that he was talking into a dead microphone while hillbilly music reverberated into the room at full volume. The noise jolted him out of his practiced routine. He shook the microphone a couple of times while his Latin eyes jerked around in frantic confusion.

The woman abandoned her curtain and wiggled out on stage. Even from a rear view, it was obvious she wasn't wearing anything. She pranced among the apparatus, pirouetting to offer peek-a-boo frontal exposure. Women in the audience let out a chorus of screams. Bingo cards spilled in every direction. Men stood up yelling at Murillo to get the dancer off the stage. He moved crabwise, waving the microphone and trying to corral her. Before any Legionnaires could climb up to help him, a mangy horde of backcountry hooligans spilled out of both wings and spread across the front of the stage. They emitted hog calls and anointed the angry crowd with beer. The boys and girls from Hickey's Hoe-down were here to settle the score. It had the makings of a great fight. It also looked like an opportunity to separate Sarah from Murillo and talk to her.

I headed for the base of the stage under a full head of steam. I grabbed a metal chair from under a woman who was alternately standing to yell then sitting down. I heaved the chair up at a bearded face under a big shapeless hat and scrambled onto the stage on my stomach. I scissored my legs shut on the first pair of cowboy boots stupid enough to try to move in on me. A hefty bitch with a face full of acne scars toppled into the angry Legionnaires. I rolled clear and left the Legion to keep the rest busy. Murillo had been sidetracked into a crotch-kicking contest. Sarah was backed up against the stairstep prize display. She was trying to fend off three drunks who thought she ought to join the girl who was still dancing to the ear splitting music. I grabbed a blender on the way to my feet and broke it over the nearest hat. A second cowboy turned around red with liquor and fury. I jammed the jagged edges of the glass into his face and twisted hard to leave him a reminder to mind his manners in the future. Number three's eyes got sober in a hurry. He backed into the tumbler cage trying to get away from me. I cracked his kneecap with a snap kick and gave him another in the teeth when he went down.

I did everything but yell, "Banzai!"

I scared hell out of Sarah. She fought like a baby tiger when I got her around the waist and headed for the wings. Her flailing legs combined with my momentum to convince the locals to give us room. Backstage I tried doors until I found one that led to a small office. I shoved her through. She jackknifed over a desk and gave me time to hit the light switch and shut the door behind myself. I slapped her hard when she came at me with her claws.

"Cool off!"

I discovered I didn't have the breath to say anything else. I put both hands up in a placating gesture and panted for air. Sarah eyed me with an animal wariness. Her off the shoulder frock was ripped wide open and her breasts were heaving inside a sheer bra. She realized how exposed she was. She pulled the frock closed and held it with both hands. We faced each other across the small room.

"Sarah," I managed to gasp. "We've got to talk."

She took two steps back in response to the one I took toward her. Her back hit the wall and terror welled up in her eyes.

"All right," I conceded hastily, retreating the one step. "All right. I won't hurt you. I promise. But we've got to talk. We've got to talk about the Doomsday Book. And we've got to talk about Walter Brixner. We've got to do that now. Before you get yourself badly hurt. All right?"

I couldn't tell whether I was getting through or not. Loud music reverberated everywhere. Scuffling shook the old building like a rotten porch. A siren wailed up outside and she tried to back right through the wall.

"Sarah, I know Tod Grayson told you about the Doomsday Book. You asked him because I told you to. That was a mistake. I made a mistake. You asked him and he told you. You probably told each other a lot of things and it got out that you were a bingo hostess. It got out, and Grayson asked you to see Brixner about the Book. That was another mistake, Sarah. It was a bad mistake. Brixner was murdered three nights ago."

She was confused. Murillo had probably already implied he would take her to see Brixner.

"Murillo will take you to see a man named Danny Rupert," I said. "Rupert is a professional killer."

She didn't know what to believe. She wanted to be anywhere else in the worst possible way.

"Tell me about the Book," I ordered. "How much does Grayson know about the woman who took it?"

Her eyes implored me to understand why she couldn't tell me. Things were out of my hands. More sirens were checking in by the minute. The growing riot squad would gain control of the situation in nothing flat. Indoor melees were made to order for saps and aluminum knucks.

The music cut off as if it had never existed. The sudden silence made a tense snarl of my voice.

"If you want any hope of keeping your secrets, you'll tell me what I need to know. Otherwise, I'll give what I do know to the police and Grayson can take his chances."

"Mr. Drew said one of the girls took it for Guy Hamilton," she cried. "The night Mr. Osborne had his attack. Mr. Brixner knew a lot of the girls. Mr. Drew wanted me to…"

She may have said more. I didn't hear it if she did. The door burst open behind me and knocked me half the width of the room. Two uniform bulls saw Sarah backed up against the wall holding her frock together. They saw me on the floor against the desk. They were a couple of sharp investigators. It took them all of a second to put two and two together and come up with five years for attempted rape. They were on top of me like the smell on dog droppings.

"Goddamn pervert!" one of them growled in my ear.

"The woman," I begged as they dragged me to my feet. "Bring the woman. She's in serious trouble. She…" I think one of them hit me in the kidneys. Whatever it was, it shut me up in a hurry.

When the world quit doing cartwheels, I was sitting against the back wall of the stage. I looked one way and got a nose full of brewery breath. On the other side was a scrawny witch with a size forty rack sagging out of the remains of a flannel shirt. She gave me an elbow in the ribs and glared malevolently through drooping wisps of hair. The three of us were part of a line of people, all sitting against the back wall of the stage. There were a lot of jeans and cowboy boots. Only a couple of Legionnaires had gotten rambunctious enough to warrant arrest, if that was what this was.

The Legion Hall looked like the aftermath of an atomic disaster. No one had arrived to check for radiation yet, but there was a first aid station setting up in the rear with business already lined up for it to do. The rest of the crowd wore police uniforms, except for a skeleton crew of purple garrison caps beginning to collect and fold scattered metal chairs. I heard cars starting up at a rate of two or three a minute out in the parking lot. I didn't expect to see Murillo or Sarah. Bingo was over for the evening. The layout was a total loss.

A Sheriff's Sergeant crunched ping-pong balls underfoot crossing the stage.

"On your feet!"

It took a little time to register through the bumps and bruises that he meant the people in the line up. Several deputies waded in through broken bingo prizes to emphasize the point. When they had us up, they herded us down off the stage in a ragged line. I had visions of a wheezy old bus that smelled like a locker room and a slow ride to some understaffed precinct. That was a trip I couldn't afford to take. I didn't think much of my chances of persuading the police to go after Sarah before it was too late. The good news was that I didn't see handcuffs on anyone in the line. It was probably too much hassle for a routine Friday night fracas. I steeled myself and moved close to brewery breath.

"When we get outside, run for it. The cops won't know us once we're gone. Pass it on."

I whispered the same advice to the witch before a tall, rawboned deputy put a stick into my ribs and told me to shut up. I was left without much hope the idea would catch on. There was only vague muttering while the line crossed the foyer.

We trudged out into the rain. It was a bad time to be having my usual luck, and I was sore as hell about it. I needed to blow off some steam.

I yelled, "Run for it!" at the top of my lungs, mostly because that was the only thing in my head.

Before I could blink people were going every direction but up. I was caught as flat-footed as the law. I shin-hacked a beefy deputy and sprinted the parking lot with heavy feet hammering behind me. I tore open the palms of both hands vaulting a hurricane fence into a dark back yard. I heard someone panting to climb over after me. I didn't wait to find out who it was or how long it would take him.

I ran like I remembered running as a kid in Hollenbeck. Over the fence in back of the pool hall, down the hill past the culvert, along the river like a bat out of hell. I ran until my lungs turned to old leather and my legs to rubber. I ran until momentum was the only thing keeping me upright. When that was gone, all I could do was collapse.

Chapter 29

Lightning groped down through the black sky like the fingers of Satan and set fire to sheets of rain that raked a cul-de-sac of dark houses. I sat slumped against someone's rockery, a sodden, discarded scarecrow, and imagined Murillo and Sarah driving through the storm. He would have had an easy time talking her into going. I had made sure of that. Spain? Sure, Baby, I know him. A real flake. Goes around telling people he's a private cop. Pathetic, you know what I mean? You think it wouldn't be in all the papers if a main man type like Brixner got whacked? Come on, Baby. I'll take you to see him right now. Murillo would keep up his soothing Latin lilt until Sarah saw her dreams starting to work again. Then he would help her into the van, and they would be gone.

Danny Rupert would be waiting for them at the warehouse. Murillo would tell him about the riot. He would tell it in his cool Latin voice, between draughts of cigarette smoke. He could afford a casual facade. With the police that close, a wise boy like Rupert was sure to fold his hand and wait for a better deal. Murillo would figure that out on his way in and keep thinking it right up until he finished talking. Rupert would hear him out and smile and put a pocket scanner on the TAC frequencies. He would have a good one. He was a professional, and he would have professional tools. Then he would ignore Murillo's fidgeting and talk to Sarah and she would tell him about me. She would be scared. She would tell him I knew where she was being taken. She would tell him I would be coming to look for her if they didn't let her go. She would throw it in his face, to warn him not to try anything. That would be just fine with Rupert. Rupert would know from Lipton that I was a loner. Lipton had hired me because I was a loner. A man who could be isolated and taken out quietly if he came to know too much.

And now Rupert and Murillo would be waiting to do the job. Murillo sweating from every pore, telling himself over and over about the heavy dues he had to lay down to get the right boys to trust him. Rupert savoring every moment of the tension, like a jaded playboy working his way slowly toward an inevitable orgasm. It was all there in my mind's eye, just as real as the climax on the night owl movie. In another minute Aserinsky would come on, backed up by a chorus line of dancing refrigerators.

The police were history when I finally found my way back to the Legion Hall. I dragged my keys out of a soggy pocket and started for the warehouse. A throbbing welt had replaced my wristwatch, but the Mars light of a locomotive oscillating in the distance gave me a fair fix on the time. Railroad schedules hadn't changed in thirty years. Links of streamlined diesels dragged mile long freight trains down out of the Cajon Pass into the classification yards at San Bernardino where angular GP-9's broke them up and muscled the first twenty car manifests to the destination yards in L.A. a little after midnight. When I came down the ramp off the Santa Ana Freeway steeple cab switch engines were shunting out the piggybacks and the LCL's with a noise like a regiment of derelicts rattling through a thousand dumpsters. Intermittent strings of freight cars rumbled along the tracks paralleling Alameda. The limit was five miles an hour. They were stacked three deep where I had to turn. I had to wait an eternity. Passing trucks were few and far between.

After I turned there was no traffic at all. Wind driven rain sluiced across the rutted street and machine-gunned empty asphalt around the dark, dripping bulk of Aserinsky's. Murillo's Ford van stood like a billboard against the loading dock, faintly shiny in the blur of a security light. I parked in the next block and fished the Army Colt out of the glove box. It was a cold alien lump of metal in my hand. I got out and fought a quartering gale back to the warehouse. The rain soaked me through again and washed the salt of old sweat down into my eyes and mouth. My legs had rusted stiff. I couldn't have gotten over the hurricane fence with a stepladder. I didn't need to. They had left the main gate unlatched.

Murillo's Econoline was as empty as his dreams. I could see the glint of the ignition key through the curtain of water running down the driver's window. He probably hadn't expected to stay long. I pushed on the wind wing. It wasn't fastened. I reached in, took the key and put it in a coat pocket. Behind the loading dock I found a sleek new Lexus sedan. The kind of car that would look right at home in the country club parking lot and still do a hundred and forty miles an hour when the Banshees started to scream inside the owner's head. It seemed about right for Danny Rupert. I couldn't make out anything resembling an alarm system. Maybe Mr. Rupert liked to live dangerously. More likely the sedan was so full of mercury switches you couldn't lean on a fender without setting something off. Nothing loud. Probably just a dull glow in one taillight. The big lenses would lend themselves to an extra bulb. Just any little something to tip Mr. Rupert off. He'd enjoy taking it from there.

I went round and round the car, working on each tire valve a little at a time to beat the system. Furious gurgling from a nearby downspout covered any noise I made.

Rain made the loading dock as slimy as a fishing pier. I banged my knee climbing up. I pushed the muzzle of the .45 through a wire cage and poked out the security bulb over the man door. I smothered the knob with my free hand. It wasn't locked. My throbbing knee reminded me of a night in Half Moon Lane, and of Walter Brixner sitting lifeless with four bullets in his chest. Brixner had been a loner, too. He had been about my age, with a past he probably talked about as infrequently as I talked about mine and a future he was probably still coming to terms with. Until he stepped through a door into a hail of sudden death.

I had no sense of going through the man door. One minute I was out in the rain paralyzed with fear, the next I stood inside with my back against the planks of a big sliding door. A powerful return spring helped me ease the man door shut against the wind. With the door closed the only sound was the rain trying to claw its way through the walls. My entrance had probably let in enough railroad noise from Alameda to tell everyone down to the warehouse cat that I had arrived. Nothing moved. The only light diffused down the long aisles from the far end where the elevated offices were. My pulse was the slow relentless hammer of a pile driver.

I crossed the width of the warehouse before I turned toward the offices, to come up behind anyone waiting to ambush me. Good luck. I couldn't take a step without squishing like a Roll-A-Matic mop. Clogged sinuses had me breathing like a steamroller. Wet clothing clung to my skin and a stiff, silent Frankenstein shadow lumbered along beside me, rising twenty feet up the wall. I couldn't have been any more obvious if I had been walking my pet tyrannosaurus. I could feel every nerve ending in my body when I turned down the far aisle. Stacks of framed cartons rose three stories to the shadowy iron roof trusses, hemming me in on either side. Any one looked heavy enough to kill me if it fell, or was pushed. Down at the far end I could see a segment of the plank stairs, rising half lit to the offices above. Walter Brixner was up there. He was cackling insanely that it was my turn to die. The cackling frightened me, and wouldn't stop frightening me.

I stopped and listened. The noise was real, not my imagination. It wasn't laughter. It was the small syncopated whining noise of a hurt animal, echoing distortedly up among the shadowy roof trusses. It had to be Sarah. I hadn't exactly forgotten her. I just hadn't any idea what I was going to do about her. It was time to have one. I yelled her name. I made it loud. I made it reverberate through the whole warehouse.

"Sarah! This is Henry Spain. I want you to do something. I want you to come down the stairs. Do you hear me, Sarah?"

The whining turned to muffled sobs. A hard slap made the sobs louder. One of them was with her. It wasn't Danny Rupert. His voice came almost immediately, from high up in the roof trusses somewhere behind me. It wasn't the warm, quiet voice I remembered. It was the breathless ecstasy of a teenage boy doing nasty things down in the basement.

"Frank! He's trapped himself in the last aisle. Move out where you can get a shot at him."

Nice going, Spain. Why don't you maneuver yourself out of options then give away your position? That way we can get this over and go home and curl up with a nice gory DVD.

Murillo wasn't in that much of a hurry. Angry nerves reverberated in his Latin voice. "What if he's carrying, Mr. Rupert? He wouldn't have yelled like that unless he had a piece."

No reply. Rupert had certainly moved as soon as he'd spoken. He wasn't risking his new position to discuss something he already knew. Rain drummed on the roof. Sarah went on sobbing. It was Murillo's play, and the world would stand still until he made it.

"Spain!" he yelled. "I know you can hear me. I got the girl here. Throw the piece out and walk into the light or she gets hurt. Bad."

I wondered if he knew how silly he sounded. There was a brief scuffle up in the office, but all he could get out of Sarah was a change in the rhythm of her crying. I used the time to work the stiffness out of my gun hand and ease along toward the lighted end of the aisle. Danny Rupert used it to run out of patience.

"Frank, Spain can't kill you from where he is, but I can from where I am."

It was time for Murillo to start thinking about heavy dues again. I put a parked forklift between my back and my last fix on Rupert's voice and hunkered into the crevice between two stacks of cartons. I put my eye to the narrow gap between the cardboard and the two by four framing. I could see only the stairs and a few feet of the landing immediately at the top. I heard the scrape of a door out of my range of vision. I watched and didn't see anything. Then I saw the top of Murillo's head. He was on his stomach on the landing. He was an easy mark for anyone underneath who wanted to empty a magazine up through the planking. But that wasn't the shot I wanted. I waited while he came cautiously to one knee, pointing his snub nosed gun down into the dimness. I waited while he crept down the stairs until he could peer the full length of the aisle. I could afford to wait. I knew the fluorescent lights had left him night blind. No matter how he strained, he would see only shadows.

I waited until he stood full height with an expression of relief on his Latin features, saying, "He ain't there, Mr. Rupert. I can't see him no place."

I shot him twice in rapid succession. The first round turned his legs to jelly. The second caught him as he clawed at the railing for support. It had about the same effect as pitching a baseball into a pile of rags. He went down and I didn't see him any more. I never did see the flash of Danny Rupert's .22. I felt the shock after the first round clipped my jaw. A second round threw splinters into my face. I had been pulling my head up from behind my gun sights when the shots came. Otherwise I would have taken both in the temple.

I jerked back under cover, sweating fear. Danny Rupert had acquired a target in poor light, aligned his sights and squeezed off two highly accurate shots. All in the time it had taken me to dump two quick rounds into an illuminated target at no more than half the range. If that weren't enough, I was night blind from staring at the lighted landing. All Rupert had to do was stay in the shadows and work around until he had a clear shot. I could wait to die. Or I could make a run for it. Into the light where he could see me clearly. Or back down the aisle where he would have a straight shot. I was in enough trouble without Sarah appearing on the stairs where I had shot Murillo. She was still crying. She was all but naked. She stepped gingerly over the body and stumbled down the rest of the way.

"Sarah!" I hissed. That was a mistake. A man's voice was the last thing she wanted to hear. She took off at a run I couldn't have matched if I had been foolhardy enough to try.

Rupert didn't shoot her. Maybe he was close enough that I could have spotted him and got off an accurate return. Maybe he just didn't want to risk anything on short acquaintance. It had to be something. Sarah was the only real threat to him. I couldn't even identify him in court. I had never seen him face to face. He could step out of anywhere in a day or a week or a month to kill me. I wouldn't recognize him. A loose iron ladder rattled back in the direction Sarah had disappeared and made that a real possibility.

I took the aisle at a dead sprint going back. I was more careful crossing the width of the warehouse to where the man door jittered in the throes of a struggle between the gusty wind and the return spring. The vague glow from a distant street lamp shimmered in a growing puddle just inside. I didn't see Rupert or Sarah. I flattened against the planks of the big sliding door and listened. I thought I could hear the muffled noise of a struggle over the steady raking of rain on the parking asphalt. It was a chance Rupert might be distracted for a minute against a certainty he wouldn't once he finished Sarah. I dropped to my stomach in the puddle, slithered quickly out across the slimy planking of the dock and dropped into the space between the outer timber and Murillo's Econoline. Rupert and Sarah were close. I could hear her crying. I could hear Rupert's low, ecstatic profanity. The truck was pointed toward them. I would never have a better opportunity.

The interior light came on the instant I pulled on the driver's door. Rupert's shot popped through the windshield just above the dash and drummed into the seatback. I was down low. All I got was a small shower of glass from the innermost layer of laminate. I poked the key into the ignition. The engine was not fully cooled. It caught immediately. I pulled the shift lever into Drive and released the parking brake. The truck started rolling. I squirmed back out the door into the blackness among the support timbers of the dock, pulling every knob on the dash as I went. I got two good headlights.

Rupert and Sarah materialized out of the rain. Rupert was smaller than I expected, not much bigger than Sarah. His suit was soaked and shapeless; his hair was wild and matted. He had pulled Sarah back close against him as a shield. He had his hands full dragging her out of the path of the advancing truck and the open driver's door. When it was abreast of his position, he turned to put Sarah between himself and the truck. He unleashed sharp little tongues of fire into the cab where I should have been. One at the floor, one at the seat.

I shot him once, high up in the side, to catch the armhole of any armor he might be wearing. I hit him hard, but he was too tough to fall or let Sarah go. He twisted, putting the struggling woman between us again. I rolled out of the support pilings, gained my feet and ran sideways. I fired again as soon as I had an inch of room. I was doing better. Sarah was able to jerk free. Rupert blew a wild shot into the asphalt and began a staggering run in the general direction of cover. I shot him between the shoulder blades. He took two more steps and flopped down in a clutter of trash cans beside a Dumpster. I was over him in a dozen rubber legged strides. I inclined the .45 and began firing. The gun went through two pulsing cycles and died on me. It was locked open, empty.

I heard the van clank into the hurricane fence across the lot. I kicked a long barreled .22 automatic away into a puddle. It was a pointless gesture. Danny Rupert was gone. Crumpled in death, he looked like an altar boy who had been hit by a car and left at the side of the road.

The adrenaline swirled out of my system like the last dirty water out of a bathroom basin. It left me feeling light headed and empty. I had an attack of mindless giggling. The harder I tried to stop it, the worse it got.

Chapter 30

It was late morning and the sun through the thin slat blinds hurt my eyes. My jaw was a dull ache under the surgical tape and my face itched from prickly stubble. I was exhausted from ten hours in and out of interrogation. I was beyond caring whether Acting Captain Earl Snyder could have my investigator's license revoked.

"Thanks to your hijinks, I have a meeting with the Prosecutor this afternoon," he went on in his crisp business voice. "I expect to be asked to summarize the currently available evidence against Terrence Stafford."

"It's about time someone took a look at it."

"Meaning we should have taken him out of circulation before now?"

"I don't understand why you haven't."

"Stafford isn't a racket boss in the popular sense of an autocratic thug. He is the de-facto heir of a pawnbroker and political fixer who challenged the national syndicate for control of Los Angeles gambling in the late forties and early fifties. When Stafford consolidated what his predecessor left behind, he limited his gambling activities to bingo. He constructed a vertical monopoly behind the veneer of churches and charities. The profits appear only as operating results of his legitimate businesses. He hasn't been to a bingo game himself in forty years. He leaves day to day supervision to an intermediate layer of management, insulating himself from all direct contact. As you may know, the testimony of a co-conspirator isn't enough to convict without independent evidence to substantiate at least some material part of what is said."

"What is it you want from me?" I asked.

"I read the transcript of your homicide interrogation. You got a lot of mileage out of the Bill of Rights."

"I'm entitled. I was wounded twice defending it."

"I think the facts you shielded may be useful in linking Stafford to one or more prosecutable offenses."

"Vietnam cured me of volunteering, Captain."

"You had killed prior to last night," Snyder reminded me. "Your personality profile indicates that .45 is your way of hitting back at a world you can't cope with. The investigative consensus is that you charged into that warehouse under a full head of frustration and killed two men to vent your own hostility. That's enough to qualify for second degree murder."

"I went because I was worried about Sarah Trapnell. I was boxed in by two armed men and forced to defend my life."

"That kind of worry is police business."

"I had no specific information that a crime was in progress or might happen, which is the only thing that would have required me to notify the police. Neither my possession of a gun nor police opinion of my reasons for possession of a gun are evidence of crime. My past activity is irrelevant. Under the law, the case must be tried on its own merits."

Snyder smiled his alligator smile. He opened a manila folder on his desk and began making notes. *The Battle Hymn of the Republic* wafted faintly from the air conditioning duct. A faraway voice began pitching yet another motivational video program. Wherever this system is in regular use, morale is up and stress is down. In test precincts the divorce rate fell by an average seven point two percent. Proven results, from a format tailored to the twenty-minute roll call. It sounded like the boys in blue would be a few minutes late driving out to the fire station to chew over what they were going to do when they retired.

"I got a call from an attorney yesterday," Snyder said matter-of-factly, without looking up.

"Anyone I know?" Behind my tired poker face I had icy visions of Charlie Watrous cutting a deal on the Hamilton killing and leaving me to face obstruction charges for not reporting our little conversation.

"Perhaps. She wanted to know what, if anything, I could tell her about a private investigator named Henry Spain."

I started breathing again. "I haven't been using you for a business reference," I assured him.

Snyder interrupted his writing. "How well do you know Connie Moore?"

"A man I killed before last night was a junkie she liked."

"I gather she wants you as a go-between to buy a film she appeared in."

"Am I being warned off?"

"The Department takes no position in private transactions."

"Didn't you confiscate a film from Charlie Watrous?"

"We impounded it for investigative viewing," he corrected.

"You'd better look fast. At sixty thousand dollars a copy, Watrous is sure to be in court Monday to challenge your probable cause and petition for return of his property."

"That's his privilege," Snyder said significantly, "as long as he doesn't mind putting his name on the public record."

My brain dropped into gear with a sudden lurch. "This business with the striptease films isn't a criminal investigation at all," I realized. "It's an effort to protect some well placed people who wish now they'd never been involved. People who have made enough money over the years to be blackmailed over their juvenile embarrassments. If the Police can maneuver an owner like Watrous into identifying himself in a common pleading, private attorneys can cut quiet deals to buy the films back."

"What are you planning to tell Connie Moore?"

"Quote her my standard rate against five percent for a successful recovery."

"If there's going to be trouble, I want to know about it before it happens. And I want to know enough to keep things from going sour."

"If I had an eye for spotting trouble before it happened, Captain, I wouldn't be sitting here now."

"I'll always be sitting here, Spain. Remember that when you discover how bad a mistake you're making."

I bailed the Volvo out of impound and stopped at the gourmet burger emporium two blocks from my office to wash down the eight-dollar pig-out with a glass of draft. It was the first meal I had eaten that day. I was still in interrogation when they fed breakfast in the investigative detention cells. They brought me in soaked and scared and shivering and put me in a cage with a skinny blond kid loaded screaming full of uppers and cheap wine. He lost his stomach all over a Marine Corps field jacket. I pounded at the heavy wire, stammering angrily for an attendant who never came. In time I was taken to a windowless cubicle. Angry detectives fired questions at me. Instead of answering, I told them about Danny Rupert. I told them he had killed Midas Turner. I told them he had certainly switched guns, but that he had killed Turner anyway. (The .22 must have grown on him. It was the same one he tried to use on me. The police eventually traced it to the murders of a union business agent and the husband of a dancer Rupert was interested in.) I told them Rupert was the enforcer for a bingo racket. I told them he killed Turner because Turner had killed an accountant named Walter Brixner. They demanded to know how and when I knew what I knew, and how I was involved. I declined to answer. After an eternity of sounding like a Sicilian at a senate hearing, I was told my attorney had arrived. I didn't know him, of course. He was smooth and correct and far beyond my ability to pay. He introduced himself and showed me where to sign on the representation agreement. Nothing more. After that it was just a matter of time until the writ would come.

The detectives relented. They gave me a big Styrofoam cup of coffee. They told me Tommy Lipton had hired me to investigate Jean LaBostrie's background. A midnight warrant served on my office would have turned up Lipton's contract. Jean, they seemed to believe, was just a suburban girl come in innocent pursuit of her life's dream. They had no idea she and I were present when Brixner was killed. They told me only in a vague sort of way how I had blundered into charity bingo backtracking her and run afoul of Danny Rupert. Snyder or one of his investigators would have filled them in on Lipton's organization. They had gotten nothing from Sarah Trapnell. It had taken six uniforms to hem her against the hurricane fence to get her into the ambulance. They never mentioned the Doomsday Book or the Temple shooting. (The shooters had been caught by then. Two of them belonged to a street gang, which is why you see Jeffrey Haven being gurneyed out of the Temple every time some TV station needs a few feet of lead tape for yet another up-to-the-second featurette on gang activity.) If they were holding back a few key bits of information to check against anything I might give them to fill in the gaps, they were wasting it. I was in no position to tell them anything. They were not Gods, who could listen to my great outpouring of truth and grant me forgiveness for my sins. They were real policemen who were tired and cranky and who had to explain their actions to real supervisors. When they heard about misprision of felonies, they filed charges against the people responsible. There were no exceptions. I couldn't talk to them, but I had to talk to someone.

I paid the waitress, drove to my office and dug the phone CD out of the disarray left by the police search. I listened to the line ring with the irritable fidgets of fatigue.

"Cedars Sinai Medical Center. May I help you?"

"You have a C. Benton Osborne in your cardiac care unit. Would you connect me with him, please?" I had to spell the name and wait while she checked her computer screen.

"I'm sorry, sir. Mr. Osborne cannot receive telephone calls. I have his office number, if you wish."

"It's not an office matter. When are his visiting hours?"

"I'm afraid his visits are limited to immediate family, sir."

"My name is Henry Spain. I'll be there about four. If I can't talk to Osborne, I'll talk to his doctor, or the resident, or the duty nurse. Whoever is available. It doesn't matter."

I stalled a few minutes to browse the noon edition. A paragraph in the local violence sidebar told me there had been a shooting in the industrial district. A San Pedro real estate broker had been DOA at White Memorial. A man with a minor police record for bookmaking had died in surgery. Two witnesses were being interviewed. The summary at the bottom contained a couple of sentences on an arson fire at Hickey's Hoe-down. It had broken out about two thirty. The building had been leveled. Nothing spectacular, folks. Just another ho-hum Friday in greater L.A. I went home to clean up and change.

Cedars Sinai was the high end of the health care system. Womb to tomb medical attention dispensed to the upper brackets in the private rooms of an architecturally impeccable high rise. The cool main lobby was carpeted, the furniture tastefully upholstered. The elevator that took me up to cardiac care scarcely seemed to move.

Winston Drew was waiting at the main nursing station. He had thrown a pricey yellow cardigan over a white polo shirt. Judging from the rest of his outfit, plus two knickerbockers and argyle knee socks were back in style at the better golf clubs. From the look on his face, his beeper had gone off while he was putting and cost him a nice bet.

"Come with me," he ordered in a low, taut voice. "I want to talk with you in private."

I stood my ground. "What room is he in?"

Drew glanced nervously at an elderly woman in a floor length mink being assisted by a couple of grown children. "Mr. Spain, I do not want a scene here, but I do have security officers standing by if you try to force the issue."

"Mr. Drew, I shot and killed two men last night. I just got out of police interrogation. If I'm involved in one bit of trouble today, I'll be right back in front of those same detectives. This time I don't think I'll be able to leave you out of my story."

Frustration compressed Drew's lips into a tight line. He probably knew more about my interrogation than I did. He could send Grayson out with orders to promise Sarah Trapnell anything to keep her mouth shut, but all he had left to use on me was executive bluff.

"Mr. Osborne is in no condition to receive…"

"Show me."

I didn't like the way he said, "Very well." His smile was as cold as liquid nitrogen and his voice was pure silk.

The halls we walked had a morbid elegance. The air was tainted ever so faintly with medicinal alcohol. Silence hung everywhere, as fragile as life. We walked softly so we wouldn't break any of it. Drew nodded us past a satellite nursing station and opened a door for me.

The room was an antiseptic place of machines and gauges and dials, of burnished bullet shaped tanks and complex valving, of tentacle wiring and neoprene tubes like stiff opaque umbilical cords. They were life to a pitiful wasted figure on a flat heavy bed. What I saw beneath the plastic oxygen bubble bore little resemblance to my vague memories of pictures of C. Benton Osborne. Random patches of his shock white hair were missing. Only the structure of his skull gave shape to a face otherwise degenerated into pasty flesh splotched with liver yellow discoloration. His lips were without color or clear definition from the surrounding skin. His eyes were closed. His position was the sole result of static inertia, and not at all controlled by the tension or resistance of muscle tissue.

"Not going to be chasing the girls any more, is he?" I said.

Drew pushed the door closed with a sharp, disapproving click. "Gratuitous satire is most inappropriate here, Spain."

"How far gone is he?"

"His mind remains active," the executive assured me.

"What does that mean? Does he speak or see? Or is he just a blip on an oscilloscope?"

"The medical staff is unanimous in agreeing that his condition does not fulfill the requirements for brain death."

"He's dead for his purposes," I decided.

"His purposes?"

"He gave the Doomsday Book to his daughter. He knew he was dying, and he passed on his legacy."

Drew stepped close enough to give me a delicate scent of expensive liquor on his breath. His voice was shallow, eager.

"You've found the girl who…?"

"I found his daughter. I can prove the relationship, if I have to."

Drew was in no mood to split hairs. "If you found the girl, you found the file. It must be returned. Immediately."

"She didn't have it."

"Then she gave it to Guy Hamilton."

"Hamilton is dead. He has been since the night he offered to sell it to you. He's on the bottom of Catalina Channel, with three bullets in him."

"Who killed him?" Drew accepted Hamilton's death with only a flicker of annoyance, as if it were something he had already come to suspect. "Who has the file?"

"I don't think Hamilton ever got hold of it," I said.

"Nonsense. He described it accurately."

"Hell, I can describe it. Black vinyl binder holding three computer tape cassettes. The tapes are a listing of property owned in phantom names culled from the computerized tombstone register Osborne used to influence elections."

Drew threw a nervous glance at the figure on the bed. "Mr. Osborne's political work was begun during corrupt times," he informed me with quiet indignation. "The auxiliary electorate program was developed as a matter of the purest necessity. To give the people of California the first clean government in the history of the State."

"If this was ancient history, the names would've been destroyed long ago. Any one of them could send you to prison."

"You, of all people, should know there are still criminal elements trying to influence politics in Los Angeles."

"I think I've met more than one."

"Just tell me who has the file, Spain."

"Your guess last night wasn't bad. Walter Brixner did have it, when he was alive. His safe was cleaned out the night he was killed."

"By whom?"

"Frank Murillo. One of the men your meddling forced me to kill at the warehouse."

"Brixner. Murillo. Those were Lipton's men, weren't they?"

"You self appointed leaders are a hoot. Doesn't it ever occur to you that the sheep may have ideas of their own?"

"Then Murillo was free-lancing?"

"I don't know for sure what Murillo was doing. But if Lipton was still looking for the Book last night, he obviously didn't have it."

"Then Murillo had it," Drew concluded impatiently. "Where did he hide it?"

"Any secrets Frank Murillo had, he took to the grave."

The executive's voice was cold, skeptical criticism. "Didn't you talk to him before you shot him?"

"They had guns, Mr. Drew. They were trying to kill me."

I watched his face dissolve slowly into a sick, incredulous expression.

"You bungled it!" he screamed at me. "You and your stupid violence! You may have lost the last chance to find the file!"

"All right. I bungled it. Sue me."

I drove home exhausted and lay down on the couch. Nervous energy crackled through me like static electricity and wouldn't let me sleep.

Time passed and it got to be supper, so I got up and made some. I knew before I had it out of the microwave that it would taste like reheated cardboard.

There had been more truth than syphilis in Guy Hamilton's brain when he called it the Doomsday Book. Nothing was going to be right as long as it hung over my head.

I made a telephone call. Then I showered again and put on my good suit.

Chapter 31

Jean LaBostrie was working into a chilling rendition of the old Chuck Willis standard: *What Am I Living For?* when I came down from the hushed foyer of the Crown Colony. The straight-backed maitre'd stopped a conversation in mid-sentence. His remote blue eyes were a silent, irresistible summons. I used the door behind the ginger tree and rode the padded elevator to the sepulchral elegance of the penthouse lobby. My palms were damp when I opened the outer door. I didn't dare wipe them off under the eye of the TV monitor in the dim reception area. I knocked and opened the door to the inner office.

The room lights were turned low, the gas fire cold. A muted clarinet carried the manic-depressive melody line of *Shrimpboats*. Lipton was ensconced in a high-backed executive swivel chair behind his big old desk and his carved lions. He was faultlessly turned out in the soft executive blue flannel I remembered from our first meeting. Seven people had come to violent ends in the interval, and he hadn't changed a millimeter.

"Come in, Spain. Nice to see you again."

I didn't return his amiable smile. His carefully cultivated manner was used Kleenex as far as I was concerned. I closed the door and went over to the desk. A bronze lamp laid a bright square of spot illumination on a leather-cornered blotter. There was a financial calculator on the pad, and a designer pen. Some sort of intricate calculation was inked partway down a single sheet of vellum letterhead in Lipton's angular cuneiform. There was also a sleek gray Luger to insure my good behavior.

"You won't need the pistol," I said. "I'm past the age where it's important to hit back at people I can't hurt."

"No hard feelings?"

"I didn't say that."

He watched me sink stiffly into a side chair, favoring a couple of tender spots. I could get up all right, but not fast enough to pose any threat to him. He put the Luger away in a drawer, out of sight but not out of reach.

"You might be interested in the results of a two and a half hour meeting in the Prosecutor's office this afternoon," he said. "Among other matters it was decided that the interests of justice would not be served by either a criminal filing or a license revocation proceeding against one Henry Spain."

"I was pretty sure when you sent the lawyer that you wouldn't leave me in a position of not having anything to lose by telling what I knew."

"Don't get any exaggerated ideas," Lipton cautioned politely. "I've no influence in the Prosecutor's office, and had no part in the decision. Between your bullet nick and what happened to the girl, any shyster worth his pinstripes could make it look in court like you were forced to defend your life. Whether it really happened that way or not."

"This isn't a shakedown."

"I never imagined it was. As I recall, you promised me the whereabouts of a man named Guy Hamilton."

"Hamilton never had the Doomsday Book."

Lipton didn't bother acting surprised. "And you found no clue to who might have it," he said to relieve me of the burden.

I took a folded sheet of computer printout from my pocket and tossed it carelessly on the desk blotter. I unkinked myself from the chair and wandered over to one of his tall windows to give him time to inspect it. It was a clear night, and an endless grid of streetlights spread like regiments of fireflies doing close order drill on the bottom of a huge paper plate. Twenty stories below, Wilshire Boulevard throbbed with a slow beat as regular as a pulse. It was easy to imagine Lipton standing here night after night with the lights turned down and the fires of empire smoldering in his soul.

A thick fervent voice behind me breathed life into the picture. "By God, Spain, they told me you were the best, but I never believed it until now."

"That's not what they told you," I said irritably. "They told you I was a disillusioned loner who would do a job if the money was right." Another reasonably well-adjusted psychotic cut in the mold of Danny Rupert and Walter Brixner.

The point was trivial, and Lipton didn't argue. "I presume you know what you've got here?"

I went back and lowered myself into the chair. "A list of dead people. People who died alone, with nothing to show for their years on this planet but a Social Security number. Each of them now owns an interest in some piece of real estate he couldn't have dreamed of owning when he was alive."

"Hundreds of millions of dollars. You'd laugh if I said a billion."

I thought the lower figure was optimistic and told him so.

"Do you know why Osborne bought the properties originally? Why a man who thought he was holier than God would raid his candidates' campaign treasuries to buy real estate under stolen identities?"

"That's between Osborne and his shrink."

"He bought to frustrate development. Whenever a project didn't fit his ideas of what L.A. ought to be, he would buy a key piece of property and stop things cold."

"He did a good job. Some of that property hasn't changed since World War I."

"The value of real estate is created by its location and zoning, not it's appearance. It is priced on its potential, not on its current use."

"The Book is only a catalog," I warned. "There are no deeds."

"A list of owners' names is all that's needed. Under California law, only the seller of property signs a deed. As buyers, Osborne's dead people don't have their signatures anyplace in the chain of title. A notarized scrawl on a statutory warranty deed will transfer any property in the Book, with no one the wiser."

"Osborne had to have real people fronting his identities," I pointed out. "Someone to collect the rent and write the checks and such."

"Most got instructions by mail, and thought they were representing legitimate clients. The few who know the score can't challenge the transfer without risking legal action for collusion in Osborne's original scheme."

"I guess you know Osborne's original reason for collecting dead people's identities."

Lipton shrugged impatiently. "Sooner or later everyone in politics discovers a dead voter is more cooperative than a live one. All you need is a little identification and a mail drop for the absentee ballot. Osborne's computers could organize things so a few trusted people could cast several thousand votes in one block without much risk of discovery."

"But with a signature on the voter registration records," I reminded him.

"L.A. County isn't equipped to do that kind of cross check. Even if they were, it wouldn't be evidence against whoever received title. Could he help it if some anonymous swindler sold property he didn't own? The recipient is an innocent victim."

"Three innocent victims, if you want to get technical."

"You and who else?" he asked sharply.

"Jean LaBostrie."

"Bad move. I've watched the girl for six weeks. She's cold rolled steel. Any man who gets his hopes up is due for a trip through the grinder."

"That's not the reason she's in."

"Why, then?"

"Osborne gave her the Book."

"She's the girl who pretended..?"

"She's his daughter," I said. "Illegitimate, of course, but his daughter all the same."

Lipton didn't believe a word of it, but having so obviously improbable a statement thrown at him deadpan made him too suspicious to respond immediately.

"I know it sounds like too much coincidence," I said, "but ask yourself if a man like Osborne would have given the Book to just anyone."

Lipton had some thinking to do. He took one of his long, green dappled cigars out of the desk humidor, fired it and sat back in his chair. The low music had shifted to the mournful violins of *The Tennessee Waltz*. He seemed to drift away with it, until an idea took root.

"Ben Osborne was a do-gooder. At least by his definition of the term. It was all right for him to rig elections, because he was only doing it so the best man would win. It was all right for him to siphon campaign contributions to buy real estate on the q.t., because he was only positioning himself to frustrate selfish interests. But when he saw his family, his associates and the men he put in office cutting corners for what they thought were good reasons, they became in his mind just another corrupt element of the society he was trying to purge. You see, don't you, Spain, how he could turn to the girl? She had been raised outside his sphere, raised pure. She was the last chance for his blood to prevail."

"I can't improve on it," I said, neither knowing nor caring how true it might have been.

"Which brings us to you," he said. "Why are you bringing the Book to me?"

"Real estate is financial roller derby. The winner is supposed to finagle his way into a deal with no investment, skim a fortune in fees and commissions, bail out with the equity safely recorded in his name and leave the other sharpshooters paying each other off in Confederate money. If I got mixed up in some maze of assignments, reconveyances and double escrows, I'd probably wind up swindling myself."

"That explains why you need me if you're going to use the Book," Lipton said. "Not why a man with twenty some years exploiting one side of the law suddenly decides to jump the fence."

"What did you expect me to do? Take it to the police?"

He sat back and considered me through a bluish haze of cigar smoke. After a while he smiled softly. "You're right, of course. Not even the Feds could handle this. As long as the book keeping was set up to show a loss, there wouldn't even be any income tax due. With Osborne dead in all but name, there is no one to prosecute. The only issue is the ownership of property, which is a civil, not a criminal matter." He stopped smiling and his eyes held mine hard and tight. "But you could have destroyed the book."

"I'm not totally fatuous."

"I don't recall suggesting you were."

"Everything you've said to me so far has implied that you thought so. Everything from day one."

"How so?"

"You didn't expect some tin whistle skip tracer to find the Book for you. You're not the type to sit around waiting for the Lottery to pay you ten million dollars. If you were, you'd be playing bingo instead of running it. You sent me looking for the Book to misdirect the opposition. You pointed me at Hamilton. I expect you knew he was dead. Hamilton was connected to charity bingo. Brixner would have told you he'd found Hamilton murdered and ordered the body disposed of to avoid any kickback. A month or so later, when you heard about the Book, you knew Osborne's men were chasing a ghost. You hired me to make it look like you were chasing the same ghost, to buy yourself enough time to check up on all the real estate lawyers and management companies in town to get an idea which ones might have fronted Osborne. You knew that when correspondence went unanswered, Osborne's front men would begin to wonder. Eventually they'd catch wise and take over the property themselves. You'd move in before the ink was dry on the deeds.

They couldn't go to the authorities without being disbarred or ruined. They would become your front men. Over time you would consolidate the property as you consolidated bingo."

Lipton smiled slowly, without pleasure. "You're middling smart, Spain, but do you really think that's enough to separate you from the rest of the industrial hooligans in this town?"

"What separates me from them is the same thing that separates you from your two bit bingo callers. I own the game."

"You don't, of course, but say for the sake of argument you had a playable hand. What would your bid be?"

"You won't be able to lay back and play Chairman of the Board on this one. I wouldn't have come if I didn't need your expertise out front."

"I don't mind a little exposure if the price is right," he said, too easily. "How many properties are we talking about?"

"You'll know that when we get to the last."

"That could take years. There's a limit to how fast we can move. Investment analysts watch real estate trends like gold prices. We could wind up as the feature story in the Bank of America's economic newsletter."

"At least I'll be alive to read it. The minute I turn the Book over, or destroy it, I become a liability to you. I wouldn't last out the day."

Lipton raised his hands in a placating gesture. "All right, all right. I happened to need a patsy, and I hit on you. It was nothing personal. I had to make a show of looking for the Book. Hamilton was five weeks dead when I heard Osborne had lost it. The chances of anyone actually finding it were nonexistent. Osborne's people were watching me. They would have tumbled to what I was planning just as you did. But now that we've got the Book, that's all changed. We can do this right. Look the whole Book over. Skim the cream before anyone else knows it exists. Leave the small fry for the sharks."

"I'm not trying to salvage Osborne's empire," I said. "I'm trying to dismantle it."

"Come again?"

"I'm counting on the sharks to bite off sizeable pieces. I'm counting on Osborne's people to turn up significant remnants. I'm dealing myself and Jean in to make sure no one shark gets too big a bite."

Lipton blew cigar smoke down his nostrils in an exasperated gust. "For Christ's sake, Spain. This kind of an opportunity comes once in a lifetime."

"My lifetime is at least half gone. I could write my autobiography on a paper napkin."

"What the hell am I supposed to do? Just go along for the ride until your mid-life crisis subsides and you get religion again?"

"If you don't like it, tell me 'no' and hope I don't hook up with someone else. Or use the gun. That ought to fool the police for two or three seconds."

Lipton ground out his cigar in a crystal ashtray. He ground it out slowly, relentlessly, completely. "Well, this business has cost me plenty. I guess I either see it through or lose any chance to recoup."

I knew then as I knew riding down in the elevator a few minutes later that he had agreed only as a matter of expediency. He would take what he could get from me. He would find what he could on his own. He might even cut a deal with Drew, if the payoff looked good. I knew it and he knew that I knew it and there wasn't anything either of us could do but play the cards we held.

The last thing he had done was ask me where I found the Book. It hit him visibly when I told him. That was the sole and only legitimate emotion I ever had from him.

Sick, twisted Walter Brixner. He was good people. Everyone had liked him.

Chapter 32

The show was over when I got down to the basement. I found a musician losing an argument with a soda machine. He believed my harmless grin and my story about working for Tommy Lipton enough to point me to Jean's dressing room door. He watched from a distance while I knocked.

"Who is it?" a gusty contralto wanted to know.

"Henry the Lizard Hearted. I'm holding a special on futile efforts and empty gestures."

The old lock made small scraping noises and Jean's face showed in a narrow crack. She drew the door inward with an urgency that sucked me in after it. She glanced out to make sure the immediate hallway was empty. She had unzipped the evening sheath halfway down her back so it hung loose on her shoulders. Residual droplets of perspiration were visible down her spine. She closed the door and put her back to it so I couldn't have gotten out if I'd wanted to.

"The police woke me up this morning. They said Frank Murillo was shot. They asked me a ton of questions about him, and all what I knew about you." She waited for some glib explanation.

"Murillo and another man tried to kill me. I don't know that Murillo wanted it that way, but he tried anyway."

"Then it was you who shot him. They never would say, but it was, wasn't it?"

She circled warily around me and sat down on a small padded bench. Wilbur the cat sat in the circle of his orange tail amid a clutter of bottles and jars and spray cans under the warm lights of a dressing mirror. He had probably adopted Jean when Albert Cooper went on to bigger and better bookkeeping. His mission in life still seemed to be giving me the evil eye.

"It's an awful, helpless feeling knowing someone you've known just is not going to be there any more," Jean said. "Two people I've known have died in the last week." It was my fault. I had disappointed the poor girl who had depended on me.

I drew a rickety cane chair across the small room and sat down so that my knees were almost touching hers. "Let's talk about the man who died seven weeks ago."

Jean fumbled a sweating can of soda off the table. I reached behind the cat and lifted her purse off the dressing table and opened it. The tiny .25 Browning was parked nose down in its pocket. I took it out and put the purse back. Jean just held the can and watched me and didn't say a word.

"I'm talking about a night in September," I told her. "Before you started at the Crown Colony. Back when you were doing boat shows and bingo games to pay the rent. It was primary election night. Bingo was shut down by State law, but there were lots of political rally hostess jobs available. The Hamilton Agency got you a hostess job with Osborne Associates. Sometime during the evening a crazy old man told you he was your father. He gave you a binder of computer tapes. Then he keeled over from a stroke. You took the binder and left. You weren't known by the Osborne people. You don't fit the pattern of losers who hook up with hack agencies so you weren't known by the other hostesses who worked the rally. But Guy Hamilton had your name on the list of hostesses he'd sent. Hamilton called you the next day. He told you what had happened, just as I am telling you now. He told you he wanted the binder. You went to his house north of Malibu that night. You went there and you shot him dead."

I bounced the little gun on my hand and said, "You shot him with this automatic," and watched the blood drain out of her face. Her eyes had a sick, glassy look.

"Walter Brixner saw it," I said before she could faint on me. "I'm not sure why he was there. Maybe he had been invited to another kind of party and Hamilton forgot in the excitement to call him and cancel. Maybe Hamilton did cancel and Brixner got to wondering why. But Brixner was there, Jean. He saw you shoot Hamilton and he covered for you. .25 caliber bullet holes could easily pass for twenty twos, professional caliber, if nobody saw the shell casings. In Brixner's circle professional killings were buried and forgotten. No questions asked. Brixner dressed yours up with all the trimmings and had it buried for you. That was his hold on you. From then until the night he was killed himself. He took the binder of tapes and got you the job here, where he could keep an eye on you. When you heard I'd been hired to investigate you, you hustled out to warn him."

Jean put her soda aside as carefully as a drunken dowager trying to juggle dignity and a Manhattan cocktail. She buried her face in her hands and cried with quiet, brutal sobs that shook her entire body. I put out a comforting hand and drew it back without touching her. She kept on crying and shaking and I couldn't think of any way to stop her. I felt clumsy and useless.

I tried to draw the magazine out of the little automatic. My fingers were thick and lacked coordination. I smothered the gun in one paw and said, "Jean…?" in a bright, cheery voice.

That did me a lot of good. Her sobs grew more savage, racking her from head to foot. I put her gun away in my pocket and slouched in the rickety cane chair. I put out a finger to stroke Wilbur under the chin and got the back of my hand raked open for my trouble. I had a long, uncomfortable wait before her sobbing fell away to a low grade of shuddering. When she finally did look at me, her eyes were red and full of despair.

"Finished?" I ventured cautiously.

She sniffled and nodded.

"Want to tell me your side of it?"

"W-what?"

"I'd like to hear your version of what happened."

"You don't care. All you care about is snooping in people's lives and finding out dirty little things and..." She sniffled, found a tissue on the dressing table and began to dab at her eyes.

"It's important, Jean. You see, Hamilton couldn't have known the binder was at large unless someone told him. And he couldn't have guessed you had it unless someone gave him some background on how Osborne had disposed of it. I can tell you a little about the someone. Osborne's people couldn't go to the police, so they would have hired private detectives. With an unidentified young woman involved, the detectives would have checked the hostesses as a matter of routine. I can just see a couple of national agency gumshoes giving Hamilton one of their righteous grillings. Their technique is early Sherlock Holmes. They'd ask just enough questions to let him know he was on to something big, then lay back and follow him to see if he tried to cash in. At least one of them was watching Hamilton's house when you killed him."

She shook her head a quick, emphatic 'no'.

"You didn't see me the night Brixner was killed," I reminded her.

"That was different."

"Where did you park?"

"Up the road. The stupid houses were all down where you couldn't see the numbers, and I parked and walked along until I found the right one."

"That's why Osborne's investigators never traced you," I said. "They had no license number."

"How come they didn't do anything when they heard me shoot Guy Hamilton?"

"A miniature automatic fired inside a solidly built house below grade wouldn't have been heard at any distance over the surf and the traffic. That is how it happened, isn't it?"

"He was drunk." She sniffled. "He grabbed me. He was shaking me and tearing at my clothes. I still don't know how I got the gun out of my purse. I…"

"Stop it, Jean. You don't have to lie to me. I don't care what you've done. I don't want to hurt you."

"How would you know? You weren't there."

"It was the binder Hamilton wanted, Jean. Not so much as a spot commodity, perhaps, but knowledge of whom he sold it to would be worth plenty in cash payoffs and political protection in the future. I can only guess how he came to know what it was. If I'm right, he was one of those people who hang out on the fringes of the exclusive cocktail circuit, collecting cast off girl friends and listening to rumors and salivating over the schemes that were making other men rich. When Osborne's detectives came hinting around, he put what they said together with what he'd heard over the years and knew who and what he was dealing with. I know that he knew, because he called Osborne's man and told him enough to convince him. Then he called you and threatened your career if you didn't give him the Book. The man had been in Hollywood for more than forty years. That's the first vulnerability that would occur to him. What didn't occur to him was your reaction. When things don't go the way you want, your first move is to steam out and get nose to nose with someone over it. You went after Brixner when you learned I had been hired, and you came after me when you didn't find Brixner in the papers. And the night Hamilton called, you went after him. I don't imagine you meant to shoot him. Probably just read him the riot act and tell him to back off. I can imagine the two of you arguing over it. Hamilton making nastier and nastier threats and you with your hand around the gun in your pocket getting madder and madder, until you finally slipped the safety and canceled his ticket."

"I never asked that stupid Guy Hamilton to call me. You should have heard him on the phone, dripping menace all over the place like he thought he was scaring me."

"Did Brixner actually see any of it?" I asked. "Or did the shots bring him from another part of the house?"

"I never knew he was there until he caught me at the door. He had to slap me to stop me laughing. He told me all what I did inside. Then he drove me to my car and told me to go home and wait for him to call."

I had a picture of Osborne Associates' high-priced gumshoes sitting in a dark car across the road, nursing cold coffee and talking into a microcassette recorder. They would still be watching the house when Charlie Watrous' big Lincoln pulled down into the garage an hour or so later. Within a day they would know that Watrous was Hamilton's attorney, that Brixner worked for Tommy Lipton and that Hamilton had called Drew. After Jean's late night visit, it had to look like Hamilton had the Book and was getting ready to play Lipton and Drew against each other to get the best price. They probably blew thousands wiring the house for sound. And thousands more turning California upside down looking for Hamilton himself. When they couldn't find him, Drew suborned Ricky Calland to make sure Lipton hadn't stolen a march on them. Lipton hadn't even known the Book was at large, until Calland told him. When Lipton did find out, he overlooked Walter Brixner, and put the rest of his high powered organization into overdrive. All the big operators on the circuit outsmarted themselves. They left a four-eyed nobody holding the Doomsday Book.

"What kind of deal did you have to make with Brixner?" I asked Jean.

"Walter wasn't the person you think he was. He had heard me sing and he said he could help my career and stuff. I would have sold my soul for a chance to sing at the Crown Colony anyway, forget the recording part. I didn't have to sign a contract to give him any money I earned or anything. All he wanted was the stupid binder. I never even knew what it was."

"Osborne didn't tell you?"

"He said something, but it wasn't even words. I got scared when he fell down. I went to get help. Some people found him first and then there were police and ambulance guys and everything was all confusion and they were telling everyone to leave. I didn't even remember I had the thing until I got to my car. I just put it in my trunk so I could give it back later or something. I was pretty shook. I..."

She had reached for a fresh tissue and happened to notice herself in the mirror. She was horrified. Crying had reddened her eyes and smeared her makeup. She turned immediately to the table and the bottles and jars to begin salvage operations. Wilbur had to move a couple of feet to keep from being wiped or powdered or sprayed.

"The binder was the key to Osborne's wealth and power," I said. "I guess I should say your father's wealth and power."

"Mom said it was true when I called her," Jean said without interrupting her work. "I mean, I always knew my father at home wasn't my real father, but he was the one who always did all the dad stuff with me, and I never wanted anyone else. I didn't even know that old Mr. Osborne. How come he thought I cared about that stupid binder?"

"He cared about it. Whatever plans he had for it didn't work out. When the end came, all he could do was hand his legacy to a daughter he had cast off as excess baggage a generation earlier." A daughter who was too wrapped up in her own crazy dream to care anything about his.

"I hope the stupid thing is gone forever," she said.

"Lipton and I are going to use the binder as Brixner probably planned to use it. We are going to include you, because you are Osborne's daughter and he gave you the Book and that's as close as we can come to a legal foundation for what we're doing, if we're ever caught. How much do you know about Lipton?"

"He was a gambler once, or something."

"Boss gambler," I corrected. "Gambling operator. Once, still and always. He was Brixner's boss in the charity bingo racket. He's also a hijacker and a fence and a killer, all by executive order. The other man who tried to kill me last night was his enforcer. Not because Lipton had anything personal against me. Circumstances beyond either of our control made me a risk to his organization. Lipton is as effectively trapped by his circumstances as you and I are by ours. He's hot as jalapeno just now, so I don't think we're in any immediate danger. But we both know what trapped people are capable of."

"What about the part where he makes all the girls sleep with him?" she asked quizzically.

"Men of Lipton's standing don't become men of Lipton's standing without learning to control their libidos."

She stopped inspecting herself in the mirror and looked at me oddly. "You want to be like him, don't you?"

"No, I don't."

"Yes you do. That's really why you're doing whatever you're doing with that stupid binder. All you've done all your life is snoop on people doing important things, and now you want to do something important yourself. You didn't buy that Porsche because it was a neat car. You bought it because people who do important things drive them, and it made you feel important."

I thought of Albert Cooper, tired of waiting for a chance to prove something. And Walter Brixner, getting discouraged and doing something stupid about it. And Frank Murillo laying down heavy dues. Jean made me feel like I was joining the Conga line.

I grinned feebly. "You forgot pond scum."

"I'm not going to bed with you to make you keep quiet about this," she said without looking at me.

"That's not why I came."

"That was really stupid, what you did the other night. I could have got knocked up or caught AIDS or God knows what."

"I'm too tired to argue," I said.

I put the little Browning back in her purse. It didn't amount to anything but a concealed weapons violation. The law required a body to make it a murder weapon, and Catalina Channel was too deep for that kind of fishing expedition. Only three witnesses had seen Guy

Hamilton's body. Walter Brixner was dead himself and Charlie Watrous and Harv were unlikely to implicate themselves. There would be no case against Jean. As far as I was concerned, Guy Hamilton had died of complications from acute ambition and greed.

"I'll call you tomorrow," I said, knowing it wouldn't be enough time to reconcile my yearnings with the fact that Lipton was right about her being too much for me to handle.

"Okay," she said. She was looking at me oddly. The turmoil inside had probably started to show on my face. I needed to get out of there before I came apart completely.

I was shaking when I eased the Porsche out into traffic on Wilshire Boulevard. I hadn't slept in thirty-six hours, and my contact with reality was getting tenuous. C. Benton Osborne appeared in the windshield. Not the wasted old man in Cedars Sinai, but a younger Osborne, vigorous and dimly seen through the fog of time. The kind of man who could assemble the power that would eventually become the Doomsday Book. His intentions were as pure as the dreams of the first men who set out to harness the power of the atom for peaceful purposes. The residue of his life's work was as persistent and deadly as radioactive waste. The daughter he had denied thought I saw it as a way to make myself a big man. The truth was it had swirled up and engulfed me and left me feeling scared and small. All I could do was try to break it into pieces too little to be dangerous. I was going to try alone because that was part of a habit pattern that went back more years than Jean had been alive.

When I was sixteen I told a high school principal that I would be doing things my way from then on. To a teenage punk with no discernible future, the rules and the people who enforced them were only a malignant backdrop to life. Malignant not in any sense of being mean spirited or fundamentally corrupt, but just because I was an immediate and perpetual sacrifice they could, and probably would, make to any 'i' they wanted to dot or 't' they wanted to cross. All these years later I couldn't put them in any different focus.

Time had passed, but nothing had changed. When it came to the core decisions, I was still a teenage punk cruising Wilshire in a V8 Ford, with the grumble of scavenger pipes to tell the world that I was bigger and more fearsome than I felt.

I knew myself a little better now, but I didn't see anything to do about it, except drive home and have a drink with the cat from next door.

CPSIA information can be obtained
at www.ICGtesting.com
Printed in the USA
FSHW010707011120
75453FS